THE MOUNTAIN MYSTIC

THE MOUNTAIN MYSTIC

by Russell W. Johnson

"Russell Johnson has packed more twists and turns into *The Mountain Mystic* than you'll find in the West Virginia backroads his characters roam. The mystery that plays out keeps you turning pages at top speed. It's one hell of a thrilling ride."
—**Wes Browne**, author of *They All Fall the Same*

"It's in the cards: Many mystery fans will enjoy this twisty page-turner."
—**Kirkus Review**

"In *The Mountain Mystic*, an explosive rural noir, brassy WV sheriff Mary Beth Cain blurs the line between lawman and outlaw in the search for justice. With a plot like a mountain road, twisting and winding to its jaw dropping peak, Johnson has braided an irreverent thriller, a legal drama, and a meditation on motherhood into a fuse and lit it on fire."
—**Meagan Lucas**, author of *Songbirds and Stray Dogs* and *Here in the Dark*

"*The Mountain Mystic*'s propulsive story grabs you on the first page and doesn't let up until the end. Russell W. Johnson pulls the reader around unexpected curves like the West Virginia back roads his characters traverse trying to solve a cold case that has been reheated by a psychic. Sheriff Mary Beth Cain and her deputy Izzy jump off the page with humor and heart. An entertaining sequel that is on par with Johnson's remarkable debut, The Moonshine Messiah."
—**Brett Lovell**, author of *A Bad And Dangerous Man*

"Russell W. Johnson's *The Mountain Mystic* thrums like the novelization of a Steve Earle song, capturing a thoroughly modern cast of West "by God" Virginians in all their messiness, pride, and defiance of historic wrongs and contemporary expectations. Prickly Sheriff Mary Beth Cain and her crew watching over Jasper County are the real McCoy."
—**Zakariah Johnson**, author of *Mink: Skinning Time in Wisconsin*

"*The Mountain Mystic* is a formidable addition to the growing collection of Appalachian crime literature."
—**Chris McGinley**, author of *Once These Hills* and *Coal Black*

More Praise
FOR THE MOUNTAIN MYSTIC

"*The Mountain Mystic* dynamite blasts the reader right back into Sheriff Mary Beth Cain's hands and by gawd don't Russell Johnson make it one helluva good return! Reads faster than a Camaro burning rubber over mountain blacktop and slams barrel proof down your gullet for the entire ride as Mary Beth spotlights for truth in a forest of dark so deep not even the Haints can see through it! Bang-a-fucking-rang!"

—**Ashley Erwin**, author of *Grit, Black, Blood*

"Pour a strong drink, kick back, and savor this Appalachian-set murder mystery that's full of surprises and intrigue. Leading this story is Sheriff Mary Beth Cain, a strong, complicated protagonist sure to make you cringe and root for in equal measure. Leave no doubt, Johnson has a winner with *The Mountain Mystic.*"

—**Curtis Ippolito**, Anthony-nominated author of *Burying the Newspaper Man*

"*The Mountain Mystic* is Russell Johnson writing in top form, creating memorable characters in Sheriff Mary Beth Cain, the first woman to ever be the top cop in Jasper County, and diminutive Chief Deputy Izzy Baker. With a ton of panache and expert skill at unspooling a story, Johnson has penned another must-read for fans of grit-lit and Southern/Appalachian noir."

—**Bobby Mathews**, award-winning author of *Living the Gimmick* and *Magic City Blues*

"Russell Johnson's *The Mountain Mystic* comes out of the gate like a cannon on page one and doesn't take a breath until its expertly-wrought conclusion. Johnson continues to carve out a niche in rural noir that feels distinctly his own, painting a detailed portrait of small-town West Virginia life rich in both beauty and tragedy, and filled with characters who immediately feel like old friends. Best of all is Sheriff Mary Beth Cain—funny, fierce, and nearly unstoppable in her pursuit of justice—who deserves to stand alongside Ace Atkins' Quinn Colson and Craig Johnson's Walt Longmire."

—**James D.F. Hannah**, Shamus-winning author of *Because the Night* and *Behind the Wall of Sleep*

RUSSELL W. JOHNSON

THE MOUNTAIN MYSTIC

A MOUNTAINEER MYSTERY

SHOTGUN HONEY

2024

Published by **Shotgun Honey Books**

215 Loma Road
Charleston, WV 25314
www.ShotgunHoney.com

Cover by Bad Fido.

First Printing 2023.

ISBN-10: 1-956957-73-1
ISBN-13: 978-1-956957-73-0

9 8 7 6 5 4 3 2 1   24 23 22 21 20 19

This book is dedicated to my favorite Appalachian men: Dad, Bo, and Joe.

THE
MOUNTAIN
MYSTIC

SHERIFF MARY BETH CAIN was good—damn good—if she did say so, herself. Since succeeding her dearly departed husband, Bill, to become Jasper County's first female sheriff, she'd closed more cases than any three of her male predecessors combined. But nobody bats a thousand in the cop game. Nobody. And, ovaries aside, Mary Beth knew she was no different. There'd been a handful of *unsolveds* during her tenure, victims and families denied their justice, and each and every one of them gnawed at her soul. Mary Beth thought about them late at night as she sipped her whiskey, counting her regrets like sheep. But what she realized on that sweltering June morning, as her college-age son, Sam, spread old newspaper articles across her usual table at the Waffle House, was that the case that haunted her most was one that went cold before she was even on the force—the unexplained disappearance of Maria Ruiz.

"Where'd you get all these?" Mary Beth asked as she ran her fingers across the yellowing news clippings.

"Saved them," Sam said.

Mary Beth shook her head and a curl of strawberry blonde

1

hair caught the corner of her mouth till she blew it away. Sam was just a kid when Maria disappeared. He was now nineteen, so he'd been hanging on to the clippings for more than a decade. "You saved them all this time?"

Sam had his mom's pale skin that concealed embarrassment about as well as a pair of chaps could cover your ass. When he turned red, Mary Beth thought, *Well, there you go. Some detective.* All these years she'd missed the fact that Sam must have had a super-major crush on Maria back in the day. But then again, who didn't? A Mexican immigrant in their small, lily-white, West Virginia town, Maria had been the kind of exotic beauty that reduced grown men into giggling idiots whenever she'd pass by.

"I'll never know why Guadalupe gave the press that photo to use. She looks like a damn beer commercial," Mary Beth said, staring at a picture of Maria seated on the hood of an old Ford, a denim shirt draped around a halter-top that barely contained her cleavage, wearing a skimpy pair of Daisy Duke cutoffs and laughing like she'd just heard a joke so funny she was about to pee what little there was of her pants. A yearbook photo would have been Mary Beth's choice but Maria's grandmother, Guadalupe, who'd been the Cain's housekeeper at the time, had chosen this one because it was the most recent.

JASPER CREEK JOURNAL
September 30, 2008
LOCAL WOMAN MISSING

Maria Ruiz, age 19, has been missing since last Thursday evening when she went for a jog at the Jasper Creek City Park around 7:00 pm. Her grandmother, Guadalupe Angeles, reported that Maria was wearing a black tracksuit and driving a red Chevrolet Cavalier. The vehicle was later discovered in the City Park's visitor's lot and did not reveal any signs of foul play.

Maria, pictured below, is five-feet-five-inches tall, with dark brown hair and brown eyes. Anyone who may have seen her or has information about her whereabouts should contact the Jasper County Sheriff's Department.

As Mary Beth read, Ralph Sherman, the portly proprietor of the Waffle House waddled up to the table and reached to refill her coffee. "Well, I'll be," he said, flexing a furry forearm. "There's a blast from the past. You reopening the case, Sheriff?"

"Nah. Just taking a trip down memory lane."

Ralph made a move toward Sam's cup and Mary Beth covered it. "Decaf for him," she said, inviting an eye roll from her son who was manically fidgeting, tapping out a staccato rhythm against the Formica tabletop. Ralph gave Mary Beth a quizzical look, like decaf coffee didn't make no sense. "Uh … gotta go brew a pot." He turned to leave, apologizing about the air conditioning. "She's just not kicking like she used to. Got a serviceman coming, should be here any minute."

Sam wiped a sheen of sweat from his forehead. "That's actually what I was wanting to talk to you about," he said to his mother.

"What is?"

"Reopening the case."

Mary Beth groaned. The last thing she had time for was a dusty old lost-cause investigation. "Sammy, baby. My deputies are stretched so thin right now. You know they annexed McCray County into Jasper, right? Now I'm responsible for all of McCray's opioid addicted-nonsense and whatever backwoods bullshit they've got going in the old burned-out hollers of coal country–on top of everything else. I just can't pile anything else on my guys right now."

"But it would mean so much to Bela Lu."

Bela Lu was Sam's childhood nickname for Guadalupe, Maria's grandmother, who'd graduated from the Cains' housekeeper to Sam's nanny when Bill died and Mary Beth stepped in to serve out the rest of his term as sheriff.

"Guadalupe understands that unless there's some new evidence, there's no justification for reopening the case. Why put her through all that heartbreak again?" Mary Beth said.

"Because she needs to know what happened."

"Maybe she's better off not knowing."

Guadalupe might still cling to the possibility that Maria was alive, but, as a cop, Mary Beth knew the odds of that were about the same as hitting the lottery while getting struck by lightning.

"You think she's dead, don't you?" Sam said, his voice cracking a little.

He really was a sweet kid, Mary Beth thought. Frustrating as all get out—enough to make a preacher cuss—but sweet. "Sam," she said, "your father worked Maria's case hard. Left no stone unturned."

"Sure, but he was only, what, like twenty-eight when he got killed? That's not all that much older than me, and I know what a goofball I am."

"Sam, your father was—"

"I know," he interrupted. "Dad was a very different person than me."

Mary Beth felt a pang of hurt over the truth of what Sam had said. There'd rarely been two men more different than the strong, silent, dutiful Bill Cain, whose idea of leisure was lifting weights or splitting logs, and the skinny little bookish Sam, who saw less sunshine than a vampire, and had worn his thumbs down to nubs from obsessive video gaming.

"Sometimes it's better not to know the truth," Mary Beth said.

Sam huffed. "I don't believe that for a second."

Spoken like a kid who's lived a sheltered life, Mary Beth thought. "Sam, I–"

"Whatever. Listen, the reason I wanted to talk with you is that there *is* new evidence. Take a look at these." Sam gestured to the newspaper clippings. "This is every story the *Jasper Creek Journal* ran about Maria."

Mary Beth scanned them. Most did little more than repeat the original blurb, mixing in the occasional quote from Guadalupe or Sheriff Bill Cain. She detected little to no new information other than one report of a two-tone brown conversion van witnesses saw in the area, with the letters SXL in the license plate.

"I don't get it. There's nothing in here."

Sam smiled like she'd proved his point. "Exactly. It's not what's in there. It's what's *not* in there."

"Come again?"

"There's nothing in there about the rosary beads Maria always carried with her, or the locket she wore."

"What locket?" Mary Beth remembered Maria liked her rosary beads but didn't recall anything about a locket.

"Bela Lu had just given it to her for her birthday. It was shaped like a ladybug and opened when you pressed the antenna. There was a picture of Maria's parents inside."

Mary Beth didn't get the significance. "Sam, I'm sure Guadalupe told your dad all that. It's common to hold back some details from the press so you can weed out the crackpots who call in with bogus leads and fake confessions."

"That's not the point," Sam said. "The reason it's important is because nobody else knew those details."

Mary Beth shrugged. "So?"

"So, I went to see someone yesterday who did know about them."

Now Mary Beth was mildly intrigued. "Who?" she asked.

Sam leaned back from the table like he feared his mother's reaction to what he was about to say. "Okay, don't get mad.

I know how you feel about these things. But have you heard of that psychic who lives up on Scarbury Hill, out in McCray County–or what used to be McCray County?"

"Oh, Sam you didn't."

"It was just for fun—a goof. I just wanted to check it out."

"Sammy, I've told you to stay away from that area. I grew up in McCray and I can tell you that half the folks out there are born scam artists."

"I know," Sam assured her. "But this lady really knew things about Maria. She knew about the rosary beads and the locket."

Mary Beth sighed. She could tell from Sam's longing expression he was expecting his mother to be impressed but she wasn't. No doubt the fortune teller had tricked Sam into offering up those details himself. The kid might have a 140 I.Q. but he was as gullible as all-get-out. Believed in Santa Claus until he was twelve years old, and Mary Beth used to be able to pull her Jedi mind tricks on him all day long.

"Sammy, baby. She saw you coming."

Ralph Sherman was back, carrying a pot of decaf so proudly you'd have thought it was an Olympic torch. "Found some in the back," he explained, filling Sam's cup on his way to take another order.

"I'm telling you," Sam said. "This was real. I didn't even say anything at all about Maria. But she got an image of her. And started describing her to a tee."

"Has she ever talked to Guadalupe?"

"Of course not."

"How do you know?"

"Because Guadalupe was with me."

Pins pricked Mary Beth's heart upon hearing this revelation. "What were you doing up there with Guadalupe?" she asked, trying not to sound agitated but unable to help feeling jealous. Sam and his Bela Lu had always possessed a bond that often left

Mary Beth feeling like the third-wheel, especially now that Sam was grown and rarely had time for his mom.

Sam shifted uncomfortably in his seat, aware of the precarious position he'd placed himself in. "I...got her the reading...as a birthday present."

Well, look at Mr. Thoughtful. Mary Beth's gifts usually consisted of a card and a bag of dirty laundry Sam expected her to wash when she wasn't busy fighting crime.

Sam quickly continued his story. "When the fortune teller held Guadalupe's hand, she got an image of Maria. Saw her wearing a black tracksuit—which was described in news reports, so I discounted that. But then she said, she was wearing the little locket and had rosary beads wrapped around her wrist."

Mary Beth rolled her eyes. "This should be an easy case to crack then. I bet this lady was able to tell you exactly where Maria's been all this time. Did she write down the address?"

"No, she lost connection after that."

"I hate when that happens."

"But," Sam said, ignoring his mother's sarcasm, "as we were leaving, she got an image of you. That's what I wanted to talk to you about. I want you to go see her."

A tiny snort escaped Mary Beth's nostrils. "What on earth for?"

"The fortune teller said she had a strong maternal feeling when she looked at me. Like my mother was someone who could find lost people or right wrongs—a police officer perhaps. Those were her exact words."

Mary Beth whistled. "Don't suppose you having the same last name as the sheriff might have tipped her off, do you?"

Sam's shoulders slumped. "Forget it," he said, and started hastily folding up his newspapers and started stuffing them into his book bag. The threat here was obvious. Sam was in college now and living in the dorms while taking summer classes at the local Bible college. If his mom pissed him off, he could just head back there and deny her his company.

"Wait." Sam paused. "I'm sorry," Mary Beth said. "You were saying—"

Sam took a deep breath and continued. "I was saying, the fortune teller wanted to meet you. Said if she could feel your energy, she might get a better image of where Maria is."

"And charge another fee for her services," Mary Beth added.

"I'll pay for it, okay?"

Mary Beth took a sip of her coffee, trying to think of a kind way of explaining to her precious son just how re-God-damn-diculous this all sounded. "How much was it, anyway?" she asked.

"Five hundred," Sam said without batting an eye.

Mary Beth nearly lept out of her chair. "Five hundred! Dollars?"

Sam cowered and Mary Beth didn't wait for him to answer. She was up on her feet so fast she nearly forgot her trademark floppy-brimmed Stetson hat. Mary Beth snatched it up and put it on her head.

"Where are you going?" Sam asked.

"I'm going to see this scam artist you just paid $500 to," Mary Beth said. "And trust me, she won't have any problems reading my energy."

2

BEING THE ONLY BLACK OFFICER on an otherwise all-white force in an overwhelmingly white county, Chief Deputy Izzy Baker was bound to stand out. But more distinguishing than his skin color was his height, or lack thereof–standing just shy of five feet, even with his boots on. The small stature was something Izzy compensated for by toting an extended barrel forty-four Magnum handgun and driving a monster-truck-sized Chevy Blazer with a jacked-up suspension, super-big tires, and a nitrous-boosted engine that roared like a jet plane. Izzy was descending from the cockpit of that massive vehicle via a rope ladder, while bumping his gums about the reason Mary Beth called him back to the station in the first place.

"You know we don't have time for this nonsense. If we start arresting every little small-time scam artist in old McCray–."

"We aren't arresting anybody," Mary Beth interrupted. "We're just gonna put a little scare into the old lady and get Sam's money back."

Izzy hopped down off the rope ladder's final rung and turned to face Mary Beth, who, at a wiry five-foot-seven stood considerably taller than the chief deputy. The two had been best friends since high school and tended to bicker like siblings when no one else was around.

"Fine," Izzy said. "Do what you want–if you think that's a proper use of your position and resources–but why do I need to go?"

Mary Beth gestured to her vehicle, a low-riding Camaro that was ill-suited to the mountain roads of old McCray, many of which were still washed out from recent flooding. She needed four-wheel drive to get up on Scarbury Hill and Izzy's Blazer could climb Mount Everest.

"You don't want to go, that's up to you," Mary Beth said. "Just give me your keys."

"No way." Izzy was protective of his vehicle. Part of the Jasper Creek way, where a person's value was often measured by the machine they drove and how clean they kept it.

"Then saddle up, Tonto," Mary Beth said.

Izzy palmed the top of his head, pushing a handprint into his high-top fade.

There were others on the force with four-wheel drive vehicles Mary Beth could commandeer, but she secretly craved Izzy's company. Seeing Sam always left her feeling out of sorts, reminding her of how grown he was and how alone that made her. Since Bill died, she'd pretty much led the social life of a cloistered nun, dutifully raising and protecting her son and her county. For whatever reason, she had never been the type to have a lot of girlfriends. So Izzy wasn't just her best friend, he was her only one, and she could really use some Izzy time.

"Okay," Izzy said. "Let's go."

Mary Beth tried to hide how pleased she was as she walked around to the passenger side of the Blazer where Izzy kept a metal rod clasped to each running board. It had a hook on the end that could be used to free the rope ladder that hung just below the door frame, tightly rolled and secured by a nylon strap. Mary Beth pulled her metal rod free and waved it high above her head until she hooked the strap. There was a simple snap button that she undid with one hard yank and the rope ladder came clanging down.

Mary Beth was already seated and belted by the time Izzy made it to the top. She was noticing with admiration how the guys down at Bobby B's Body Shop had configured the Blazer to suit Izzy. In high school, she used to tease him that he'd need to tie blocks to his feet in order to reach the pedals, but Izzy's younger brother Bobby, who was a whiz mechanic, had installed pedal extensions that allowed Izzy's short legs to operate the truck with ease.

As Mary Beth secured her rope ladder she said, "You should get one of those lifts, like the ones that help old people go up the stairs."

Izzy fired up the engine and said, "You should learn how to talk nice to people. Then maybe you wouldn't be so damn lonely."

"Fair point." Mary Beth put on her seatbelt and admired a photo of Izzy's wife, Princess, mounted on the dash. She was a former beauty queen who was now a reporter for the local news station. The photo showed Princess in a sleek violet chiffon dress, wearing large gold, hoop-earrings, and really popping her hip.

"I'll never know how you landed a stunner like that," Mary Beth said, pointing to the photo.

"Shut up," Izzy said. "You're just jealous."

He pulled them out of the station parking lot. They roared down College Avenue, past the Dollar General and an impressive field of shiny new vehicles at Moyer's Chevrolet. From there they cruised past Yeager Stadium where the Jasper Creek Cougars were holding unofficial two-a-days, violating all kinds of rules, running their players up and down the stadium steps a solid month before practices were allowed to begin.

Twenty minutes later they were winding their way through

the twisty mountain roads into what until recently had been McCray County, a former coal mecca whose population had dwindled to the point it had to be consolidated into Jasper.

Mary Beth pulled out the newspaper clipping of Maria she'd been looking at earlier that morning and Izzy took his eyes off the steep switchback he was descending, long enough to glance at it.

"Nice set of lungs," he said.

Mary Beth punched Izzy in the arm with enough mustard that the deputy nearly lost control of the vehicle. The behemoth Blazer barely fit on the narrow mountain road as it was and skidded to a stop on the shoulder where a warped, rusty guardrail was all that separated them from a precipitous drop.

"Goddamn, woman! You trying to make me wreck?"

"I'm trying to teach you some manners," Mary Beth said. "That *set of lungs* was a person. An actual, goddamn human being. With feelings and hopes and dreams and people who cared about her—including me." Tears welled up in Mary Beth's eyes remembering the time Maria stopped by the Cains' house for senior prom pictures. She thought about how beautiful Maria looked in that strapless blue dress, and how Bill had delighted in scaring the shit out of her escort by donning his sheriff's uniform while cleaning his gun.

Izzy pressed the extended gas pedal and eased them back onto the road. "Take it easy," he said. "I was just messing around. What's got you so worked up?"

Mary Beth sighed and stared out the window at vines of honeysuckle and kudzu covering a jutted rock formation. "The stuff about Maria just stirs up a lot of stuff, you know? The case put a lot of strain on me and Bill, and I maybe said some things to him I regret."

"Can't imagine that," Izzy said, giving Mary Beth a little side-eye. Ever since the Old Wengo Mine fiasco months earlier, where Mary Beth was tasked with heading off a bloody

Waco-style confrontation between the Feds and her crazy brother, Sawyer's, half-baked but heavily-armed militia, Izzy'd been on her ass to see a therapist. During the dust up's aftermath, Sawyer had ambushed Mary Beth and Sam and they were forced to kill the conspiracy guru in self-defense. Since then, Izzy said Mary Beth, had "become the poster child for PTSD." But the sheriff subscribed to her mother Mamie's philosophy that shrinks were for cry-babies. Sure, maybe she'd been a little crotchetier than usual, but she would work through things in her own way, and in her own time. Until then, her deputies could just keep giving her a wide berth if they didn't want to get their heads chewed off.

"Hey, you need to turn up here by the old drive-in," Mary Beth said, anxious to change the subject.

Izzy was still learning his way around old McCray, but Mary Beth was born and raised there up until age sixteen, when her father died and her mother sent her to Jasper Creek to stay with her grandparents.

Jesus, what kind of dark star was I born under? Mary Beth wondered, looking around at all the empty storefronts, the old timey soda shop and an abandoned theater with a formerly grand marquis—skeletal remains of a once vibrant community. Loss was everywhere she looked. And loss was something Mary Beth knew all about. Both her father and her husband having died in the middle of a drug bust. Different busts that occurred decades apart—and of course Bill, the former Jasper County Sheriff, had been the buster, whereas Mary Beth's father, a career drug dealer, was the bustee. But still, that was some kind of bad luck, or coincidence, or irony perhaps. Mary Beth wasn't really sure, but she knew it sucked ass.

"MB? Hello?"

"What?" she said, stirred from her reverie.

"I was saying, driving through here must bring back a lot of memories for you."

Mary Beth shrugged. "I suppose."

She took one last look at Maria's picture, kissed her finger and pressed it to the dead girl's image, before turning it over. Then she pointed to a gravel road up ahead, marked by a painted wooden sign. FORTUNE TELLER. "Turn there," she said. "Right now, I'm more interested in finding out my future."

3

THE FORTUNE TELLER'S PLACE of business was a double-wide trailer with white vinyl siding that was in desperate need of power-washing. Izzy parked by a sagging carport next to a mud-covered four-wheeler and an El Camino with pancake flat tires. Mary Beth jumped down from the Blazer while Izzy took his sweet ass time, carefully descending by rope ladder.

"Whenever you're ready," Mary Beth said, arms crossed.

Izzy skipped the last couple rungs, hopping down, and saluted Mary Beth with his middle finger. "After you, boss."

They traversed a path of mismatched pavers overgrown by tall grass, beneath the canopy of a row of oak trees that formed a kind of tunnel leading up to the mobile home. The front porch was guarded by a fat, multi-colored cat who was snoozing and snoring like a warthog. A crooked tin sign hung from the door knocker.

COME IN.
I'VE BEEN EXPECTING YOU

"Cute," Mary Beth said. She raised her fist to knock but before she could rap on the door a woman's voice called out from inside. "Just come on in."

Izzy shot Mary Beth a look.

"She heard us coming," Mary Beth whispered.

"Come on in," the voice called out again. "Both of you."

Mary Beth looked around, trying to figure out how the old lady managed to see them. The drapes on the front windows were solid and completely drawn. Maybe there was a hidden camera somewhere. She shrugged and turned the knob. The door opened with a creak and they entered into a dark foyer, lit just barely enough to make out a honey pot full of wilted sunflowers and a large framed photo of an old, bearded man with snow-white hair, saying grace over a silvery loaf of bread.

"Over here." The woman's scratchy voice came from their left, behind a curtain of hanging beads.

Mary Beth and Izzy pushed through the beads into the living room where they saw the old lady sitting in a rocking chair in the corner, next to a wood stove. Being summer, the stove wasn't in use, but the room still had an odor of wood smoke, and a tiny whiff of something rotten, like maybe the trash in the kitchen needed to be taken out.

The woman's gnarly fingers were steadily at work, crocheting a black, white, and red afghan with a zig-zag pattern. She looked up at them, revealing cloudy blue eyes, webbed with cataracts so severe Mary Beth wondered whether she was blind.

"Sweetheart," the woman said, "you've got just about the reddest aura I have *ever* seen."

Mary Beth looked around, not sure what the woman was talking about.

"Good mercy, there is a lot of anger in you."

Izzy chuckled. "Well, I'm sold already. She's got you pegged, MB."

Mary Beth elbowed Izzy, meaning to get him in the shoulder, but accidentally hitting him just below the jaw.

"Ow! See," he said, rubbing the side of his face. "That's exactly what she's talking about."

"Shut up," Mary Beth said.

The old woman craned forward. "He's right though, isn't he, dear? I can see it clear as day. Very, very angry."

Mary Beth huffed.

"What else do you see?" Izzy asked.

The old woman opened her milky eyes wider. "You have a burning need to create order out of the chaos."

"So, what you're saying is: I'm a cop." Mary Beth was wearing her floppy brimmed Stetson and tapped the shiny gold star pinned to its wine-colored band.

"Yes," the old lady said. "But you want it so badly that you very often break the rules yourself, don't you?"

"Damn. This lady's good," Izzy said.

"Or she just reads the papers." Recently, the Charleston newspaper had done a whole exposé on Mary Beth called *Rough Justice*, reporting on her "extra-legal methods" and falsely insinuating she was connected to the McCray County mafia, a hillbilly crime syndicate her mother Mamie had led since Mary Beth's father died. The sheriff had since disabused people of that notion by running her mother clear out of the state, forcing Mamie to set up shop across the Kentucky border.

Mary Beth fired a thumb at Izzy. "Do him."

The old woman sat her crochet hook in her lap and leaned forward. "You've got a good bit of anger as well. I can see why you two are partners. You understand one another. But you are much more grounded. Cautious. The anchor. Your aura is mostly pink."

Now Mary Beth laughed. "She is pretty good, Pinko." Just the other day Mary Beth had started calling Izzy a "pinko commie" because he was one of about three registered Democrats in all of

Jasper County, and thus couldn't vote for her in the upcoming Republican primary.

The old woman rocked back in her chair and said, "It will be five hundred dollars for a formal reading."

Mary Beth tossed a pair of handcuffs on a round table in the middle of the room where they clanged down between a crystal ball and a thick, wax-dripping candle.

"That's the only thing I brought for you today, lady. I came to get a refund of the five hundred you charged my son for your bogus reading. You can either fork over the dough, or else go ahead and put those on."

The old woman resumed her crocheting. "You don't believe," she said, more as a statement than a question.

"What tipped you off?"

The old woman stopped rocking, dropped her afghan into a wicker basket, then stood, hunching over as she hobbled toward the table at the center of the room.

"Let me see your hands, dear?"

Mary Beth replied, "Funny. I was about to say the same to you."

"Please, just indulge me for a moment. No charge unless you're convinced." The woman took a seat at one of the three-legged wooden stools surrounding her table.

"Listen—" Mary Beth started to say but Izzy nudged her.

"Go on," he said. "What can it hurt?"

Mary Beth rolled her eyes as she extended her arms. The fortune teller turned her hands over and ran her fingers across Mary Beth's palms.

"You have quite a bit of intuition yourself. Do you ever find that you'll be thinking of someone right before they call or pop up somehow?"

Mary Beth shrugged. "Happens to everybody. It's called coincidence."

"Perhaps. But it happens to some more than others. You see, I believe that everyone has some degree of what most people would refer to as psychic abilities. For instance, have you ever noticed how people can tell when you're staring at them?" The old woman closed her eyes. "Try it sometime," she said. "Get in a position where there's no way the other person can see or hear you, and just stare at them thinking some really intense thought, and I bet you they turn around."

"Why is that?" Izzy asked.

"I believe it's a natural ability we've lost over time. Back when we had to worry about being attacked by lions and tigers and snakes in the grass, we were much more adept at using our mind's eye."

Mary Beth pulled back her hands. "Okay, enough of this."

The old woman said, "You sometimes have dreams that come true too, don't you?"

Mary Beth gasped and clapped the sides of her face. "Oh, my God," she said. "Now that you mention it, yes. I did have a dream. Just last night, in fact. I was here. Right here in this room. With both of you. And...."

"What?" Izzy asked.

Mary Beth closed her eyes tightly, really straining. "And... and...you...gave me the five hundred you hoodwinked from my son." She shoved her hand in the old lady's face. "Now fork it over, granny, before I haul your ass in."

The old woman remained unaffected by the threat. "There was one dream in particular," she said. "A brutal, terrifying dream you had when you were a child. Do you remember?"

Well, shit, Mary Beth thought. As much as she hated to admit it, there actually was one that came to mind. She almost mentioned it, but reminded herself how this scam worked. A cold reading, where the psychic kept throwing things at the wall until something stuck, constantly watching for a reaction they could pass off as a "hit."

After a long pause, the psychic filled the silence. "You do

remember, don't you? How could you ever forget? The emotions were so intense."

Mary Beth was determined not to play along but what the woman said next sent a chill down her spine.

"It was the first time you'd ever seen anyone murdered."

At the mention of the M word, every ounce of cynicism left Mary Beth's body for a moment. "How could you know that?" she asked.

"I feel it, dear. I feel the terror you felt. Now, tell me. What is it that you saw in your dream?"

Another probing question. Mary Beth recognized it but had to really steel herself to keep from answering. "You're the psychic," she said. "You tell me."

The old woman moved her top dentures out of place then pushed them back to the roof of her mouth, securing them with her thumb. "I don't pretend to see everything," she explained.

That's right, Mary Beth thought, her cynicism returning. "I guess your spirit guide crossed back over?"

The woman cackled with witchy laughter. "No. No. No spirit guides. When I'm with folks, I just get feelings and mental images. Sometimes I can make sense of it. Sometimes I can't. But right now, I'm getting a feeling I always get when someone's been killed. And I can see a little pale-faced girl with curly reddish-blonde hair, waking up in a cold sweat, and running into her parents' room. I'm right, aren't I?"

"Yes." Mary Beth couldn't help confirming the truth of what the lady said. She was exactly right. One hundred percent. Mary Beth had been that little girl with the murderous dream.

"What did you tell them, dear? Your parents—when you woke them."

"That I'd dreamed of our neighbor, Mr. Pearson, lying in a pool of blood. That he was…" Mary Beth heard a slight crack in her voice that surprised her. She'd seen a number of dead bodies since but it was like she'd reverted to childhood. "He was dead," she whispered.

The old woman nodded. Her cloudy blue eyes rolled back in her head. "Ahh, yes. It wasn't just a dream though, was it?"

"No."

"What do you mean?" Izzy asked.

Mary Beth said, "We found out the next day that the Pearsons had a fight and Mrs. Pearson stabbed her husband with a butcher knife."

"Did your parents believe you?" The old woman asked. "When you told them?"

"Not at first. They told me to just go back to bed. But I remember my mom seemed worried. She came and laid down with me to help me get back to sleep, which was something she never did. After we found out about the murder, they told me never to speak about the dream. Afraid people would think we were crazy...or maybe involved somehow."

Mary Beth was officially floored. She had no idea how the woman could have known about a dream from more than thirty years ago that she'd never spoken of since that night.

The fortune teller stood, stretched her back, then picked up the handcuffs and handed them to Mary Beth. "Why don't we call it even, for today? Shall we?"

Mary Beth watched silently as the woman hobbled to her rocking chair and rummaged around in her wicker basket until she found her crochet hook. Just before she plopped down on the rocker and resumed her yarn work, she announced out of nowhere, "Pregnant bullfrog."

"Excuse me?" Mary Beth said.

"You came here wanting to know the location of the missing girl—the one your son was asking about, right?"

"Yeah," Mary Beth said. "But I don't understand. What's that got to do with a pregnant bullfrog?"

"I have absolutely no idea. But I'm getting an image of a large, dead frog, being cut open, and it's full of eggs. Pregnant."

Mary Beth and Izzy looked at each other, both bewildered.

"Think on it," the woman said. "Try to clear your mind, then pay attention to what materializes. I'm sure that little girl who had that special dream all those years ago, can figure it out."

4

ONCE OUTSIDE, IZZY SAID, "You know, I didn't recognize Maria's name when you first mentioned her, but come to think of it, when I first joined the force I remember there was a case Bill was all consumed with."

"That was probably Maria's," Mary Beth said. "Bill just about killed himself trying to solve the thing. Guadalupe was basically family, and we weren't all that much older than Maria, so she was like a little sister. Bill worked nights and weekends scouring the earth."

"Did he ever talk about the case?" Izzy asked. "Tell you about any favorite suspects."

Mary Beth rolled her head around, cracking her neck. "All I remember was Bill was real suspicious of Maria's ex-boyfriend. They were recently broken up and he had a reputation as the jealous type. But the guy had an alibi. I think he was away at school at the time."

Izzy stroked his chin. "Maybe we should take another look at him?"

When Mary Beth didn't answer, Izzy looked up at his boss and found her deep in thought.

"What do you think?" he prodded. "Feel like taking a peek through the old file? MB?" Izzy waved his hand in front of her face.

"Away at school," Mary Beth said. She snapped her fingers. "That's it!"

"What's it?"

"Pregnant bullfrog."

"You feel okay?" Izzy asked.

Mary Beth looked down at him with a crooked grin. "I'm better than okay. I think I know where we need to go."

The next thing Izzy knew, he was back to chauffeuring Mary Beth through coal country, barreling down another windy-ass mountain road in the middle of nowhere, with madam sheriff badgering him to "step on it."

"I don't even know where I'm going," he complained.

"It's just over Hawk's Nest Hill. Then cut down past Squeeze Creek."

"Oh, well, why didn't you say so?" Izzy said, having no F-ing clue where either of those places were. It was just one of the many things he hated about old McCray. Not only was GPS a no-go in the deep hollers, and the roads so curvy they always left him pining for Dramamine, but the locals were the absolute worst at giving directions. Half the roads didn't have names, and directionally decipherable terms such as north, south, east, west, or even left or right, were practically non-existent. It was all, head over yonder for a stretch, then cut thisaway or thataway. You'd have to be as much of a mind reader as the Mountain Mystic to know what in the world they were talking about.

"Left, or right?" Izzy asked as he eased the Blazer down a thirty percent decline back onto some nameless rural route.

"Left."

"Thank you." Izzy hung a Louie and asked, "What's the big hurry, anyway?"

Mary Beth looked reluctant to share her thoughts. "You just watch the road," she said. "We're headed into the area that got washed out by the floods and some of the roads still haven't been repaired."

No problem, Izzy thought. His baby, Beulah, not only had four-wheel drive and a turbo-charged engine, but 66-inch tires. Fording a couple streams would be no problem. Still though, he'd like to know where they were headed.

"Come on, MB. Tell me what's going on."

She frowned. "Promise you won't laugh?"

"I promise I'll try not to."

"Okay," Mary Beth said. "I know this sounds crazy, but when I was in seventh grade I had to dissect a frog."

"So what? I'm pretty sure I did too."

"Yeah, but the one I dissected was full of eggs. A pregnant bullfrog, just like the psychic said. I remember because the sight of the eggs, combined with the smell of formaldehyde, totally grossed me out and I threw up right there in class. It was very embarrassing. Got sent home, and everything."

Izzy was waiting for more. When it didn't come he said, "Okay. That still doesn't tell me where we're going."

"Cierra Junior High," she said as though it should be obvious. "That's where I dissected the frog. And the school closed back in 2000. Was just sitting there abandoned by the time Maria went missing."

Izzy was tempted to laugh but held to his promise. He hadn't said anything about avoiding sarcasm, however. "So your spidey sense is telling you that's where Maria is?"

"Look, I know it's a long shot," Mary Beth admitted. "But we're out here anyway, right? Might as well go check it out. The building's been condemned forever, it would be a pretty good place to stash a body."

Izzy traversed a dip in the road covered by standing water a foot deep. "Okay, fine," he said. "We'll head over there. But what's the hurry?"

Mary Beth took off her floppy brimmed Stetson and placed it in her lap, which was usually a sign she was about to say something important. "That's what's got me so weirded out. The school was just in the paper the other day. A story about how it's finally going to be demolished. Was supposed to happen years ago but got held up by some classic McCray County corruption, bribes and such, trying to score the contract, then the floods came, and then there was no more money until the annexation. I mean, what are the odds that the school gets a story in the paper just days before this psychic lady starts spouting her pregnant bullfrog business?"

Izzy honestly wasn't sure what to think about that.

"Demolition crews could be out there already, wrecking shit," Mary Beth said. "We need to get the move on."

"Okay, okay, I'm going."

After a few more turns, cutting "thisaway" and "thataway" they eventually arrived at the final resting place of the Cierra Junior High. It was a wide two-story brick structure that sat atop a plateau in the bottom of a deep valley straddled by a massive elevated train track with steel legs the color of pea soup. They'd beaten the demolition crews there, but not by much. The area was already surrounded by orange plastic fencing and some heavy equipment was assembled but no workers were present.

"Must have been quite a sight at one time," Mary Beth said, "but this school was already ancient when I was here. The whole place used to shake whenever the train came rumbling through the valley, carting coal off to the world."

Izzy parked and Mary Beth immediately hopped down and started trudging through a muddy field of knee-high weeds, without waiting for him to make his descent. Izzy climbed down from the big Blazer as quickly as possible but Mary Beth was already halfway across the muddy field by the time he got to the ground.

"Wait up." Izzy charged after her, keeping his head on a swivel to look for snakes, while worrying about ticks.

Mary Beth finally stopped when she got to the foot of the long staircase leading up to the school entrance.

"Geeze, how many steps is that?" Izzy asked, eyeing the steep incline.

"Sixty-five, if I remember correctly. We used to say it was so steep, you'd just about touch your nose."

Izzy groaned.

"Come on," Mary Beth said. "It's a lot easier coming back down."

They made the long climb up to the school and were both out of breath by the time they reached the top and discovered the double door entrance was chained shut.

"Don't suppose you've got a pair of bolt cutters in your truck?" Mary Beth asked.

"Dang it, I came off without them today." Izzy was ready to call it quits on this adventure. The old abandoned school gave him the creeps and even if they could get inside, the only thing Izzy expected to find would be some rusty nail positioned right where he'd accidentally step on it and contract lockjaw.

Mary Beth examined the windows reflecting the bright sun. Izzy was afraid she was going to try and bust one out, when she pointed to a window that was boarded up, with the words STAY OUT spray-painted on it.

"We aren't the first ones to try getting in here," she said.

"Yeah," Izzy said. "Thus, the STAY OUT. Whoever's responsible for this ruin doesn't want trespassers—like us—going in there and getting hurt."

"No, look." Mary Beth pointed to the edges of the board, a

single piece of plywood nailed to the window frame. "Come closer." She bent down and indicated to the board's lower-right corner. "Someone's pried the nails out down here. Over here too." Mary Beth manipulated the board which proved to be attached by only a single nail in the middle-top so that it could be rotated around in either direction enough to squeeze through.

"Open sesame," she said smiling.

Izzy sighed. Looked like they were going in after all.

Mary Beth went first, while Izzy held the board to the side. Once she was through, he heard her yell, "Holy shit!"

"What? What's wrong?"

Mary Beth didn't answer right away but he could hear her breathing heavy.

"MB? You okay?"

"Yeah," she said finally.

"What happened?"

"Nothing. Just come on through. I'll hold the board for you from in here."

"Why did you yell?"

"I said it was nothing. Now, come on."

"First tell me why you yelled," he said.

"It was *nuh*-thing."

"If it was nothing then—"

"Izzy, Goddammit, just get your ass in here."

Izzy groaned and muttered under his breath. He really wasn't feeling this, but it wasn't like he could back out. That was one of the problems with being best friends with a daredevil shit-kicker, who just so happened to be a woman. His male ego compelled him to try and keep up, even when his instincts told him to turn the other way.

Mary Beth reached through the window and had the plywood rotated to create a space for Izzy to wriggle through. He awkwardly tried going at it feet first, but the bottom of the window was higher than his waist, which required him to attempt it one leg at a time and his legs weren't long enough. He got his right leg through as far as his ankle and was stuck there like he was holding a high kick in his Taekwondo class.

"Just give me your hands and I'll pull you through," Mary Beth said. "Head-first."

"I don't want to fall to the ground on the other side."

"Jesus Hieronymus Christ, Izzy. I won't let you fall. Let's just do this, Susie."

Izzy pulled his leg back and stuck his head through.

"Give me your arms." Izzy did. Mary Beth seized them, releasing the plywood board that dropped down, hitting him in the center of his back as she tugged and lifted him off the ground and through the window.

"Okay, I'm in. Now let go of me."

Mary Beth released Izzy and he did a turn, taking in the dark, empty hallway, with its chipped, black and white, checkerboard floors and hole-ridden walls.

"So what were you yelling about?"

Mary Beth shone her flashlight down on a pile of brown pellets, clustered near the wall. "When I came through, I looked over and was eye to eye with a rat about this big," she said, holding her hands eight inches apart.

Izzy's heart fluttered. He hated rats. *Hate-ed.* Last fall, he'd been taken captive by a local militia headed by Mary Beth's late-brother Sawyer, a conspiracy Guru dubbed the Moonshine Messiah, who staged a showdown with the Feds that would have killed hundreds if Mary Beth hadn't intervened. During the process, Izzy had been held hostage in an underground mine for days, imagining rats crawling all around him the entire time. Since then, he'd slept with the light on and jumped at the mention of any rodent.

Izzy pulled his forty-four Magnum revolver that had an extended barrel as long as his forearm. "I swear to God, MB. If I see a rat, I'm shooting it."

"Put that away. They're more scared of you than you are of them."

"The hell they are."

"Well, whether they are or not, I don't want you hitting me with the ricochet. Now, put it away. That's an order."

Izzy reluctantly holstered his weapon but didn't snap the safety strap, just in case he had to pull it again. Sometimes he had to remind himself that Mary Beth suffered just as much as he did during the militia ordeal. She and her son Sam had also been held captive by her brother who there were forced to kill in self-defense. Mary Beth tried to act resolute about the whole thing, telling anyone who asked, how Sawyer had it coming, but Izzy knew a large chunk of Mary Beth's soul died along with the Moonshine Messiah.

"Come on," Mary Beth said. "Let's check this place out."

Izzy pulled his flashlight and followed behind, kicking aside a wad of old printer paper with bubble tracks.

They cleared the first floor without discovering anything more interesting than a long overdue copy of *Where the Red Fern Grows*, then made their way up a grand staircase with a peeling mural of the Ten Commandments painted on the wall. On the second floor they similarly checked each room until they got to the end of the back hall to the class where Mary Beth had once dissected a frog. It was the final one to be inspected, and the only room they'd encountered that was locked. Mary Beth tried peering through the door's mail-slot-sized window.

"See anything?" Izzy asked.

"Just some scattered junk. Looks like there's something lying over in the corner but I can't make it out."

Mary Beth took a few steps back and gave the door a vicious kick. It shimmied but didn't give way. "Shit!" she said, rubbing her hip.

"Let me try," Izzy said.

Neither he nor Mary Beth had a whole lot of weight to put

behind any door busting efforts, but Izzy was a third-degree black belt in Taekwondo and could muster the kind of strength that often surprised people. He backed up until he was flat against the far wall, took off at a run, leaped into the air and yelled like Bruce Leroy as he struck the door left of the handle with a flying kick that broke it clean off the hinges.

"Yeah," Mary Beth said. "Well, I loosened it for you."

Izzy had landed in an awkward split and was pretty sure he'd just torn a hamstring. "Appreciate it," he said.

Mary Beth helped him to his feet and they gave the room a look around. Didn't take long to determine there was nothing of note, other than some old roll-up wall maps over a missing chalkboard. The something Mary Beth had caught a glimpse of in the corner of the room was a double-bed-sized section of ceiling that had fallen in.

Mary Beth's face sagged. "I'm sorry," she said. "Sorry for dragging you out here. This was really stupid." She looked about as dejected as Izzy had ever seen her and he realized just how much Maria Ruiz must have meant to her. "That fortune teller's good," she said, shaking her head. "She really had me going."

"You want to pay her another visit?" Izzy asked. "We could run her ass in."

"Nah. Forget it. I don't want to give her the satisfaction. We've wasted enough time on this nonsense."

That suited Izzy just fine. The sooner they got back to civilization, the better. He followed Mary Beth back down the long hall and the main staircase near the front of the school and they were almost to the entrance when Mary Beth stopped and smacked her forehead. "Of course," she said. "The fallout shelter."

"The what?"

"It's an external basement, like a storm cellar. The entrance is out back. That's where they kept the frogs. Had them in cases inside a big refrigerator down there. I remember Ray Carson and I had to go help Mr. Tillerson bring them up to class."

"Come on, MB. You said yourself this was stupid. Let's get going."

But Mary Beth had that gleam in her eye again. "It'll just take a minute," she said. "Come on."

Izzy reluctantly followed Mary Beth to the rear of the school. They pushed the panic bar to open a fire door that they propped open with some rubble from the hallway to keep from getting locked outside. The back of the school was a narrow walkway on the edge of the plateau that looked down on some overgrown ball fields. They followed the path until they came to two large storm doors atop a triangular slab of concrete. It was the entrance to a fall-out shelter that Mary Beth said dated to the school's original construction in the sixties when the Cold War was at its hottest and everyone feared an imminent nuclear attack.

Mary Beth used two hands to lift one of the heavy doors while Izzy started getting hives, thinking about going down into a dark basement that reminded him way too much of his prior captivity in the Old Wengo Mine. He was struggling to think up a face-saving excuse not to go down into that black abyss when they heard the screams.

5

IT WAS CRAZY. INSANE. Totally nuts. But Mary Beth couldn't help it. Her first thought when she heard the screams coming from somewhere down in that fallout shelter was that it sounded like Maria.

Instantly, the sheriff's head flooded with images of her long-lost friend chained up down in that dank basement, somehow kept alive all the years since her disappearance. Mary Beth's heart thumped as she threw the heavy storm door aside, pulled her flashlight and shone it down into the black, revealing nothing but empty stairs.

"Sheriff's department!" she yelled. "Who's down there?"

A woman's voice cried out in response. "Help me! Please help! Hurry!"

The voice sounded different to her, this time. Less like Maria's, but in obvious need of rescuing, nonetheless. Mary Beth moved briskly down the staircase, with Izzy close behind. She maneuvered through a labyrinthine basement, serpentining around rectangular brick columns, panning left and right with her flashlight while doing her best to follow the screams past piles of broken desks and athletic equipment that loomed in the dark. She ducked below low-hanging exposed pipes and rounded a rusted boiler before she spotted the soft glow of burning candles near a lover's nest of sleeping bags.

Curled in the corner was a young, strung-out couple propped up against a warped bank of discarded lockers. The girl looked like she was maybe eighteen, scary skinny, with long, stringy brown hair and eyes that were deeply set in a gaunt face covered with cold sores. She continued screaming like her hair was on fire as she shook her comatose boyfriend. He appeared to be about the same age, was wearing a pit-stained tee-shirt and Hawaiian shorts, and had hairy, pimpled legs that flopped like a ragdoll as his girlfriend tried to rouse him.

"He's not waking up!" the girl yelled.

Mary Beth got close enough to see the drool dripping down the boy's chin. "What did he take?" she asked.

The girl was too frantic to answer intelligibly but pointed to a rusty spoon and needle lying near the sleeping bags.

"Heroin," Izzy said.

Mary Beth looked back to him. "Gimme your Narcan," she said, referring to the medication that, if administered soon enough, could counteract opioid drugs like heroin and oxycontin whose relaxing qualities were so effective they sometimes caused the body to forget to breathe. Since assuming jurisdiction over McCray County, with its all too frequent overdoses, Narcan had become standard issue amongst Mary Beth's deputies. She required them to keep it on them at all times.

Panic blazed in Izzy's eyes. "It's in my truck," he said.

Mary Beth received the news like a kick in the gut. "Shit." It could take fifteen, twenty minutes to get all the way there and back, even if you were really hauling ass. This boy didn't have that long. "You're supposed to keep it with you!" she shouted.

"Well, where's yours?" Izzy asked.

Mary Beth's was in her car, too, but that was beside the point. "Go!" she yelled.

Izzy spun around to leave but she seized his shoulder.

"No! Wait! I'm faster. Give me your keys."

Izzy reluctantly but quickly scrounged in his pocket, pulled out his keys, and slammed them into Mary Beth's outstretched hand. "It's in the back seat," he said.

"Lay him flat," Mary Beth commanded. "Rescue breaths until I get back. Two short, then one long one. Every five seconds."

Izzy made a pained face. He obviously wasn't going to enjoy giving the young man the mouth-to-mouth, but didn't dare delay. He got the boy in position, pinched his nose, pushed down his jaw, and went to work.

Mary Beth took off at a dead sprint.

Her flashlight beam bounced rapidly as she ran, making it hard to see. She rounded a turn and her shoulder clipped a brick support beam. It spun her around, but somehow, she managed to maintain her forward momentum, backpedaling then swiveling. When she reached the stairs, she took them three at a time. Driving up, up, up, until she erupted out into the daylight. From there Mary Beth re-entered the rear of the school through where they'd propped open the fire door. She flew into the dimly lit hallway, sliding on some loose papers. Mary Beth gathered herself, crouched into a sprinter's stance and dashed forward as fast as her legs would carry her.

Jesus, her chest burned. She hadn't run like this in years. Her legs already felt heavy, like they'd been tethered to a ball and chain. Every muscle fiber in her body screamed for her to slow down, stop and rest, but she managed to push through. Just four minutes without oxygen and brain damage could start to set in. Death would not be far behind. And who knew how long that boy had been lying there, not breathing before she found him. All Mary Beth could do was press on and pray that Izzy's rescue breaths would be enough to keep him alive until she got back.

But as she neared the entrance to the school, Mary Beth realized she had another problem. The only way out was back the way they'd come, through the window covered by a plank of plywood hung from the outside. There'd be no one there to hold it for her this time so she could wriggle through. Christ, just getting enough of a hold on the board from the inside to twist it open would be difficult. Mary Beth didn't have precious minutes to waste on trying to manage a graceful exit.

Instead, she lunged at the board, leaving her feet and twisting in the air so that her back struck the wood. It instantly broke free from the window frame and Mary Beth crashed down onto the school's stone porch, falling from a height of about four feet—more than enough to knock the wind out of her. But that wasn't the worst part. Her momentum was such that she tumbled forward, down the long stone staircase, having to cradle into a ball to protect her head as she bounced along like a runaway boulder, plummeting faster and faster, until ejecting into the air off the bottom landing and coming down hard in the soft mud.

There she laid in the weeds, gasping for air, bruised and battered, and thankful to be alive. If only she could lie there and rest. But an unforgiving summer sun beat down from between the mountain walls like God shining his spotlight on her, telling the sheriff: *Thou shalt get your bony ass up and move.*

Mary Beth growled as she struggled to her feet. She lurched through the muddy, weed infested field, managing only a slow trot at first, but picking up speed, slopping and splashing forward. She pulled the keys from her pocket and mashed down the remote button until she heard the little chirp and doors click open. With difficulty she scrambled up into the elevated driver's seat then collapsed inside the cab, feeling like she might vomit from exhaustion. Her chest heaved so hard it felt like her lungs might explode.

Izzy broke in over the walkie with a burst of static. "Hurry, MB. He's dying!"

Mary Beth glanced in the backseat and saw the medical kit. She seized it. Then she looked up at the school, all the way atop that daunting hill. She didn't have it in her. There was no way she could climb all those steps. Not in time.

"We're losing him!" Izzy shouted.

Mary Beth tried fecklessly to catch her breath but she was panting like an overweight bulldog on a hot day.

That's when a crazy idea struck her. One that Izzy certainly wouldn't like.

"Fuck it," Mary Beth mumbled. She slammed the key into the ignition and cranked the powerful engine to life. "Sorry, Izzy," Mary Beth said, then mashed the gas pedal to the floor.

The Blazer took off like a bull out of the chute, tires spinning and mud flying as it charged angrily across the field. When Mary Beth hit the long staircase, the front tires popped up into a massive wheelie that would have made Colt Seavers proud, then crashed back down where the four-wheel drive grabbed hold and propelled the Blazer upward, climbing the staircase so quickly Mary Beth wasn't able to stop in time to avoid smashing through the front doors of the school and wedging the truck inside the archway.

"Fuck." One thing was for sure, Mary Beth realized, she'd better save this boy's life, because Izzy would kill her for what she'd just done to his truck.

She tried to open the driver's door, but the front of the cab was flush against the entryway. Mary Beth thought about throwing the truck in reverse and gunning the engine to free the Blazer but feared that if she pulled loose, she'd end up reversing all the way back down the steep staircase again.

Instead, she cut the engine, climbed into the back seat, opened the back door and dropped to the ground. From there she crawled beneath the monster truck, between the front tires and into the school.

And then she ran.

Mary Beth ran without stopping until she reached the back stairs, readying her flashlight as she approached. Once she got to the fallout shelter, she hopped down the stairs, four or five at a time.

"Hurry!" Izzy yelled from off in the distance. Mary Beth tore through the dark basement, winding around and bouncing off pillars, following the girl's screams and Izzy's shouts until she caught sight of the still burning candles. Once there Mary Beth collapsed to her knees and handed the medical bag to Izzy like a relay baton, before she began to dry heave.

Izzy wasted no time administering the Narcan shot. He quickly inserted the needle into the boy's arm and pushed down the plunger.

Then they waited.

Mary Beth collapsed and rolled onto her back. Her body shook from exhaustion as she stared up at the ceiling.

The girl shouted, "It's not working!"

"Just give it another minute," Izzy said.

"No! I can tell. It's not working," she said,

"Just a minute, it—" Izzy's voice trailed off, then he said. "MB, I'm not getting a pulse."

Mary Beth managed to push herself up onto her elbows, just enough to see the boy and the sad look on Izzy's face.

"No!" the girl screamed.

"Ma'am, I'm—" Izzy started to say, but the girl charged at him, trying to snatch her boyfriend away. Izzy held out an arm to block her and it was at that moment that the boy sat up.

He coughed twice, spit out some bile and black liquid, then made a gurgling noise, followed by a gasp, and several failed attempts to swallow. The boy's hands moved toward his throat but didn't make it past his collarbone before his eyes rolled back in his head and he collapsed onto Izzy.

"He's aspirating," Mary Beth shouted. "Heimlich!"

Izzy was lying on his back with the boy on top of him. He

wrapped his hands around the boy's waist and began violently pressing in on his stomach while Mary Beth helped get them both to a seated and then standing position.

Izzy was really giving it all he had but nothing was dislodging. "It's not working!" the girl screamed again.

This time she was right. The boy's face and lips were turning blue.

"Do something!" the girl shouted.

Mary Beth tried to think. She went to the medical kit while Izzy continued to try and clear the boy's airway. She looked to see if there was an EpiPen. There wasn't. But there was an ink pen, kept there to record any emergency drug usage and it gave Mary Beth an idea.

"Izzy, lay him down on his back."

"What are you going to do?" he asked.

"Just do it," Mary Beth commanded.

Izzy gave the boy one last really good Heimlich compression, lifting him up with it, but when that didn't work, he complied, laying the boy on the ground.

The girlfriend fell to her knees and prayed.

Mary Beth knew the boy had choked on some of his own vomit, forming a plug somewhere down in his throat, through which no air could pass. The only way to save his life was to give him another airway. Mary Beth unscrewed the ballpoint pen, taking off the hollow cap and dropping the rest to the floor. Then she pulled out her pocket knife and flipped it open with her thumb in one smooth motion.

"What are you doing?" Izzy asked.

"Just hold his head back."

Mary Beth brandished the knife. The girlfriend covered her eyes.

If there'd been more time, Mary Beth would have sterilized the blade over the candle flame, but she figured infection was the least of this kid's worries at that point.

"Do you know what you're doing?" Izzy asked.

No. Not really, Mary Beth admitted to herself. She had read about emergency tracheostomies before, but she'd certainly never done one. Sharing that truth would not engender confidence, however, so she lied. "Of course," she said. "Now hold him still."

Izzy tightened his grip on the boy. Mary Beth felt his neck. She searched for the indentation between the boy's Adam's apple and Cricoid cartilage. *Shit, is that where it's supposed to go?* She wasn't entirely sure but prayed to God she was right as she jammed the knife in and made a half-inch incision.

There was surprisingly little blood. *That's good,* Mary Beth thought. That meant she'd avoided the jugular vein.

Now for the moment of truth. Mary Beth flexed the flap of skin to create an opening. Then she inserted the pen, put her lips to it, and began to blow.

6

"TWO PUFFS OF AIR AND THE KID just opens his eyes like he's waking up from an afternoon nap. Can you imagine?" Izzy was leaned up against a vending machine at the Jasper County Hospital, sipping on a styrofoam cup of black, burnt-smelling coffee, shooting the shit with his brother Bobby, who despite being six-foot-two, still was, and always would be, Izzy's little brother.

"That's crazy," Bobby said. "That Sheriff Cain is something else." Bobby was wearing some grease-stained coveralls, having come straight from his auto body shop after getting a 911 text from Izzy. "Do me a favor though, would you?"

"What's that?" Izzy said.

"Next time you message me to come to the hospital for an emergency, how about you let me know that it's your truck we're talking about. I thought you were hurt."

"I am hurt," Izzy said. "Did you see what Mary Beth did to my baby? She busted it all to hell."

Bobby waved off the comment. "All cosmetic, man. A little body-work. Fix up the front end. She'll be good as new."

Izzy spotted Mary Beth, marching down the hall alongside a bearded, white-haired doctor in OR scrubs who was untying his face mask. She pointed at Izzy and motioned for him to follow.

"Be back in a sec," Izzy said to his brother. He followed Mary Beth and the doctor through some automatic glass doors to the outside, where the girl they'd found, whose name they now knew was Julie, was seated on a park bench. She was chain smoking a soft pack of crumpled Kools. When Julie saw them she dropped her limp smoke on the asphalt without bothering to stomp it out and rushed to meet them.

"Well?"

"He's stable," the doctor said.

"Does that mean he's gonna be okay?"

The doctor sighed. "He went a long time without oxygen. We can't be sure yet what the long-term effects of that will be but early signs are good. He's responding to stimuli … I'm optimistic."

Julie wrapped the doctor in an overbearing hug. "Thank you, doctor. Thank you so much."

The doctor blushed as Julie released him. She turned to Mary Beth with tears in her eyes. "Thank you too, Sheriff."

Mary Beth tipped her hat like it was no big deal. Julie came at her for a hug but Mary Beth seized her hands. "You're welcome," she said, then nodded to Izzy, who slapped on the cuffs.

"What the hell?" You're arresting me? For what?"

"For the drugs we found," Mary Beth said. "Plus, breaking and entering."

Julie jerked her shackled hands free of Mary Beth's grip and Izzy grabbed hold of her collar to make sure she knew she wasn't going anywhere.

"This is bullshit!"

"Listen," Mary Beth said. "I know you can't make bail so you're gonna get three squares a day for a couple of weeks and a chance to get clean. And we'll make sure you have some methadone to take the edge off the nausea and the shakes. You ever tried to kick before?"

"Yeah," the girl moaned. "It was awful."

"Well, we're gonna be there to help you through it this time. You're eighteen now, Julie, and could be looking at real time if convicted. But I'm gonna talk to the DA for you. He's getting ready to retire in a couple weeks and is cutting a lot of deals right now. I'm sure he'll agree to get you into a drug treatment program in lieu of prison as long as you keep clean."

The tears started pouring down the girl's face like she'd just been tasked with the impossible. Mary Beth pushed her chin up. "Don't you give me that cry baby shit. You hear me? You've got your whole life ahead of you and you're gonna beat this, right?"

The girl nodded tentatively.

"Julie, if you don't, I'm gonna kick your ass. And you know I can do it too," Mary Beth said.

Julie smiled slightly, tears still streaming down her cheeks, and nodded more convincingly this time. "Yes, ma'am."

"That's better." Mary Beth turned to Izzy. "Goforth should just be coming on duty. See if you can get him to come pick Julie up. I know your ride's got some … issues … right now."

A couple smart-ass remarks occurred to Izzy that Mary Beth would have appreciated if nobody else was around. But since they were being all official at the moment, he simply said, "Will do, Sheriff."

He sat with Julie on the park bench and let her cry it out on his shoulder until Deputy Goforth came and took her away.

When he went back inside to check on what Mary Beth was up to, he found her still lingering around the waiting room, talking to Bobby, who said, "Yeah, sure Sheriff. I've got a sledge hammer."

Soon after that the three of them were in Izzy's busted-up truck, stopping by Bobby's garage to pick up a sledgehammer, for reasons Mary Beth wasn't sharing, then heading back to the Cierra Middle.

"Look," Izzy said, as they pulled into the muddy, weed covered lot outside the school, "we've come all the way out here, in my poor injured vehicle, in the middle of the night. Before we go back in that creepy-ass school, I think we deserve to know what's going on." Izzy pointed up to the dilapidated structure that towered over them like a gothic torture castle, backlit by a full moon.

"Quit bumping your gums, and let's get a move on," Mary Beth said.

Izzy folded his arms. "Not until you tell me what this is all about."

Mary Beth switched on her flashlight and held it beneath her chin like a camp counselor telling a ghost story. "I'd rather show you," she said, employing her Count Chocula voice.

Izzy looked to his brother Bobby for backup but he just shrugged and said, "We're already here, right?"

Bobby opened his door and dropped the heavy sledgehammer kerplunking down into the mud, then hopped down after it. Mary Beth jumped down as well and Izzy cursed them both under his breath, while doing his best to catch up after descending more slowly, by use of his rope ladder.

He really wanted to give Mary Beth an earful as they trudged up the steep staircase leading to the school, but since Bobby was carrying the sledgehammer, didn't feel he had a right to complain. Once they finally reached the landing, though, as everyone paused to catch their breath, Izzy couldn't resist remarking on the gaping hole in the wall Mary Beth had created by crashing his Blazer into it earlier that day.

"Surprised you didn't want to just drive on up the steps again and save us some time."

"Well," Mary Beth said, pointing to the smashed entranceway, "at least we won't have any trouble getting inside this time. You're welcome."

She led them over splintered wood doors and broken glass, across the threshold and down the long hallway to the rear of the school where the fallout shelter was located.

"Back down there?" Izzy groaned.

"Yep," Mary Beth said.

Bobby sat the sledgehammer down, and wiggled his tired arm. Izzy picked it up, to give him a break, and bit his tongue as he followed Mary Beth back down the stairs, through the catacombs below until they reached the spot where they'd found the overdosing boy.

Izzy dropped the sledgehammer, making a loud ping against the concrete floor. "Okay," he said. "Now what?"

Mary Beth shone her flashlight on the curled up sleeping bags the young couple left there. She stood next to them, then turned her flashlight on the warped bank of lockers leaned against the wall and ran the beam all the way up to the ceiling. "Remember when we were sitting at the hospital, waiting for the doctor to come out?"

"Uh, yeah," Izzy said. "We were just there."

"Remember how I told you that I kept seeing it in my mind, how that boy sat up all of a sudden and his eyes rolled back in his head?"

"Yeah, I guess so. What about it?"

"Well, it didn't register with me at the time but as I was lying there trying to catch my breath from where I'd run to get the Narcan shot, I was looking up at the kid, and staring right at this." Mary Beth panned her light past the lockers again to the bare gray wall just below the ceiling.

Izzy didn't see what she was talking about.

Bobby didn't either. "What are we looking at, Sheriff?"

"Look around," Mary Beth said. She panned the basement with her flashlight. "The walls all the way up to here are cinderblock. Until you get to the end here. The lockers mostly cover it, but you can see this part here is drywall."

Bobby moved closer. He was tall enough to reach above the lockers and ran his hand over the section of drywall Mary Beth was illuminating. "Pretty shoddy work too," he said. "They didn't even bother doing the seam. Looks how it's separating over there."

"Kind of like somebody threw this up awful quick, wouldn't you say," Mary Beth added.

Izzy saw it now too. "And why drywall this one little section when the whole rest of this place is exposed block?"

"Exactly what I was thinking," Mary Beth said.

Now Izzy knew why they'd brought the sledgehammer. "You're thinking you're gonna find Maria Ruiz's body behind this wall, aren't you?"

"I don't know," Mary Beth said. "Could be as empty as Al Capone's vault. But I thought we'd at least take a look."

Izzy smiled, and nodded to his brother.

"Oh, okay. Right now?" Bobby said.

"No time like the present," Izzy said. "The sooner we get out of here the better."

Bobby lifted the sledgehammer, holding it with two hands, one at the base of the hilt, the other up just below the hammer.

"Wait a second," Mary Beth said. "Izzy, help me move these lockers first."

She and Izzy pushed the bank of lockers, screeching like fingernails on a chalkboard as they scraped along the floor, and leaned it up against the adjacent wall.

"Go high," Mary Beth said. "Right in the middle. Just in case there is a body lying on the other side. I don't want to disturb it any more than we have to."

Bobby gave the wall a solid whack about six feet off the ground. The hammer sank into the drywall, leaving a hole big enough to stick your head into. He reared back with the hammer, ready to give it another go before Mary Beth stopped him.

"Hold on," Mary Beth said. "Can you see in there?" She handed Bobby the flashlight.

"Yeah, I think so." Bobby stood on his tippy toes shining the light into the hole.

"What do you see?" Izzy asked.

Bobby was moving the flashlight back and forth, trying to stand tall enough to peer down.

"Not much."

"Nothing?" Mary Beth asked.

"It's…"

"What?" Izzy demanded.

"It's just more hallway."

"How far back does it go?" Mary Beth asked.

"Not far, Sheriff. Few feet is all. I can see the back wall."

"Can you see anything else?" Izzy asked.

"No," Bobby said. "Just a concrete floor and cinder-block walls."

Bobby came down off his toes and handed the flashlight to Mary Beth. "What do you wanna do now, Sheriff?"

Mary Beth looked disappointed, but said, "Might as well tear it down and take a closer look."

"You got it," Bobby said.

He gave the wall six more whacks before Izzy and Mary Beth started tearing at the sides of the holes he'd made and cleared a space big enough to squeeze through.

Mary Beth went through first, followed by Izzy. Bobby was right. Or at least it appeared so at first. The only thing Izzy saw initially was a few extra feet of hallway. But at the back, on the left, was a little alcove the size of a phone booth. Mary Beth shone her light around the corner, then took a step back, clapping her free hand to her mouth. Izzy caught up to her and saw it too. A petite skeleton, still mostly intact, positioned sideways inside the alcove, arms hugging knees, wearing what appeared to be a soot covered tracksuit. There was still some long dark stringy hair attached to the skull.

"Holy shit!" Bobby got a glimpse at the corpse and turned away like he might be sick.

"What's that around the wrist?" Izzy asked.

Mary Beth bent down to get a closer look. "Rosary beads," she said. "Maria always carried them around with her." Her voice sounded unusually gruff, like she was doing her best to keep it together.

"Guess we better get forensics in here before we contaminate the scene," Izzy said.

"Yeah," Mary Beth agreed. "Just one thing I need to do first." She reached in her pocket and pulled out a pair of medical gloves she must have snaked from the hospital. She snapped them on and delicately reached underneath the collar of the corpse's shirt. She pulled loose a necklace of some kind.

"What is it?" Izzy asked, suspecting he already knew the answer.

"It's the little ladybug locket Maria used to wear."

It was just like the fortune teller predicted. Izzy didn't know what to say or think.

Mary Beth stood and wiped a tear from her cheek. "Goddamit," she said. "I hate always being right."

7

WITHIN AN HOUR, MARY BETH had four more deputies at the old abandoned school. They were taping things off and searching the grounds but Mary Beth wouldn't let any of them near the basement. She knew her best, and perhaps only, chance of finding Maria's killer was to recover some minuscule deposit of DNA evidence from the corpse and Mary Beth wasn't taking any chances on her guys bungling this with their typical dipshittery. They'd need the most cutting-edge scientific techniques law enforcement had to offer. So as Mary Beth and Izzy sat in the cab of his big Blazer, they started discussing the possibility of bypassing the always backlogged state crime lab and going straight to the top, by having dispatch connect them with the FBI center in Clarksburg.

"You think they'll be willing to help?"

Under normal circumstances, maybe not, but after the way Mary Beth saved the Feds from disaster during the Old Wengo brewhaha, she had some serious sway with the g-men.

"I got some favors I can call in," she said.

Izzy slowly nodded in agreement. He pressed in the side

button of the CB. "Forget the crime lab," he told dispatch. "Hook us with Clarksburg."

It took over an hour before they finally got to the right person. Once they did, Mary Beth was able to light some sufficient fires under butts to get a team in-route that night. ''No piddle-assing," she told them. "I'm not leaving till y'all get here."

By the time the techs made the three-plus-hour drive and finished up their work it was after four am, which, late as it was, still hadn't been enough time for Mary Beth to figure out how she was going to break the bad news to Guadalupe. For nearly a decade, the old lady had faithfully made weekly trips to the Iglesia, lighting candles for her granddaughter, praying she was still alive.

"Want me to break the news?" Izzy asked.

Mary Beth patted his hand. That was a sweet offer. "Nah, I need to do it," she said.

"Well, when you do, remember the lab techs said we'll need to swab Guadalupe for DNA to make a positive ID that the body in there is Maria's."

Mary Beth nodded. She understood, though that all seemed like a formality. Considering where and how they'd made this discovery, and the fact that the body was found wearing a black tracksuit—the same clothes Maria was last seen in—along with rosary beads and the ladybug locket, with what appeared to be a photo of Maria's parents in it, there wasn't much question as to whose remains they'd found. Might as well have had a birth certificate pinned to her chest.

"Guess the whole pregnant bullfrog thing wasn't so crazy after all," Izzy said.

"Yeah. Guess not." Mary Beth shook her head in disbelief.

She was really mystified. How had the fortune teller known about that pregnant bullfrog? And how in God's creation did she know mentioning it would get Mary Beth thinking about the abandoned junior high school where she'd done that dissection all those years ago? More importantly, how did the old lady know they'd find the body there? The whole thing was blowing Mary Beth's mind.

"Maybe we should start using a psychic on all our cases," Izzy said.

Mary Beth frowned, not sure how to feel. "Don't know about that," she said. "But I'm definitely planning on talking to her again."

She may not have known how in the hell the so-called "Mountain Mystic" knew what she seemed to know, but one thing was for sure, Mary Beth wasn't willing to just chalk it all up as genuine clairvoyance. At least not yet.

As the lab techs packed up their silver metal cases, she ordered Deputy Goforth to go pick up the fortune teller and bring her in for a sit down.

"But it's not even dawn, Sheriff," Goforth complained.

"So? You should be able to get the drop on her, don't you think?"

Goforth looked like the only place he wanted to go was to bed. "What if she don't wanna come?"

Mary Beth was too tired to explain the subtleties of police procedure right then, especially to someone who should know better. "Then arrest her."

"For what?"

"Shit, Goforth, I don't know," Mary Beth said in the middle of a yawn. "She just led us to a dead body, didn't she? Use your imagination."

"You actually want me to book her?"

Mary Beth rolled her eyes. It was really grating how dense some of these guys could be. "No. Just do whatever you have to do to get her to the station. Then keep her in the box until I have a chance to talk to her on my turf. We'll cut her loose after that."

"How long will that be?"

Mary Beth stretched out her arms, feeling like she might sleep for a week if she ever got the chance to lie down. "Until I catch a little shut eye."

"S'pose she calls a lawyer?"

Mary Beth snorted. "Take a look at where you are, Goforth. You think anybody living out here knows a lawyer? Now get moving."

Goforth waddled off, muttering under his breath and Mary Beth turned her thoughts back toward Guadalupe. She really was not looking forward to that conversation. Checking her watch again she decided that given the hour she'd be more than justified in procrastinating a little while longer by catching a few hours of sleep first.

The sun was already peeking over the tree-covered mountains by the time she caught a lift back to the station to get her Camaro. She rolled down the windows on the drive home, catching the smell of fresh bread cooking up over at Mitzy's Bakery and started rehearsing in her mind how she'd tell Guadalupe the news. *Sit her down and hold her hand and just give it to her straight in your most calm, compassionate voice. Then go in for the hug and let her cry it out.* It would be tough, but in some ways Mary Beth felt it was an honor to be the one to do it. She was the sheriff. The rock. The one everybody else could depend on.

When Mary Beth finally got home, she knew she needed to sleep but there was still too much adrenaline pumping through her veins so she set an alarm for ten a.m. and fished a half-empty whiskey bottle out of the trash can. Since the Old Wengo fiasco and the death of her brother, Mary Beth had been hitting the bottle a little too regular, so the night before she'd decided to take a week off from it. But if the events of the last twenty-four hours didn't call for a little shot of hooch, then what did? Mary Beth poured herself a double, knocked it back, then poured another just to be sure she could get to sleep. Then she returned the bottle to the trash can, where it belonged, determined to now go at least ten days before her next drink, just to make sure she wasn't developing a problem.

When Mary Beth awoke a few hours later she felt like she'd barely slept at all. She stood and stretched, her bruised and swollen limbs reminding her of every one of the stairs she'd rolled down the day before. She hobbled to the kitchen and took a seat at the breakfast nook, surveying the damage her body had absorbed. As she did so, she also realized she was shaking off a feeling of Bill—a presence so intense she could almost smell his musk in the room. Must have dreamt about him, she figured—though it would have been the first time in years. Maybe her subconscious was reaching out to her, wanting to tell Bill about this major discovery in the case that had tortured him so.

What a creature of habit Bill had been, keeping to routines like they were religious rituals. Every morning he'd get up while it was still dark to work out with the weight-set he kept in the garage—the cheap kind with gray plastic dumbbells full of sand. Then by seven a.m. he'd be showered and dressing while Mary Beth was still lying in bed, trying to steal some extra sleep before facing the drudgery of another day. That's when Bill would usually slip in behind her and start feeling her up—his idea of foreplay.

She felt a little guilty now about how she'd usually rebuffed those advances. It wasn't that she found Bill unattractive, mind you. It's just that in the scales of her heart, if you weighed the opportunity for a few bonus minutes of shut-eye versus some nookie, it was no contest. Mr. Sandman would slam his side of that balance to the table every time.

At least that was what she used to tell herself.

But there were also the evenings when Bill would try a per-functory back or foot rub for a few seconds before sliding his hands to the more interesting areas, and even then, she'd usually fight him off with an assault of the unending to-do list, the business of the upcoming schedule, or all the things they needed to buy and didn't have, which Bill would inevitably take as an attack on his manhood—his ability to provide—and thus would soon sulk off to the living room to spend the evening in front of the TV drinking beer. It was no wonder they'd never managed to give Sam a sibling.

Looking back on it, she'd denied Bill to the point that if she'd ever caught him up at Mountain Flowers rolling around with one of the trollops who worked the trailers out back of the strip club, she could hardly have blamed him.

She'd have fucking killed him.

But she wouldn't have blamed him.

Mary Beth never had to worry about such things with her Bill though. He was as reliable as April rain. The book on him was simple. Just three chapters: Work, family, community. One of the things she loved about him: he was as simple as she was complicated.

As Mary Beth sat at her kitchen table sipping her coffee and rubbing her sore calves, she started feeling more and more guilty about it all, like she'd never really loved Bill the way he deserved.

Why was that? She wondered. Bill'd been quite the catch by Jasper Creek standards, an all-state football player and son of the sheriff, who'd basically inherited that vaunted position at a young age following his father's disabling heart attack. And, despite a broken nose that was never set quite right, Bill was ruggedly handsome. By contrast, Mary Beth was just the cute, skinny little hillbilly girl with a twangy voice and way too much pluck for most men's taste. From the outside looking in, Bill was out of Mary Beth's league, yet it was always him reaching out for her and her pulling away.

With the enhanced perspective of time and distance she

realized part of her frequent denials had been due to a simple lack of comfort. Something inside that told her things were temporary. If she'd ever gone to see the therapist Izzy kept pushing on her, she'd probably trace it back to a fear of male abandonment, having lost her drug dealing daddy to a police sniper's bullet when she was just thirteen. And that may have been it. Regardless of the reason, though, Mary Beth just always had a nagging feeling in her gut that it wouldn't last.

In her more masochistic moments, she'd admit part of her had always harbored a secret fantasy that her first love, Patrick Connelly, who'd gone on to Georgetown and become a big-time lawyer in DC might one day ride back into town and sweep her away from her life of domestic servitude. But that was mostly pipedream. She never would have honestly guessed she'd lose Bill so young, and to a bullet, the same way she'd lost her father. The gaping wound that kind of loss left inside a person was one thing she understood all too well. Which was probably why she was still dragging her feet on delivering the news about Maria.

Putting it off wouldn't make it any easier, though. Mary Beth decided it was time to rip off the band-aid. Shoot, the way gossip spread in a small town, if she didn't get to Guadalupe soon, the rumor mill might beat her to it.

So, after showering and dressing, Mary Beth set out, cruising through town, still feeling kind of dreamy as she took in the sights.

It was going to be another hot day. Some ladies were setting up big Gatorade coolers on a card table at the corner by the library and the tiny amphitheater, indicating temperatures expected to climb past ninety, which was a rare enough event in that high elevation town that the Chamber of Commerce gave out free lemonade. They'd done so twice already that summer, which was a record for June. *Maybe there is something to all that global-warming talk*, Mary Beth thought, as she rolled past

Jasper Creek's first Starbuck's—proof to the city planners their little town was officially on the map.

From there she headed out of Jasper Creek proper toward where Guadalupe lived on the other side of the railroad tracks—an area that was still the non-white part of the county despite the official end of segregation generations earlier. There was a trailer park there near the old one-room Cool Rock post office. The park was officially named The Oaks, but everyone called it the Barrio now, as it was mostly inhabited by members of Jasper County's growing Latino population.

Guadalupe had a nice double-wide near the back, under the canopy of a weeping willow tree. Her lot stood out by how extremely well-kept it was, owing to the fact that half Guadalupe's grandsons worked landscaping jobs and made sure their *abuela's* lawn stayed professionally manicured. Mary Beth parked next to a faux marble bird bath surrounded by white rocks and planters full of posies.

It was supposed to be Mary Beth's day off so she was in plain clothes, thin linen pants and a white cotton top that she now thought was too low cut for this occasion. She felt a little naked without her uniform.

When Mary Beth got to Guadalupe's door she swallowed twice, letting her fist hang in the air for a moment before she knocked.

No answer at first.

Mary Beth thought about leaving and trying again later. She hadn't noticed Guadalupe's car out front, but knew the old lady usually parked her Monte Carlo in back. Mary Beth gave the door another gentle rat-a-tat and heard some movement inside. She took a deep breath as she heard the deadbolt slide open.

The door swung outward.

What Mary Beth saw next made her stomach drop.

8

"SAM?"

Mary Beth was staring at her college-aged son in his T-shirt and boxer shorts, hair all a mess, crust in the corner of his eyes, standing there in the home of his eighty-year-old former nanny.

"Mom?" Sam had a guilty, deer-in-headlights expression. As disgusting as it was, Mary Beth's first thought was that he looked like he'd been caught shacking up.

"What in the hell are *you* doing here?" she asked.

Sam was on summer break from college but *supposedly* had decided to stay on campus to take some extra classes, despite Mary Beth's pleas for him to return home.

"Um …," Sam stammered and started fidgeting, nervously tapping the side of his leg.

He had always been a weird kid–bookish, socially awkward, and probably a little on the spectrum. Growing up, he had been much closer with Bill, with an affinity that went much further than the typical allegiances of gender. Bill got to come home from work each day like a conquering hero and throw him so high in the air it had to feel like flying. Meanwhile, Mary

Beth was the beleaguered housewife, a task master who yelled a lot and made sure Sam kept up with his chores and ate his vegetables.

"I'm waiting for an answer, Sam," Mary Beth said.

"Oh...I...um.... Well, Guadalupe's not here. She went to the store, I think."

"Good to know," Mary Beth said. "My question is what are you doing here? I thought you were taking summer classes."

"I was. I am. I just...."

"Just what?"

Sam's fidgeting intensified. Mary Beth seized hold of his hands, forcing him to stop tapping and look her in the eyes. "Just what, Sam?"

He pulled away and glared at her. "God, nothing. I just got a little homesick, that's all."

That was the lowest of low blows. Mary Beth felt like a horse had kicked her in the chest. It would have been better to find her boy shacking up with his octogenarian former nanny than to be confronted with the fact that he simply preferred her to his own mother.

"So come home, then." Mary Beth said, unable to prevent the crack in her voice or the tears welling in her eyes.

"Come on, Mom. Don't cry." Sam moved toward her and she pushed him away. The little bastard wasn't going to hug his way out of this one.

Mary Beth had never been Miss Popular, but the last eight months since the Old Wengo Affair, she had felt especially lonely. Her always-sharp elbows and crotchety disposition had ramped up considerably during that time, and thus her deputies—even Izzy to some extent—had been doing their best to avoid her. But Sam was the one person who should understand. They had the shared trauma. They were the ones who knew the truth of what went down the night Mary Beth's crazy brother Sawyer broke into her home seeking revenge. He'd beaten Sam that night and was about to kill Mary Beth before Sam recovered his mother's gun and shot Sawyer in the chest enough times to close the Moonshine Messiah's maniacal eyes for good. To be sure there'd be no repercussions for her boy, Mary Beth had arranged the scene and coordinated the story that she was the one to fire the fatal shots. Because she was the sheriff and Sawyer was a well-known shitbag, the shooting was deemed justified with little ado. Now this was the thanks Mary Beth got from her little ingrate offspring.

"Look, it's no big deal," Sam said. "I just wanted a few restful days, you know. A chance to veg-out a bit. And when we're together it's always…"

"Always what?"

Sam hesitated before answering. "Work."

Work? Work was the twenty-two hours of labor Mary Beth had endured to bring the little shit into the world.

"Well bless your heart," Mary Beth said." You poor thing." She was about to lay on a heaping dollop of guilt when she caught the faint whiff of something emanating from the kitchen. Her nose shot into the air like a bloodhound. A cold chill ran up Mary Beth's spine. "What's that smell?"

Terror flashed across Sam's face. "What smell?"

"Samuel Huff Cain, you know exactly what smell I'm talking about."

Sam tapped chopsticks against his leg. "No, I don't."

That was bullshit. Sam could smell it and Mary Beth could too. She felt a tempestuous fury rise up inside her.

"You know exactly what I'm talking about, Samuel. That's banana pancakes isn't it?"

Sam swallowed hard. "Uh…no."

"Yes, it is Sam. Don't tell me it's not. I can smell it. Guadalupe made you banana pancakes–*my* special breakfast."

Sam made a feeble attempt at an incredulous expression. "You're crazy."

"Crazy huh? Out of my way." Mary Beth brushed her son aside and stormed through the living room, past the sectional couch and into the kitchen.

"Well, ho-ly dog shit."

There it was. Right in the middle of the table, stacked on a plate of navy Fiestaware. Perfectly circular, silver dollar-sized banana pancakes.

Mary Beth snatched one off the plate and shoved it in her son's face. "What's this?" she demanded.

Sam stared at the floor. "A banana pancake."

"A banana pancake. And why is Guadalupe making you banana pancakes, Sam?"

"Because they're my favorite?"

Mary Beth nearly spit in his face, she was so angry. "I know they're your favorite. My question is why is Guadalupe the one making them for you?"

Sam faced his mother like a novice matador confronting his first bull. "Mom, please don't get mad. I was just feeling kind of down and Bela Lu wanted to do something to cheer me up. It's no big deal."

"No big deal," she said quietly. Mary Beth sniffled, switching from angry to wounded—the two most powerful weapons in her mother's arsenal. "No big deal. Tell me something, Sam, if it's no big deal then why are you lying to me about it?"

"Look, Mom—."

"If it's no big deal, then why is it that instead of coming to your *actual home* when you feel a *wittle* homesick, you come here?"

Sam teetered, shifting his weight from one foot to another. "Um...I don't know."

"You don't know? That's all you have to say to me? After I have devoted my life to raising and protecting and providing for you, that's all you have to say?"

Sam stuck his thumbs inside his boxer shorts and ran them

along the waistband like he wished he had some pockets to plunge his hands into.

"I guess?"

I guess. Mary Beth had been hurt a lot in her life. She'd lost her father. She'd lost her husband. Shit, she'd even taken the rap for shooting her own goddamn brother. But nothing had ever hurt quite like this. It was like she'd walked in on the love of her life with another woman, only worse. A lover could always choose someone else. *But your child?* That was the one person who had to love you. The one person you had to love. You couldn't just trade up if you didn't like the way things were going. When Sam was a little baby with colic and didn't sleep through the night for the first eighteen gawd-awful months of his life, did Mary Beth take him back to the hospital and try to switch him out for another kid? *Hell, no!* Yet here he was, in some other woman's home, asking *her* to make *him* banana pancakes.

"Well, this is just great," Mary Beth said. She could feel the moisture welling around her eyes again. She elbowed Sam out of her way and headed toward the front door.

"Where are you going?"

Mary Beth stopped. For the briefest of moments she knew she was about to say something out of anger she would later regret, but preventing it would have been like trying to stop a locomotive, and Mary Beth made no attempt to apply the brakes.

"When your precious Bela Lu gets back, tell her to come see me down at the station. I found Maria. She's dead."

9

MARY BETH STILL HAD a pretty good case of the red ass by the time she got to the station. She was in the mood to yell and Deputy Goforth gave her an excuse when he told her he'd been unable to find the old psychic lady who'd led them to Maria's body.

"Goddammit, Goforth. I gave you one fucking job to do!"

"Well shoot, Sheriff. The old lady's psychic. I guess she knew I was coming and skedaddled."

Mary Beth palmed her forehead. "You're telling me there was no sign of her there at all?"

"None that I could see."

"You sure you were at the right place?"

"Yes, ma'am. Knew right where you was talking about. I been up there before communing with my mama after she passed."

Mary Beth did her best to ignore that statement. "And you were there at what time?" she asked.

Goforth stroked his mustache. "I'd say it was around five this morning. Banged on the doors awful good. Took a long walk around, shining my light in the windows where I could.

Come back and banged some more." Goforth turned up his palms. "Nada."

"How long did you wait?"

Goforth sucked on an invisible straw. "Gave it a good hour, I reckon. Went back and sat in my cruiser."

"You didn't fall asleep did you?"

"Come on now, Sheriff."

Mary Beth was beside herself. She wanted to talk to this psychic now. "You see any vehicles around?"

"El Camino," Goforth said. "Tires as flat as a ten-year old girl."

Mary Beth didn't appreciate the simile but decided not to make a thing about it. "How about a four-wheeler?" she asked. "Would have been parked right near the old clunker."

Goforth stroked his stache some more. "Nah. I'd a seen that Sheriff. There weren't no four-wheelers around."

"Well, then I guess we got us a runaway psychic on an ATV. Think you can go find her for me?"

Goforth stretched and said through a yawn, "I been on near sixteen hours, Sheriff."

Mary Beth was feeling awfully punchy herself. Her natural reaction was to want to throw something at her deputy, but she refrained, realizing he was right. Before she could say anything else, Deputy Skipwith gave a quick knock on the office door as he rolled in a dolly loaded with banker boxes. "Got the Ruiz file out of storage, Sheriff."

"Good," Mary Beth said. "Put it in the corner over there."

"Geeze, I'd hate to have to read through all that," Goforth said.

Mary Beth looked on him more kindly, feeling less on edge now that she had something to do, namely combing through boxes of Bill's old reports. "You get on home and get some sleep, Benny," she said, referring to Ben Goforth by his Christian name.

"You sure, Sheriff?"

"Yeah. Sorry I was so hard on you just now. This one just hits close to home, you know."

"Sure, Sheriff," Goforth said. "We all know. I remember back when Mr. Bill was working it. He felt the same way you do. Said she used to babysit your boy and come over for Sunday dinners and such."

Mary Beth smiled. Something about the deputy seeing her in the same light as Bill warmed her heart. "Well, maybe we'll have a bit better luck this time around."

Goforth nodded and it seemed like they were all on the same team again.

"You get going now," Mary Beth said. "Go get some rest."

Both men turned to leave. Mary Beth said, "Hang back a minute, Skipwith."

The skinny deputy stopped and slinked into the corner as Goforth sauntered off. "What do you need, Sheriff?"

"Need you to head on up to Scarburry Hill. Stake out this fortune teller. Give it till the end of your shift. If she doesn't show by then, come back and put a BOLO out on her."

"You think she's mixed up in the girl's death?"

"I don't know what to think. All I know is, I want to talk to her. Now you go ahead and get, and let me get to reading."

Skipwith left and Mary Beth tore into the case file. She had a habit of starting a new legal pad every time she took notes, so that she'd end up having about twenty going at a time. Some might say it was a waste of paper but something about a fresh pad seemed to help her think. She pulled a blank one from a desk drawer and wrote Maria Ruiz's name at the top in all capital letters. Below it she wrote Maria's date of birth, the date of her disappearance, and her age at the time—twenty years old.

After that she began skimming through Bill's voluminous reports, writing down names and dates she wanted to remember. For a case with no physical evidence and no real eyewitnesses of any significance, Bill had managed to fill reams of paper with narrative accounts of his investigation. If the guy stopped to take a piss during his shift, he'd have written it down somewhere.

A couple of hours into her review, Izzy showed up. He was supposed to be off duty too, and thus was also dressed in his civilian clothes, which in Izzy's case consisted of cargo shorts and a Game of Thrones t-shirt. Mary Beth immediately noticed his worried expression.

"What's up?"

"Press has already caught wind," Izzy said. "And I swear it didn't come from me."

Izzy's wife, Princess, was a field reporter for the local news station. It was a connection they'd often used to their advantage by strategically leaking information. On other occasions, like this one, the relationship served as a helpful warning when things were about to hit the airwaves.

"How'd they find out?"

Izzy shrugged. "Don't know. Guess the leak is alive and well."

Last fall, when the Charleston paper was running their "Rough Justice" exposé on Mary Beth and what they called her "extra-legal" methods, she and Izzy both concluded someone within the department must have been feeding them information. The temptation by some was to point the finger at Izzy since his wife worked for the regional NBC affiliate, but Mary Beth knew better. She'd witnessed the receiving end of enough of Princess's tirades to know that Izzy didn't tell her shit. "He might as well be married to you," Princess would say to Mary Beth. "He tells you more than me."

"How much do they know?" Mary Beth asked.

"They know about the body is all. Don't think they know who it is yet."

The control freak inside of Mary Beth hated any information slipping into the public sphere without her say so. Plus, keeping things under wraps could give her an advantage when questioning potential suspects.

"Can Princess get them to sit on it for a day or two?" she asked.

"Said she'd do her best to buy us twenty-four hours, but no promises."

Mary Beth sighed. "Well, guess we better get to it then. Take a box." She kicked one of the untouched banker boxes in Izzy's direction and they both dug into the files.

The deeper Mary Beth got into the reports, however, the more she realized there wasn't much there. Three-fourths of the files recounted how Bill had exhaustively run down the possibility that Maria had taken off and was still alive somewhere. Mary Beth knew that obviously wasn't the case and put all that stuff aside. She would go back through it later because you never know what you might learn that could be useful. But for now, she wanted to focus on the prime suspects. Unfortunately, that list consisted of just one name.

"Pedro Kowalski."

"Who's that?" Izzy asked.

"Maria's ex-boyfriend. I met him once when he took Maria to the prom. Just knew him as Pedro. Didn't know his last name was Kowalski."

"What is that, Polish?"

"Yeah, I guess. Sure didn't look it though."

"What was he like?" Izzy asked.

Mary Beth shrugged. "Pretty quiet as far as I can recall. But, of course, Bill was giving him that psycho cop, pseudo-step-dad-routine. You know, all that 'be on your best behavior or else' stuff."

"You remember anything else about him?"

"Not really. I remember Maria saying he was smart. It says here that at the time Maria went missing, he was a student at Marshall."

"Thought you said he was smart."

Izzy and Mary Beth shared a laugh. The Chief Deputy's

criminal justice degree was from West Virginia University, the state's flagship institution, and although Mary Beth's only diploma came from the school of hard knocks, she too was a big mountaineer fan who enjoyed putting Marshall in its place.

"Looks like he was the only smart one in his family," Mary Beth said. "Apparently his cousins were all mixed up with some wanna-be gang bullshit. Got some drug busts, grand theft, assault. Nothing on Pedro through. He kept his nose clean. Oh, here we go, though, this is interesting."

"What's that?"

"Pedro's older brother was Raul Kowalski, a truck driver who got busted in Arizona transporting cocaine."

"Shill for the cartel?"

"Sounds like it. He cooperated with the Feds and helped them get a conviction of Alberto Diaz, a lower-level captain for the Solares Cartel." Mary Beth paged ahead in the report. "Here's the really interesting part. The Diaz conviction was just three months before Maria's disappearance."

Izzy whistled.

Mary Beth flipped through the next few pages like something must be missing. "Just ends there. Bill's report says a reliable confidential informant confirmed that Maria's disappearance was not retribution for Diaz."

"That's it? Doesn't say anything more?"

"Nope."

"Nothing about who the CI was or why they were confident it wasn't drug related?"

Mary Beth skimmed some more. "Nothing. Whoever this CI was, Bill must have been serious about keeping his identity a secret. Doesn't even name his handler. Do you know who was running drug snitches back then?"

Izzy stroked his chin. "Your old buddy Randy Law, maybe. He used to work the city park where most of the stuff went down in those days."

Mary Beth groaned. Randy Law was an ex-cop who had been Bill's best friend, but hated her guts. "You know he won't talk to us," Mary Beth said. "The guy was best man at my wedding and won't even speak to me now."

"Well, you did shitcan him."

"He deserved it," Mary Beth said.

Randy was a good-ole boy and an unabashed chauvinist who'd had trouble accepting a woman sheriff. Thus, after Bill died and Mary Beth took over, one of her first official acts was to present Mr. Law with a pink slip and two weeks severance.

Izzy shrugged. "Regardless, I don't really see this being a retribution murder. Somebody kills the snitch, fine. Then I'm thinking it's a payback hit. Maybe even if they kill a member of his family. But offing the snitch's brother's girlfriend? That seems a little too protracted."

Mary Beth considered that. "Yeah, you're probably right." She paged through the report some more, hoping to find something more promising.

"Where's it go from there?" Izzy asked

"Nowhere really. Bill's back to the Pedro angle. Got a bunch of interviews here from people who say Pedro was the jealous type. Always thought Maria was cheating on him."

"Was she?"

Mary Beth frowned. "Nothing confirmed in here. But truth be told Maria was a bit of a flirt. I could see it. She's stuck here in this small town, working as a hairdresser while her beau's off at school. Probably bored out of her mind. Wouldn't be surprised if she stepped out on him."

"Well, whether she did or not. Still doesn't mean he killed her."

"Come on, now Izzy. You've seen enough episodes of "Dateline" to know it's always the husband or boyfriend. Although Pedro's college roommate alibied him for the weekend Maria disappeared. What have you got over there?"

Izzy stuffed a stack of papers back into the banker's box he'd been working on. "There was a witness who reported seeing a conversion van parked near Maria's car at the city park that had the characters SXL in the license plate. And this box is filled with reports on basically every single van in the country with those digits. Bill ran them all down and, as far as he could tell, none of them were anywhere close to Jasper Creek when Maria disappeared.

There was a knock on the door and Mary Beth's secretary, Vanessa, stuck her head in. Mary Beth's heart sunk at the sight of her. Vanessa was another of Guadalupe's granddaughters, a cousin to Maria, and Mary Beth hadn't thought to break the news to her personally.

"Is it true, Sheriff?" Vanessa asked.

"Shit." Mary Beth stood and went to her, saying, "I'm so sorry, Vanessa. I should have come to tell you. I just got caught up with everything."

Vanessa covered her mouth. Tears rolled down her cheeks as Mary Beth embraced her.

"Thank you, Sheriff," Vanessa whispered. "At least we'll finally know what happened."

"There's still a lot of questions," Mary Beth warned. "We haven't even confirmed for certain it's Maria. But it appears to be. We'll use DNA to verify it once your grandmother gets here."

Vanessa wiped away her tears. "That's what I came to tell you. *Abuela.* She's here."

10

GUADALUPE DIDN'T COME ALONE. Sam was there too, arm wrapped around his sweet Bela Lu's waist, propping her up. He avoided making eye contact with his mother who averted her gaze as well, focusing her attention on Guadalupe instead.

Mary Beth's former housekeeper/nanny, was a short, squat woman with leathery skin that hung to her tired bones, weathered from a lifetime of hard work. She must have been at the beauty parlor when Mary Beth went by her trailer that morning because her hair was freshly cut in a short, layered kind of pixie cut that was dyed burnt orange. The old woman was doing her best to keep a stiff upper lip but Mary Beth could tell she was overcome with emotion.

She didn't know exactly how many grandkids Guadalupe had—at least twenty in the States—but she knew Maria was the one she'd been closest with, having raised her from a young age after her parents died. Losing Maria must have felt just like losing a child. Mary Beth knew she should have been the one to tell her they'd found the body—mother to mother. She owed Guadalupe that. But her jealousy and temper had gotten the best of her that morning, causing her to drop the bomb on Sam instead.

Guadalupe reached for Mary Beth's hand in an awkward gesture, turned it over like she might kiss it, then gripped Mary Beth's elbow and lurched forward, pulling her into a hug.

Mary Beth gently patted Guadalupe's back. "I'm sorry my friend," she whispered. "I'm so sorry."

Guadalupe sniffed loudly. "Can I see her?"

Mary Beth hesitated. They would need Guadalupe to identify the clothing and things they'd found with the body, especially the locket with the photo inside of, presumably, Maria's parents. But Mary Beth wasn't sure the old woman could stand the sight of her once beautiful granddaughter reduced to rotted sinew and bone.

"Please," Guadalupe said, "I need to see her."

Then again, how could Mary Beth deny her? The body was currently at the county coroner's office awaiting the FBI's expert pathologist who was en route from DC. As deteriorated as Maria's remains were now, they were about to be poked and prodded and disassembled even more and perhaps carted off to God knew where. This might be Guadalupe's only chance to lay eyes on her granddaughter's final remains.

"Of course," she said. "We'll give you a ride."

"I'm coming, too," Sam blurted.

"This is official police business," Mary Beth snapped.

Izzy gave her a disapproving look. "The FBI tech will need to do a cheek swab of Ms. Angeles while we're there, so they can use her DNA to confirm the body we found is Maria's. We'll also need to see if you can identify some personal effects recovered at the scene. But I don't think it will hurt if Sam comes along. Having some emotional support can be really important at a time like this. Don't you agree, Sheriff?"

Before Mary Beth could respond Vanessa chimed in. "I'm coming, too."

"No problem," Izzy said. "That's a good idea."

Vanessa and Sam moved next to Izzy, pulling Guadalupe to their side, all facing Mary Beth who was clearly outnumbered. She forced a polite smile. "Great," she said. "Let's all go. One big happy family."

When Mary Beth and crew presented themselves at the coroner's office that morning, they were met at the door by Dr. Bashid Patel, a bald, bespectacled man who was known for two things: smoking like a forest fire; and cursing more than an insult comic on cable.

"What's with this goddamn, fucking FBI, bullshit, huh?"

Dr. Patel was obviously unhappy about having to wait for an FBI pathologist before beginning *his* autopsy. Mary Beth knew this was gonna be a thing, so she motioned for Izzy to take Guadalupe, Sam, and Vanessa down the hallway where one of the FBI techs they'd met the night before was seated on a folding chair outside the exam room. Then she ushered Dr. Patel into his office.

"Nice to see you too, Doc," Mary Beth said.

"Don't you fucking smart-mouth me." Dr. Patel plopped down in a burgundy leather chair behind his desk, where he already had half a cigarette burning in the ashtray but went ahead and lit up another for good measure. "Little fucking, snot nose, piss ant G-Man telling me I can't work on my own goddamn corpse. Who's the motherfucking coroner here, huh?"

"You're the coroner," Mary Beth assured him. "It's your autopsy. I told them you were the best."

Dr. Patel put his second cigarette down, teetering on the ashtray rim. He noticed the other still burning there and picked it up for one last puff before smashing it out.

"So why do I need to wait for this goddamn guy?"

Mary Beth took a deep breath. She didn't like being yelled at, but knew this was just Dr. Patel's way. Back in the day, he'd actually been Sam's pediatrician—believe it or not—before a substance issue forced him to voluntarily surrender his medical license for a while. It was quite the scandal at the time, but nobody had ever questioned the quality of Dr. Patel's treatment or how much he cared about his kids—a sentiment he'd usually expressed by cussing out the parents who'd allowed them to get sick or injured in the first place. It was Mary Beth who helped get him appointed coroner, where he didn't technically need a license to apply his medical expertise. Since then he'd proved to truly be an excellent forensic examiner. But in big cases the prosecutors always shied away from letting him testify, afraid his past troubles would hurt his credibility with a jury.

"We can't take any chances on this one," Mary Beth said. "I need the FBI expert to participate in the examination in case he needs to testify."

"Fucking bullshit." Dr. Patel lit another cigarette, letting this new one hang on his lower lip as he talked. "I been clean 10 fuckin' years. And even when I wasn't I was the best goddamn doctor in this town. But you don't want me to testify?"

"It's not that, it's—"

"Don't you fucking patronize me."

Mary Beth sighed. "I'm just worried a jury may not appreciate your winning personality."

"Fuck you."

"Back at ya, smokey."

Dr. Patel stared at Mary Beth for a moment, the cigarette nearly dropping from his lip, then cough-laughed. "Good for you," he said. "You never take no shit, do you? I always liked that."

"Thanks," Mary Beth said.

Dr. Patel's attitude softened after that. He adopted a more collegial tone, saying, "You're seriously wasting your time with the Feds, though. I can tell you right now how the girl died."

Mary Beth took a seat opposite Dr. Patel. "Do tell." She crossed her arms, drawing attention to the nasty scrapes and bruises gained from her tumble down the Cierra Middle School staircase the day before.

Dr. Patel shot up and moved quickly around his desk, pulling Mary Beth's arm toward the light to get a better look. "How'd you get those marks?"

"Ah, it's nothing. Little fall is all."

Dr. Patel gave her his, you-better-not-be-bullshitting-me look. "Woman comes in all busted up, saying she fell, usually means some son-of-a-bitch smacked her around."

Mary Beth had to laugh at that—it had been so long since she'd had a man. Not to mention the fact she'd rip the nuts off any guy who ever raised a hand to her. "Well, in my case it's the truth. No sons-a-bitches in my life. None at all. Now, finish what you were saying about the cause of death."

Dr. Patel held Mary Beth's gaze for a moment like he was trying to decide whether or not to believe her, but eventually released her arm. "That's easy," he said. "Gunshot. Back of the head. Right around the crown. Angled down. Execution style." Dr. Patel put a two-finger pistol to the back of his head and dropped his thumb. "Bam. Took me about one second to spot it before that jackass out there told me I had to wait for their guy. Hole about this fucking big in the skull." Dr. Patel made a quarter-sized circle with his finger and thumb.

Execution style? That didn't sound right. Mary Beth's gut told her Maria's death would turn out to be a sex crime. She figured somebody'd snatched the fair Ms. Ruiz in the park, had their way with her, and killed her to keep her quiet. In the file Mary Beth reviewed earlier, Bill had compiled all criminal complaints taking place at the city park where Maria was last seen. They were all drug related, save for an old date rape charge against a guy who was living in California at the time of the Ruiz disappearance. No muggings or sexual assaults or other reports of women being harassed in the area as of that time. But before she left the station, Mary Beth had asked Deputy Jenkins to update

Bill's research for more recent reports of crimes at the park. And Jenkins was also supposed to pull the record of everyone who had been charged with rape or sexual assault in the past eight years. Mary Beth had a pretty strong suspicion that the son-of-a-bitch she was looking for would show up in one of those searches.

"Could it have been blunt force trauma that caused it? Maybe somebody hit her in the back of the head with a rock or a bat or something?"

Dr. Patel looked at Mary Beth like she just asked if he wouldn't mind cramming one of his lit cigarettes up his ass. "No fucking way. I know what a fucking bullet hole looks like. Besides, I saw the jawbone lying on the table out there and it's got a semi-circle gap in the bottom of it. Nice and symmetrical. Angle should match up just right. That's your exit wound. Right out the neck, above the throat."

"How can you tell which is the entrance and which is the exit wound without any skin to examine?"

Dr. Patel had lectured Mary Beth in the past that, despite what you see on the "bullshit TV," the exit wound was not always larger than the entrance wound. He'd also told her that the way you determined the entrance wound with an execution-style contact shot, where the muzzle is pressed against the body at the time of discharge, was by the tattooing of the skin from the gun's burning propellant. Here that was impossible because there was no surviving skin to examine.

"Cause there's a lot of dried blood on the chest of the jacket she was wearing. Didn't see any on the back except for a little crusted up in what's left of the hair, right around the bullet hole. And there's some scuffs around the pant knees. This lady was kneeling down when she got tapped out from behind. Real professional. Then she falls forward and bleeds out. Fucking execution."

Mary Beth shuddered at the thought of Maria down on her

knees with a killer's gun pressed to her skull, knowing her life was about to end.

"I need the slug to be sure," Dr. Patel said, "but from the size of the hole, I'd say it's consistent with a nine-millimeter. May-be forty-five. But more likely nine-millimeter cause it's a relatively small hole. But a handgun definitely. A rifle or shotgun would have blown the back of her fucking skull open."

"What about a twenty-two?" Mary Beth was thinking about how common those were with younger folks around Maria's age at the time. Kind of a starter gun for a lot of people.

Dr. Patel made a sucking noise. "Could be...but I doubt it. Not gonna have the power to go through the skull, then all the way through the brain and out the chin, chipping the jawbone." He fanned his glasses up and down on the bridge of his nose, picking up steam with his opinion. "No. Most twenty-two's use hollow tip bullets. When a hollow point penetrates the skin, the bullet's torn all to hell. Stays inside the body." Dr. Patel shook his head the more he thought about it. "No, I think twenty-two's gonna get lodged inside the brain somewhere and stay put."

Okay, so no twenty-two. That still didn't narrow it down much. Nine-millimeters and forty-fives were two of the most popular caliber bullets on the market and the myriad of hand-guns that fired them were about as common in West Virginia as finding a Gideon Bible inside a hotel nightstand.

"Fuckface out there said you didn't find any slugs or casings at the scene."

Mary Beth frowned. "That's right. At least not that the techs have told me about." She knew that without a slug, they'd never be able to match a gun to the bullet hole in Maria's skull. They could rule some out, perhaps—like rifles and 22's— but a posi-tive match would be impossible.

Dr. Patel lit up another cigarette. "See. We don't need no bull-shit FBI. Now, how about you let me go do my job?"

Mary Beth hesitated. She knew Dr. Patel really was good

and she wanted his insights on this, which is why she insisted he be able to perform a joint autopsy with the FBI's pathologist to begin with. (They'd have preferred to just cut him out of the process altogether.) But, if they ever did catch the killer, she knew an FBI hotshot would carry a lot more weight with a jury. And besides, this wasn't a typical autopsy. All the tissues and organs had decomposed. Anything the experts could learn from Maria's remains at this point would require a much more high-tech analysis than Dr. Patel's typical shoot-from-the-hip approach could provide.

"Tell you what—" Mary Beth started to say, when she was interrupted by wails coming from down the hall.

Guadalupe.

"Shit," Mary Beth said. The FBI agent must have gone ahead and let them view the remains. "Hang on." She left Dr. Patel in his office and hurried down the hall where she found Guadalupe and crew in the viewing room, peering at the remnants of Maria through a plexiglass window, her bones splayed across a metal exam table like a museum exhibit. Guadalupe had swooned and fallen backwards from the shock. Sam and Vanessa were holding her head just off the herringbone patterned floor. Tears streamed freely down all three of their faces.

Guadalupe's shaking hands were clutching a photo. When Mary Beth knelt down to try and help raise and console her friend, Guadalupe shoved the photo in her face. It was Maria at her Quinceañera, dressed like a Disney princess in soft blue sequins, a sparkling tiara perched prominently in her wavy brown hair, her smile full of silver braces.

"What they did to my baby girl," Guadalupe wailed.

"We'll catch whoever did this, Bela Lu," Sam said, hugging the old lady. "We'll make them pay." Then he looked up at Mary Beth. "Won't we, Mom?"

Sam was staring at her with an earnestness she hadn't seen from him in a long, long time. Mary Beth couldn't help it. No amount of cop could keep her heart from melting. She put her arm around Sam and joined the other three in a group hug. "Of course, we will," she said. "You can count on it."

11

MARY BETH WAS SITTING in her Camaro watching Izzy trying to tell his wife, Princess, he needed to blow off their plans to accompany Mary Beth on his day off. The tense domestic scene gave the sheriff a sense of anxiety like back when Sam was in Little League and she wished to God she could just go out there and hit the damn ball for him. Izzy and Princess were standing outside the local news station about fifteen yards away. Izzy had his hands slapped together in a prayerful gesture, pleading his case to Princess who was all hands-on-hips and shaking her head.

Mary Beth rolled down the window to see if there was something she could say to help the situation.

"But baby," she heard Izzy say, "I'm protecting the public."

"What you need to be *pro-tecting* is your *marriage*," Princess responded. "We've been planning this for weeks."

"I know, but this is a really big case."

"So?"

"So, how many times have we had to cancel dinner plans because you get called about a story?"

Izzy got his wife to pause with that one, then followed up with, "Besides you've been saying how you need to spend more time with your mama. I'm sure she'd love to go with you." Before Princess could say anything else, Izzy added, sounding extra sweet, "And you know—MB and I are gonna be up there near where they make that Fenton glassware you like. I could pick you up something real pretty."

Princess threw her head back. "Oh, you think it's like that, huh? You just buy me something shiny and that makes it all okay?"

"Maybe not *all* okay," Izzy said. "But it doesn't hurt."

Mary Beth detected a smidge of a smile spreading across Princess's face. With her pageant looks and model height, Princess would stand out in a crowd no matter who she was with, but next to her husband who was nearly a foot shorter, it was hard to take your eyes off her. Mary Beth was staring, thinking about what the fortune teller had said about how everybody had a little vestigial psychic ability that allowed them to feel when they were being watched, when Princess glanced upward and the two women made eye contact.

"Shit." Mary Beth tried to look away but knew she'd been made.

"Hiiiiiii, Sheriff," Princess called over to her.

Mary Beth gave Princess an embarrassed little wave. Then the reporter said to her husband, "Okay, here's what's gonna happen. I'm gonna forgive you breaking yet another date with me. But when you two crack this big case you're working on, you're gonna give me exclusive access to the story. Understand?"

"Baby, you know I'd only talk to the best reporter in the business."

"Ummm, hmmm." Princess was trying to look mad, but Mary Beth could tell she was letting Izzy off the hook.

He craned his neck, puckering like a kid asking for a kiss. Princess was still giving him a little stink eye but she bent down and pecked the chief deputy on the lips. "Go on," she said. "Go have fun with your friend."

Izzy wasted no time saying his goodbyes and bounding for the Camaro. He slid into the passenger seat, eyes gleaming like a teenager whose parents just left him home alone for the weekend. "Ready to roll?" he asked.

"Does the pope shit in the woods?"

"Okay then, let's hit it."

Mary Beth cranked the ignition and the Camaro roared to life. "You got the address?"

Izzy pulled out his smart phone and read it off to Mary Beth.

Prior to going to the coroner's office, the investigative plan had been to wait on the lab techs to do their thing and then see where it led them. The hope was that some DNA could be recovered from the corpse that the FBI would plug into its massive database, the Combined DNA Index System, or CODIS, which held the life combination on more than eleven million people who'd been convicted of crimes. But after the scene with Guadalupe and Sam at the coroner's office, Mary Beth couldn't just sit around and wait for the federales to save the day. She needed to get busy doing *something*, anything, even if it was just for show. So, she and Izzy decided the obvious place to start would be with Maria's old boyfriend, Pedro.

Only Pedro was no longer Pedro.

He was now Peter. And not just Peter, but *Doctor* Peter Kowalski, an orthopedist who was part of a multidisciplinary medical practice near Parkersburg, about three to four hours away, in the northern part of West Virginia, up near the Ohio border.

Once Guadalupe had calmed down some back at the coroner's, she was able to tell them what little she knew about Pedro's current whereabouts. Mary Beth had broached the subject by commenting about how Guadalupe always knew what was up with all the Latinos in Jasper Creek, which caused Guadalupe to scoff, "He's a white boy."

Guadalupe had gone on to explain how Pedro's mother, who was from Jalisco and sufficiently non-white, had married Pedro's father, a Caucasian dude who was now well into his sixties and retired after making a bunch of money selling mining equipment. Pedro had "grown up white" according to Guadalupe. It wasn't until he started dating Maria that Pedro/Peter tried connecting with his roots, hanging with some of his "Chicano cousins" who had moved there from Arizona and were a rough bunch.

"He can't even speak Spanish," Guadalupe complained. According to her, Pedro rarely came back to Jasper Creek. It was Vanessa who'd heard he'd become a doctor. Then a google search produced a hit for a Dr. Peter Kowalski. A quick look at the bio picture, and Mary Beth, who'd remembered Pedro as a teen, remarked, "Son of a bitch changed his name."

She'd showed the picture to Guadalupe who said, "See? White boy."

Regardless of his current cultural identification, if Mary Beth and Izzy wanted to interview Pedro before close of business, they really needed to get the move on so Mary Beth had her lead foot firmly engaged, taking out just enough time to swing through a Wendy's drive-thru on the way out of town to pick up the first meal she'd had all day. Her stomach alarm was growling so loud she was pretty sure she could have eaten the ass end out of a hippopotamus right about then and figured the square-shaped burger she scored wasn't all that much different, nutritionally speaking. Meanwhile, Izzy, ever frugal, opted for the dollar menu, feasting on "chickenless" nuggets and a junior frosty.

Not bothered by the interruption of driving, Izzy finished his meal by the time they hit the on-ramp for I-77, and started reading through the rest of the file on Pedro as Mary Beth serpentined through cars on the highway, while sucking down fistfuls of French fries.

"Sounds like Guadalupe's take on Pedro hasn't changed much," Izzy commented. She'd told them back at the coroner's office that despite any offense she may have taken from Pedro's "whiteness," Guadalupe didn't think he was a bad kid. A good student who was always polite, she'd said. She didn't know anything about Pedro ever getting violent with Maria and quite frankly didn't think he had it in him. His cousins on the other hand—they were a different story.

Mary Beth slurped down a drink of her Coke. "Where'd the abuse allegations come from then?" she asked.

Izzy paged back in the report until he found the name. "One of Maria's girlfriends. Laura Keenan. You know her?"

Mary Beth didn't.

"Said she saw Pedro at a party, grabbing Maria by the shoulders, shaking her and threatening to kill her."

"Well, that sounds relevant. How long before she disappeared?"

Izzy studied the file. "Just a week before. They were visiting him at Marshall. Were at a fraternity party when it happened. Instead of spending the night like they planned, they ended up driving the whole way home that evening. Laura says she tried to find out afterwards what was going on but Maria refused to talk about it. Said she was real upset."

That was a lot more incriminating than Mary Beth suspected they'd find in the old file. "So, one week before Maria disappears, Pedro threatens to kill her?"

"Sounds like it."

"What's his story about what went down?"

Izzy skimmed some more. "Doesn't really have one. He gave his alibi for the weekend Maria disappeared. Stayed at school with his roommate, Denny Williams, who vouched for him.

Then he lawyered up and refused any further interviews. And he refused to take a poly."

Mary Beth finished her last fry and curled the wrapper on her burger back enough to hazard a bite while holding the steering wheel with her knee. "That's interesting," she said, her mouth full of food. Personally, she didn't put much stock in polygraphs. The results were never admissible. But they were often an effective way to elicit a confession. Tell a perp they failed a lie detector and a lot of people thought they were cooked and would just give it up. And, regardless of their technical reliability, Mary Beth always viewed a suspect's willingness to take a polygraph as its own kind of candor test. It always got her hackles up when a person refused.

Izzy said, "Pedro turned into a brick wall after he hired an attorney. Bill couldn't get him to talk and didn't have enough to charge him with anything."

"Who was his lawyer?" Mary Beth asked.

Izzy moved his finger quickly down the page until he found a name. "Oh, boy. Your main man, Alexander Pomfried."

Mary Beth nearly choked at the name of her nemesis. Alexander Pomfried was, far and away, the most successful criminal defense attorney in southern West Virginia, and a vociferous critic of Mary Beth. In fact, he'd won a number of acquittals by attacking the sheriff's "methods" as unconstitutional.

"Well, shit my britches," Mary Beth said.

Izzy closed the file. "So, what's our play with Pedro?"

Mary Beth bit off another hunk of her square burger before answering. "The usual," she said. We'll make him think we know a lot more than we do and see if he sweats."

"I'm guessing you're the bad cop and I'm the good cop?"

Mary Beth grinned and said, "I'm not sure we're gonna need a good cop."

12

THE LADY AT THE FRONT DESK was a big country-looking girl with loosely curled, somewhat matted, sandy brown hair and a long, sloped forehead. She wore pink Hello-Kitty medical scrubs like she might be called away from her web surfing into a surgical operation at a moment's notice.

"Do you have an appointment?" she asked, clicking away on her mouse, staring at the monitor with mock confusion.

Since Mary Beth and Izzy were in plain clothes, there'd been nothing as of yet to tip the lady off they were there on official business, until Mary Beth plopped her badge down on the counter with a tinny ring and said, "Honey, I don't need an appointment."

The woman's eyes went big as silver dollars at the sight of the star. "Let … me … just see if Dr. Kowalski's still here."

When she left, Izzy cautioned Mary Beth, "Just remember we aren't in Jasper County, okay?"

"What's that supposed to mean?"

"I'm just saying we don't really have anything on this guy at this point and he is a doctor after all. The kind of guy who's got the resources to make a stink during an election year. You know what I'm saying?"

"I'm running unopposed."

"You don't know that for sure yet. The County Commission extended the filing deadline to July first and I've heard a couple of them have been out recruiting somebody to run against you."

"Whatever. If you think I'm going to back off because—"

"Look, just be professional, okay? That's all I'm asking."

Before Mary Beth could answer Izzy's insulting little reminder, Dr. Pedro "Peter" Kowalski, popped into the reception area. He was dropping off some walk-out papers from his last patient of the day and looked right at Mary Beth like he recognized her but wasn't quite sure why.

"*Hola*, Pedro." Mary Beth showed him her badge. "Sheriff Cain from Jasper County. You remember me? Maria's senior prom? You forgot to bring her a corsage. That wasn't very thoughtful, Pedro."

Pedro nodded. Now he remembered.

"This here is Chief Deputy Baker. How 'bout we go have a talk?"

In the three or four seconds that followed, Mary Beth decided she didn't like this guy, none. His eyes morphed way too quick from deer-in-headlights to smoldering contempt, then knee-deep into a metaphor-mixing, shit-eating grin.

His once thick, lush, hair, always oiled up with styling goop, had receded like the Carolina coast in the years since Mary Beth last saw him, stopping its descent near the center of his noggin—the anterior fontanelle, as it were—with a little island of twisty curls down around the forehead.

"Please," he said, pointing toward a private hallway. "Let's go to my office."

Mary Beth said, "After you."

Regardless of Izzy's warnings, she knew this was a big moment that called for a little of her particular brand of magic. Pedro had a history of lawyering up and shutting down. Catching him off-guard like this was maybe the only chance she was going to get to squeeze some new information. So, when the doc closed the door to his office, motioning for his guests to take a seat in the black leather slingbacks facing his metal desk, Mary Beth decided to kick off the questioning with something that was sure to shake him right from the start.

"You been enjoying your freedom since Maria disappeared, doc?"

Pedro looked like he damn near swallowed his Adam's apple he gulped so hard. He put his hand to his stomach like it had been sliced open and was trying to keep his guts from spilling out. "Uh … Eh … Excuse me?"

In unison, Mary Beth and Izzy lounged back in their seats, Izzy staring the doctor down while Mary Beth eyed his ego wall with disdain, showing she didn't think much of the degrees and certificates he had hanging there.

"Maria Ruiz," Izzy said.

The doctor took a deep breath. "God, not this again. I've been through this before."

Mary Beth said, "Well, things are different now, *amigo*. We found her body."

Pedro clasped his mouth. He reached behind him, trying to find his chair and still nearly missed it when he sat.

Mary Beth and Izzy stayed quiet for a minute—watching. If Pedro was acting, he was doing a good job of it. Mary Beth saw about six different emotions quiver across his face.

"My God," he said, finally. "Where did you find her?"

Izzy answered, "Found her buried in the basement of an old, abandoned school. The Cierra Junior High out in what used to be McCray County. You know it?"

"No," Pedro said.

"You sure?" Izzy asked.

"Yeah, I'm sure," Pedro said, sounding defensive.

Izzy fired back at him, "What about your cousins?"

"What about them?" Pedro snapped.

Izzy and Mary Beth looked at each other, taking note of the rise that question had elicited. Izzy said, "We know a few of them work landscaping jobs. Any of them ever cut grass out there?"

"No, I … I don't know. I don't think so."

This was the part of the interview where Mary Beth would usually push her hat back to show some exasperation, then lean forward with her "let's-cut-the-shit" question. Out of habit she reached for her forehead now, realizing her hat wasn't there, and played it off by brushing her curly bangs out of her eyes. "Well, which is it doc?" she asked. "You either know or you don't know."

Pedro was flustered. "I, uh, I think … maybe I shouldn't say anything else without my attorney present."

Ding, ding, ding. An alarm always went off in Mary Beth's mind when someone asked to lawyer up. Once a suspect invoked the right to counsel the textbook said to back off, but Mary Beth knew that the second Pedro talked to an attorney, his lips would be forever sealed. This was her one opportunity to convince him to talk.

She leaned back again, this time propping her leopard-print kitten heels on the doctor's desk. "Well, that's your right," she said. "This is mostly a courtesy call, anyway. Won't be much need for witness interviews once we hear back from the lab. Techs tell us that Maria's body was just crawling with DNA." Mary Beth turned like she was stretching her neck and shot Izzy a little wink where Pedro couldn't see it. "Once we get that. Just put her in the computer, and—beep, bop, boop—it'll spit out the name of our killer. Almost not even fair, is it Deputy Baker?"

Izzy didn't miss a beat. "Nope," he said. "There's been a lot of advancements in DNA since Maria went missing. Crooks weren't as careful back then."

Mary Beth said, "We were hoping maybe you'd get one of your nurses here to go ahead and do a little blood draw that we could take with us. Save us the time from getting a warrant and all. What do you say to that?"

Pedro looked from one officer to the other. "I really think I should call my lawyer."

Mary Beth sighed like she'd heard people make this same mistake a thousand times. "You? You probably should, Pedro. If you're guilty that is. People who are guilty always need a lawyer. What do you think, Deputy Baker?"

Izzy stared at Pedro like he was appraising a cut of meat. "I don't know. What you said is true of course. I'd probably lawyer up if I was guilty. Unless … "

"Unless what?" Mary Beth asked.

Izzy shrugged. "That's just the classic mistake people make if they're guilty of *something*—but just not guilty of *everything*. Sometimes they're just a part of the story and there's other players involved. If that's the case, they'd be much better off fessing up, and doing it before it's too late."

Mary Beth knew where Izzy was going. He was reacting to how defensive Pedro got at the mention of his cousins. His instincts were telling him that—as Guadalupe had said—Pedro might not have it in him to do something like press a revolver to a beautiful young woman's head and pull the trigger, but maybe he knew someone he could get to do it for him.

"Gets to be like a game, doesn't it?" she said to Izzy.

"Sure does," he responded. "First one to squeal wins."

Mary Beth added, "Sometimes they win immunity from prosecution, or at least a lesser sentence." Then she took her feet off the desk and leaned forward, flaring her nostrils, looking as serious as a stage-four cancer diagnosis when she said, "Everybody else, though Pedro—the ones who clam up and let somebody else squeal first. They win something too. Wanna know what they win?"

Pedro didn't answer. Mary Beth didn't care. She said, "They

win an all-expenses paid, lifetime stay at a pound-em-in-the-ass penitentiary."

Izzy shot her a look like she'd just stepped over the line. Which, maybe she had, but if ever there was a time to do so, now was it. She knew that if the Feds' search for some usable DNA came back empty, then Pedro would be the only lead they had in this case, and this was her one opportunity to squeeze something out of him.

"Pardon my language, Pedro. That wasn't very lady-like. I just hate to see someone with so much going for him make that kind of mistake. A guy like you in a place like that." Mary Beth shivered.

She could tell Pedro was scared. He also had a look like he wanted to say something but just hadn't been pushed quite hard enough yet. She asked Izzy, "You remember that Danzig fella who refused to roll over on his buddies who robbed that liquor store? The one where they killed the clerk?"

Izzy gave her a stern look. "No."

It wasn't an answer to her question, Mary Beth realized. Izzy was telling her not to go there. But she went anyway. "He was just the getaway driver, remember?"

Izzy shook his head. She knew he knew this story, but he said, "Maybe, we should get going, Sheriff. Since *Doctor* Kowalski doesn't want to talk." He emphasized the title, reminding Mary Beth that she wasn't in Jasper Creek anymore, and this wasn't some country bumpkin she was about to threaten.

"In a minute," she said, waving Izzy off. "So, anyway, Pedro, this Danzig fella, he didn't hardly have nothing to do with the killing. Weakest one of the bunch. That's why we went to him first. Gave him a chance to come clean and help himself. But he was just too scared of his friends to roll on them. Afraid they might rough him up. Guess what happened to him."

Izzy stood. "Come on, Sheriff—" he started saying at the same time Pedro asked, "Wuh … what … happened?"

Here we go, Mary Beth thought. *He's talking. Just need to keep this going.* She glared at Izzy's seat like, sit down and watch how it's done.

"It's really a damn, shame," she said to Pedro, talking real quiet—almost whispering. "He was a good-looking fella. Like to gel his hair all up kinda like you do. Fresh meat—that's what they call them."

"Seriously, Sheriff," Izzy said, tapping his watch. "It's getting late and the man's invoked his right to counsel."

"He's not answering any questions," she shot back. "Invoking your right to counsel doesn't mean I can't tell a story." She looked back to the doctor. "So, anyway, Pedro, one of the big fellas in there took a liking to old Danzig. Decided he'd like to make him his bitch? You know what a prison bitch is?"

"Sheriff—"

"At ease, Deputy, you're ruining the story now. So, how 'bout it, Pedro, you know what a bitch is?"

"Uh, I think, maybe I do."

"Sure you do," Mary Beth said. "So, anyway, the first attempt at a little romantic interlude didn't go so well. Danzig was playin' hard to get, so to speak. So, he got taken to the Dentist."

"The dentist?" Pedro asked.

"I'm gonna wait outside," Izzy said.

Mary Beth ignored him. "Trust me, Pedro. This is no ordinary dentist. This guy doesn't do cleanings, if you know what I'm saying. No, this guy uses a pair of pliers from the machine shop and pulls your fucking teeth out."

Pedro recoiled.

"So, you can't bite," Mary Beth explained. "No matter *what* they stick in your mouth."

The room fell into complete silence for what seemed like ten minutes, but was, in reality, just a few seconds. Then Mary Beth clapped her hands and said, real breezy-like, "Well, guess we gotta git. Tell your lawyer to give me a call, Pedro. Just hope it's not too late."

"Wait. Where are you going?" Pedro, who seconds earlier looked like he wanted to get as far away from these officers as possible, suddenly didn't want them to leave.

Mary Beth shrugged. She really had no plan at this point other than to yank Pedro's chain but she decided to throw a couple options up at the wall and see if something stuck. "We've got a lot to do," she said. "Need to talk to your cousins of course. And your brother, Raul. Oh, and we thought maybe we'd go look up your old college roommate who alibied you for the day Maria disappeared. If he lied, that could be aiding and abetting. We want to see if anybody else wants to play the first-to-squeal-wins, game. Take her easy, Pedro."

"Time to go, sheriff," Izzy said. As he ushered her out of the door, Mary Beth stared back at Pedro one last time and squealed like a pig. "Reeeeee."

13

THEY'D BARELY CLEARED THE OFFICE threshold before Pedro came thundering after them.

"Hold up!"

Mary Beth and Izzy spun around.

"You're going to see Denny?" he asked.

Mary Beth shot Izzy an I-told-you-so look. She wasn't entirely certain but thought Denny was the name of Pedro's college roommate who'd alibied him for the weekend Maria disappeared.

"You better believe it," she said. "Unless, there's anything else you want to tell us first."

The ladies who worked up front were watching them as they packed up their things, ready to call it a day. The sandy-haired receptionist and Pedro exchanged a glance. He nodded to her, like it was okay for them to go on, then said to Mary Beth, "Please. Let's talk some more before you go."

Internally, Mary Beth started doing her happy dance, thinking she was about to get somewhere with this major person of interest. On the outside though, she was glancing at her watch like she had somewhere better to be. "Okay," she said, "but let's make this fast. We've got more interviews to do."

Pedro walked them briskly back to his office. Shutting the door, he asked, "Is it a crime to lie to the police?"

Well, this is an auspicious beginning, Mary Beth thought. She and Izzy both looked at each other. What had he lied about? His alibi? Maybe, or whether he or his family had anything to do with Maria's murder?

Mary Beth gave him her look of maternal disapproval, pegging Pedro for a mama's boy and hoping her glare would help loosen his lips. "It's a pretty stupid thing to do," she said.

Then Izzy, said, "But you weren't under oath. So, it's not technically a crime. If you said something in your initial interviews in this case that you'd like to go ahead and amend ... you've still got a chance to do that without getting into trouble."

Pedro bit at his bottom lip.

Mary Beth tried to prod him along. "So how about it, doc? Need to unburden yourself? It's now or never."

Pedro looked around like he was trying to find the answer printed on one of the certificates papering his wall. He picked up a bronze, whale-shaped paperweight, and started nervously turning it over, passing it from hand to hand.

"Better you hear it from me first, I guess."

Mary Beth felt her pulse quicken. "Yes, it is," she said, trying not to sound too eager.

"Denny." Pedro spit out the name, then stared at them, gauging whether they already knew what he was about to say.

Mary Beth had a feeling she knew where this was going and decided to bluff him along. "You gonna tell us the truth about your bullshit alibi?"

Pedro stopped rocking and dropped his head. His jugular vein was pulsing as he tugged on the little island of twisty hair on his forehead. "It's not like what you think."

Izzy said, "Then tell us what it is like."

Pedro groaned. "Oh, Jesus."

Mary Beth stood. "I'm losing patience, Pedro."

"Okay, okay."

Mary Beth gave him a glare as she reclaimed her seat, like this was his last chance.

"It started as something really innocent," he said.

Mary Beth's ears perked. This was how a lot of good confessions began.

"Denny, I mean."

"What about him?' Izzy asked.

Pedro kept his eyes on his desk as he spoke. "I was supposed to be with him that weekend. That's what I'd told Maria, anyway. She'd wanted me to come home. Said we had things we needed to talk about. Important things, and I–well, I didn't want to— go home, that is. So, I told her that I couldn't because I'd promised to go to some party with Denny for his birthday. So, when the police first interviewed me, that's what I told them, too."

He paused, waiting for another question to prompt him along. Mary Beth and Izzy sat there quiet as church mice, not helping him at all.

Pedro couldn't stand the silence. "Maria had only been missing a couple of days at that point. I figured she was gonna turn up and once she did, she'd have been mad as hell. And she..." Pedro hesitated. "Let's just say she had a bad temper. So, I ... I just kind of blurted out that I'd been with Denny, and then that cop, that Sheriff asked to talk to Denny so I handed him the phone. He'd been sitting right there the whole time I was talking and heard what I'd said so he backed me up. We had no idea the thing with Maria was going to turn into such a big deal. And by the time we did we were stuck."

"That when you hired a lawyer?" Izzy asked.

Pedro turned up his palms. "Yeah. I was terrified. So, I called my parents and my dad called the same attorney who'd represented my brother with his...trouble. Anyway, the lawyer didn't want me talking to the police after that."

"Didn't want you to take a lie detector test either," Mary Beth said. "Must not have thought much of your story."

Pedro got his back up a bit at that. "My attorney said those lie detector tests aren't reliable and nothing good could come from taking one. Said that even if I passed it, it didn't guarantee you guys would leave me alone."

After that, Pedro went quiet. Mary Beth felt the energy in the room sag. She needed to fire it back up quick before Pedro clammed up for good. She quickly debated which direction to take the interview. There was a lot to follow up on, including several interesting allusions Pedro had made to what sounded like a tumultuous relationship with Maria.

Since he'd just blown his own alibi, the obvious question to ask at that point was his true whereabouts that weekend. But he'd be expecting that. Mary Beth wanted to hold off on that for just a bit so she could take Pedro somewhere he wasn't expecting, try to keep him off balance, and then come back to the alibi when he was less prepared to confront the issue. Also, the reference to Pedro's attorney, Alexander Pomfried, had Mary Beth's wheels turning back toward the drug angle. It was yet another connection to Pedro's brother, Raul, who'd informed on a cartel capo. Izzy may not have been hot for the drug retribution theory but Mary Beth thought it was too juicy to totally abandon. She decided to probe there next.

"You know, there's been a lot of speculation that the 'trouble' your brother got into may be what got Maria killed."

Pedro shook his head. "I never believed that for a second. That was Raul's deal. I had nothing to do with it and Maria certainly had nothing to do with it."

He seemed too confident about it, Mary Beth thought. Too quick to want to cut off this line of inquiry. It's not every day your brother rats on a fairly major underworld figure right before your girlfriend disappears. You'd think someone concerned about Maria would at least be willing to entertain the possibility that the two events were connected. There was something here Mary Beth needed to shake loose.

She pulled out her smartphone and punched up one of the photos she had taken of Maria's body all decomposed, stuffed into a hidden alcove in the basement of the Cierra Junior High. "Look at this," she commanded.

Pedro jumped back. "Jesus Christ." He clapped a hand to his mouth.

"Maria was executed, Pedro. Down on her knees with a gun to the back of the head. Then her body was hidden in a cool and deliberate manner. This was no random act of violence. It was a professional-style execution. Now are you really going to tell me there's no way there's a connection between *this* and your brother helping convict a Solares captain just three months before Maria disappeared?"

A long tear trailed down Pedro's cheek. He was shaking his head No, but his eyes weren't so sure. When he spoke his voice was shaky.

"He said it was safe."

"Who?" Mary Beth demanded.

"The attorney. Pomfried. He said it would be safe to cooperate with the Feds. He told us the Mexican cartels weren't like the mafia. Said you're allowed to rat. It's expected. Everybody rats when they get busted. You just aren't allowed to steal. That'll get you killed."

Mary Beth had heard such myths herself about the cartels. The logic was that there were so many links in the chain, so many buffers from the local *halcones* and gang bangers slinging the junk up to the real masterminds back in Mexico, that lower-level cooperation with the authorities wasn't seen as a major threat by the people who called down the hits. But Mary Beth had never totally bought that logic. Maybe it was her own personal vindictive streak informing her gut on this, but she figured retribution was a major risk any rat would run. Even if the drug lords didn't order a hit from up on high, what was to stop some lower-level goons, like the friends and family of whoever had taken the fall, from seeking some payback?

Plus, the guy Raul Kowalski helped convict wasn't a bit player. He was a capo in the Arizona territory. She made a mental note to check with the Feds out there to see what else she could learn about that prosecution. Who else had cooperated in the Diaz case and what had happened to them?

"Where's your brother now?" she asked.

"Last I heard he was in Mexico."

"For vacation?" Izzy asked.

"No. He lives there now. Moved in with my mom's family back there pretty soon after all the legal stuff."

Izzy followed up. "Got a phone number for him?"

Pedro shook his head. "We haven't really kept in touch."

Mary Beth asked, "You two have a falling out?"

"No. Not really. I'm just busy trying to be a doctor and raising two little kids. And he's busy doing whatever it is he does?"

"How about your parents?" Izzy asked. "Would they have a phone number for him?"

Pedro sighed. "My mom's deceased and my dad lives down in Florida now. I don't really talk to him anymore and I doubt Raul does either."

"Your mom's death have anything to do with your brother's drug connections?" Mary Beth asked.

"Not unless they figured out a way to give her breast cancer."

"I'm sorry," Mary Beth said.

"Me too," Izzy added.

"Yeah, well my dad was running around on her when she was sick. His way of coping, I guess. But my brother and I found out about it and never really forgave him. Haven't been too many family get-togethers since then. I'm not even sure where exactly Raul lives now or what he does for a living."

Mary Beth had a million other questions about the brother and the drugs, including what if any involvement Pedro had in that racket, but decided to table that. The talk about his family had Pedro looking sullen and she could tell he was starting to close down, emotionally. She decided now would be a good time to switch back to the alibi issue.

"So, if you weren't with Denny the weekend Maria disappeared, where were you?"

Pedro tugged on his hair some more. "With a girl."

Figures. If Pedro was stepping out on Maria, that could explain why he didn't want to tell the truth when first asked about his whereabouts.

"Will this girl back you up on that?" Izzy asked.

Pedro's answer was immediate. "Of course, she will."

"The same way Denny did?" Mary Beth asked.

Pedro covered his heart, "I swear to God, I am telling the truth. I know how it sounds, but I would have never hurt Maria. I mean we definitely went at it from time to time. And she really knew how to push my buttons, for sure. But I…" he paused then said, "I loved her. She was the first girl I ever loved. It was kind of an immature, high school sort of love, but it was real." He smiled wistfully then added, "There's nothing like your first, right?"

That all rang true with Mary Beth. Although she didn't put much stock in polygraphs, she held her own internal lie detector in high regard, and it was telling her that Pedro was being truthful—at least about his feelings for Maria. There was something in his eyes that she could relate to that had her flashing on her first love, Patrick Connelly. They'd been high school kids, too, when they got together, not knowing a thing about real commitment or the kind of sacrifices a mature, lasting relationship required, but there had never been and would never be another man who could evoke the same kind of strong, visceral reaction she used to get whenever he would walk into the room.

Izzy asked, "This girl you were with that weekend, you still in touch with her?"

Pedro sat the whale paper weight he'd been holding back down on the table.

"I'm married to her."

Mary Beth snorted. "Well, that's convenient."

"Look, I swear—" Pedro said, raising his hands.

Mary Beth watched him closely. Her internal lie detector was still telling her he was on the level, but she needed to be sure.

"Take out your phone," she said.

"You want me to call her?"

"No. I want you to take out your phone."

"O-kay?" Pedro pulled a large black iphone from his pocket. "Hand it to me."

"Why?" he asked while tentatively extending his arm.

Mary Beth snatched the phone. "So, you can't call your wife and tip her off about the story you just told."

"It's not a story," Pedro said. "Call and ask her. She's on speed dial. First number in the favorites. Go ahead. You can point it at my face to unlock it."

Mary Beth did just that and saw a beach picture pop up as the phone's background. There was Pedro looking tan and fit with his hairy chest, wearing Tommy Bahama shorts, standing next to a smiling blonde-haired woman in a tasteful, navy one-piece with a skirted bottom. They were each holding a little girl, blonde twins in flowery sun hats. Mary Beth clicked on the favorites and found Elizabeth Kowalski listed as the first contact. She pulled up the phone number and was about to make the call when she got a better idea. She switched off the phone.

"What are you doing?" Pedro asked.

Mary Beth stuck his phone in her pocket. She said, "I think this is a conversation I'd rather have face-to-face."

14

FOR A SECOND IZZY THOUGHT he might actually get a chance to drive Mary Beth's Camaro—which would have been the first time ever—after Pedro agreed to take them to his house so they could interview his wife in person.

Initially, Mary Beth said she wanted to ride with the doctor to continue the interview on the way there and make sure Pedro didn't have another cell phone stashed away in his Mercedes that he could use to get in touch with the missus. But as Izzy was adjusting the driver's seat, trying to accommodate for his short legs, he made a joke about maybe getting some payback for Beulah, his Blazer that Mary Beth busted up the day before. After that, Mary Beth decided Pedro might be more willing to open up to a man, and, in the interest of the investigation, ordered her chief deputy to get the hell out of her car.

So, Izzy rode shotgun with the doc, in his car, with Mary Beth following behind in her Camaro. Izzy was appreciating the softness of the plush gray leather seats, enjoying the smooth ride of Pedro's Mercedes Kompressor sports sedan, when he asked, "So how much trouble are we getting you into with your old lady—a couple of cops showing up at your doorstep wanting to talk about your ex-girlfriend?"

Pedro shrugged. "The cop part will shake her a little but she knows all about Maria. That's no secret."

"You and Maria were still together when you started dating your wife?"

Pedro took his eyes off the road long enough to glance at Izzy. "Sort of."

Izzy thought maybe he was going to leave it at that but after a few seconds he added, "Maria's and my relationship status wasn't really all that well defined at the time."

"What do you mean?"

"It was just one of those things—you know? We'd dated for years and were always breaking up and getting back together. But even when we were on a break there was kind of like an expectation there."

"So, you were on a break when Maria disappeared?"

"In my mind we were."

Pedro pulled the Mercedes to a stop at a redlight and pointed to the time—6:23. "You sure I can't just give my wife a heads up that I'm on my way? She's probably already got dinner on the table."

"Sorry, man," Izzy said. "No can do."

Pedro sighed. Izzy tried to divine if it was concern over what his wife might say when interviewed by the police over his claimed alibi or just knowing she'd be annoyed about him getting home late without calling. Could have just as easily been the latter, Izzy decided. Neither he nor his wife did much cooking, but if Princess had put dinner together and he showed up late without a courtesy call she'd have definitely been all up on his ass about it.

"If it helps," Izzy said, "I'll be sure to tell your wife that you wanted to call but we wouldn't let you."

Pedro nodded. "Thanks, man. That would help."

This is good, Izzy thought. He felt like he was bonding a little bit with Pedro. After enduring Mary Beth's third degree and thinly-veiled threats of anal rape, he must be relieved to be dealing with the good cop. Felt like an opportune time to keep pressing the questions but do it like they were old buds saddled up to the bar at their favorite watering hole.

"So, you said that in your mind you and Maria were on a break. Did she see it differently?"

Pedro didn't answer right away. Then said, "It was complicated."

"How so?"

The light turned green and Pedro accelerated, focusing intently on the road.

"Doc, you still with me?"

"Huh? What? Oh, yeah, sorry." He shot Izzy a half-smile. "I just a …you know, seeing that photo of Maria. I just can't get that image …. Can't get it out of my head."

"I understand. But anything you can tell me could turn out to be really helpful in catching whoever did that to her. I'm sure you want to help us do that."

Pedro tilted his head. "I do. It's just … I don't want to say anything bad about her, you know? Speaking ill of the dead. It just doesn't feel right."

Izzy watched Pedro for a moment, trying to get more of a read on him. His sentiment, when he talked about Maria, seemed genuine enough, but he was also clearly uncomfortable. That was often a sign to Izzy that somebody had something to hide. But the guy was being questioned in connection with an old girlfriend's murder, riding along with a sheriff's deputy, leading two cops to his house to question his wife. That'd be enough to make even the most innocent person seem jumpy. Still, Izzy sensed a hesitancy in Pedro that went beyond the current situation or respect for the dead. If he had to put money on it, he'd bet there was still some secret Pedro was protecting. The question was what and how to get it out of him.

Izzy decided to bump things up a notch, but still try to do it in a non-threatening way, like he was on Pedro's side. "I'm sorry we've got to put you through this," he said. "But you know how these things go. Woman is killed. The husband or boyfriend is the first person we look at? Especially if there's been some turmoil there."

Pedro shook his head like he understood.

"Now I'm gonna level with you," Izzy told him.

"Okay." Pedro swallowed hard.

"I look at you, and I don't see a killer. But we know you've already lied to the cops once. And we know that you and Maria had a rocky relationship. So, you holding back on the details, is just gonna make the sheriff back there all the more suspicious." Izzy pointed a thumb back at Mary Beth's mean looking black Camaro following close behind.

Pedro's knuckles turned white as he gripped the steering wheel. "I didn't have anything to do with this!" he said. "I swear to you. I wish to God I'd just taken that stupid polygraph back then, so you'd believe me."

Izzy gave him a friendly rap on the shoulder. "I think I do believe you, man. But you've got a problem here."

"What's that?"

"Friend of Maria's says that a week before she disappeared, they were up at Marshall visiting you, and you two had a big blow up. Says you shook Maria and threatened to kill her. Said the fight was bad enough they ended up driving all the way home that night. So now we hear that, and what are we supposed to think?"

"Jesus Christ. It wasn't like that at all."

"Then tell me what it was like, because right now all we have is that story I just told you. If you've got a different one. We need to hear it."

Pedro banged his head against the steering wheel and nearly ran the car up on the curb of the neighborhood street they were traveling down.

"Take it easy," Izzy said, "we're just talking here."

"That's all I was doing! Talking. We were just having an argument. I don't remember exactly what I said to her, but whatever it was, it was just a figure of speech. I was drunk and pissed, but I would have never done anything to hurt Maria."

Izzy stayed quiet for a bit, just watching Pedro, studying him as he rubbed his eyes. "I wasn't even anywhere near Jasper Creek when she went missing."

Back to the alibi, Izzy thought. But what he wanted to know was what Pedro and Maria had been arguing about that had gotten him so upset he laid his hands on her and threatened to kill her? Izzy watched and waited to see if Pedro would offer up an explanation. If not, he would certainly ask him but felt it was always best to just let the witness talk if they would. The things they chose to discuss, the places their mind went when undirected by pointed questions, could be just as informative as the answers they gave.

"He had assurances," Pedro said.

Izzy looked at him quizzically.

"My brother, Raul. You asked earlier how I knew Maria disappearing wasn't some kind of retribution for turning state's evidence. I should have mentioned before, he'd also gotten assurances there'd be no consequences if he cooperated."

"Yeah," Izzy said, assuming Pedro was just trying to change the subject. "You told us. The cartels don't care if you rat as long as you don't steal. But what about this blow up you had with Maria. I wanna hear what that was all about."

Pedro pulled the car into the long driveway of a red brick colonial-style home with black shutters and two chimneys. The home sat on a half-acre lot, shaded by mature oaks and maples, in an old money neighborhood—the place where the doctors and lawyers lived.

"There's more to it," Pedro said. He parked behind a silver Mercedes SUV with white, stick-figure stickers on the tinted back window, indicating it belonged to a family of two adults, two children, and three dogs.

"Let's hear it," Izzy said. "What were you fighting about?"

"No," Pedro said. "I mean about my brother. There's more to it."

Izzy glanced at Mary Beth pulling in behind them. "I'm listening." He gestured for Pedro to hurry before she got there.

"What I said is true. The attorney told us that the cartels are more likely to come after you for stealing than ratting. But we were still scared. The guy they wanted Raul to inform on was no small fish."

"Yeah...."

"So, the attorney had some connection. A past client or something who was able to get some assurances from higher ups in the cartel that Raul would be okay."

"Who?" Izzy asked, noticing in his peripheral vision that Mary Beth was out of her car and heading their way. He wanted to try and get this out of Pedro before she got there, in case her presence caused him to clam up.

"I don't know," Pedro said. "The attorney couldn't tell us. Said it was privileged. But he told us it was confirmed that Raul had no reason to worry. Like maybe some people higher up the chain wanted the guy, the..." Pedro struggled to remember the name.

"Diaz?" Izzy interjected.

"Yeah, Diaz. Like maybe they wanted him to get convicted."

Hmm, Izzy thought. That was interesting. He wasn't sure how that could have anything to do with Maria but he knew Mary Beth would be intrigued to learn that her old nemesis, Alexander Pomfried, had a back channel to some higher-ups in the cartel.

Mary Beth was standing outside the driver-side door now,

knocking on the window. Izzy signaled he needed a minute. "Was there any *quid pro quo*?" he asked. "Did Raul have to do anything for the cartel in exchange for being left alone?"

Pedro glanced out the window then back to Izzy. "No," he said. "At least not that I know of."

15

THE DOGS MET THEM at the front door. Three yappy terriers sounding a shrill bark alarm that could have woken the dead. Izzy started kicking at the one closest to him that was baring its teeth and jumping a foot off the ground each time it chirped.

Good thing Izzy's not packing his forty-four, Mary Beth thought, or they might have a canine-icide on their hands.

Pedro quickly corralled the dogs into a home office off the foyer, closing them in behind French doors where they continued to go ape-shit, barking and jumping all over each other. But at least the sound was slightly muffled.

Then came the kiddos, two blonde, bubbly little girls, cheering the return of their Daddy. Pedro stooped down to hug them, squeezing them a little extra tight it seemed, no doubt relieved to embrace his beauties after the afternoon he'd had. It was a scene Mary Beth remembered well: how Bill got to come home from work like the conquering hero and Sam would rush to his side, fleeing the homework or chores or whatever else Mary Beth had him doing.

Next down the hall came Mrs. Kowalski who announced her

presence with an obvious note of annoyance as she turned the corner, saying, "The girls were starving so we had to go ahead and eat." The second she caught sight of Mary Beth and Izzy though, her demeanor changed, smiling big and bright. "Oh, hello. I didn't realize we had guests."

She was wearing some trendy activewear, a sleek turquoise pullover with zippered pockets on the upper arms and dark-gray stretch pants, looking like she might be headed to a yoga class later. Elizabeth Kowalski hooked a thumb inside a posh silver-chain necklace and patted at her long blonde hair, like she was embarrassed by her appearance, though nary a strand of her low ponytail was out of place.

Mary Beth recognized this woman instantly, and not just because she'd seen her picture on Pedro's phone. She was the perfect mom. Young, pretty, and privileged=one of those women who approached mothering like a competition, lying awake at night, planning weeks ahead of time the all-organic, hormone-free ingredients of her dinner menus and the family crafts they'd do together to make sure the little angels didn't get too much screen time. She'd only laid eyes on this lady for two seconds, but Mary Beth would have bet her left kidney this Elizabeth Kowalski not only cut the crust off the multi-grain, gluten free bread she used to make her babies' sandwiches, but probably carved those little fuckers into some kind of cute design like tiny hearts or four-leaf clovers.

"Honey," Pedro started to say before Mary Beth stepped in front, cutting him off. "Sheriff Mary Beth Cain, Jasper County," she said, extending a hand to Mrs. Kowalski. "This is Chief Deputy Baker."

"Evening, ma'am," Izzy said.

Elizabeth Kowalski shook Mary Beth's hand timidly, saying, "Girls, go back to the kitchen and clear your plates."

"But Mom—" the slightly taller girl complained.

"Ainsley Kowalski, you heard me young lady," she snapped.

"Yes, ma'am," the little girl responded.

Mary Beth caught the agitation and stress in Elizabeth Kowalski's voice.

"Is something wrong?" Mrs. Kowalski asked.

Pedro tried opening his mouth again, but Mary Beth held up a finger. She'd warned him out in the driveway not to do or say anything to signal his wife once they got inside the house. Elizabeth looked startled at first, then slightly put off that Mary Beth seemed to wield as much control over her husband as she had over the children.

"Nothing's wrong," Mary Beth said. "We just have a few questions."

She and Elizabeth eyed each other for a moment, sizing the other up.

Izzy added, "Your husband wanted to call to let you know he'd be late and bringing guests but we asked him not to."

Mary Beth glared at Izzy, like Whose side are you on?

"I don't understand," Elizabeth said. "Peter?"

"It's okay—" he started to say, till Mary Beth shushed him.

She knew she needed to quickly separate the spouses in order to conduct her interview, and said, "Pedro," intentionally calling him by his real name, "do you have a man cave in this place somewhere?"

"Sure," he said. "Down in the basement."

"Why don't you and Izzy go check it out and let me and Mrs. Kowalski, here, have a little girl talk?"

Pedro's basement was decorated in a 1950's theme. It had a black and white checkerboard floor, a couch that sat inside the tail fins of a Cadillac, red vinyl stools surrounding a wet bar, and a jukebox in the corner that played old 45's. The lone item in this man cave that Izzy guessed had actually been selected by the

Kowalski's paterfamilias was the eight-foot, red felt, slate pool table in the center of the room.

"Rack 'em," Izzy said.

After taking the tour and punching up some Jackie Wilson on the jukebox, he'd helped Pedro collect the balls from the drop pockets around the table. Pedro was distracted and nervous. He kept checking his watch and glancing at the stairs like he was hoping to hear what the women were talking about up there, but he eventually managed to arrange alternating solids and stripes for a game of eight-ball as Izzy chalked his cue stick, singing along to Lonely Teardrops.

Izzy liked his chances here. Pedro might have the home field advantage but Izzy had spent much of his childhood in pool halls and had watched *The Color of Money* at least fifty times.

When Pedro removed the triangle, Izzy cracked a strong break that dropped one of each. He then opted for solids with a smooth little stroke that nipped the one-ball just hard enough to nudge it into the side pocket.

"Nice shot," Pedro said.

"Thanks."

Izzy put two more solids in before scratching on a missed bank shot at the six.

Then Pedro took his time moving the cue ball into position, still looking distracted. He hit the ball way too hard, with a choppy stroke. Tried running it down the bank where the eleven was basically covering the corner pocket but he cut it too close and the cue ball ricocheted off the rail before it got there, pushing the eleven farther from the hole.

"This just isn't your day," Izzy said.

"You can say that again."

Izzy was rounding the table, eyeing a way to knock the four into the opposite corner while bringing the cue ball back to a place where he'd have a decent shot at that six again, when Pedro asked, "What do you think they're talking about up there? I didn't think it would take this long."

Izzy looked up at the ceiling. "Man, it's hard to say." He chalked his stick. "In my experience though, you got two women sitting around talking about you. It's usually not good." Izzy stroked the four ball just right, the cue bouncing back past the middle cluster of balls, leaving a long but makeable shot at the six.

He started chalking again as he moved in position for his next shot. "So, if you've got a more exculpatory version of events from the last time you saw Maria, it'd probably behoove you to go ahead and share it with me."

"Exculpatory?" Pedro asked.

"One where it doesn't sound like you were really threatening to kill her."

Pedro leaned his stick up against the wall and rubbed his temples. Izzy hoped he wasn't giving up on the game. He'd thought playing would relax Pedro and make him more talkative.

"You've got to understand something about me and Maria. She was a real jealous type. Even when we weren't together."

Izzy gave Pedro a disbelieving look. "No offense but—pretty girl like that?"

"Yeah," Pedro said. "She was pretty—sure. She had plenty of guys like my cousins hitting on her all the time who'd have been more than happy to bang her. But I was like her ticket to the life she wanted. That's how she saw it. My family were members at the Hogan Hills Country Club where she could hang out with us and pretend to be a small-town debutante."

"Ok. So, what were you two arguing about that night Laura Keenan says you threatened to kill her?"

Pedro rolled his eyes. "I don't remember saying that, first of all. And if I did, I certainly didn't mean it. Not literally. She and Laura just showed up that night, totally uninvited. I had no idea they were coming. And I was there with Liz," he said, pointing up at the white drop ceiling.

"Did Maria know you were seeing somebody else?"

Pedro listed from side to side like a cruise ship on rough seas. "Kinda, maybe," he said. "I mean we weren't technically together at the time. Maria and I would argue and break up all the time. But whenever I was about to move on with somebody else, it's like a little bell would go off in her head and she'd show up and try to ruin things for me. And I just wasn't having it that time. I knew the thing with Liz was different."

Izzy leaned his pool stick against the table. He stroked his chin, considering what Pedro said, while still eyeing his shot at the six. "Okay," he said. "So, you're at a party with your new girlfriend and Maria shows up. Walk me through what happens."

"I hadn't gone through the whole long Maria story with Liz yet—how it was always kind of complicated with us—and I didn't want her to find out that way. So, I just needed to get Maria out of there, but she was refusing to leave. And I don't know what all I said to her—like I told you, I'd been drinking. But whatever I said, I just wanted her to leave. I didn't want to hurt her. I didn't want her to disappear. I certainly didn't want her dead. I just wanted her to leave."

"You did put your hands on her, though?"

Pedro shrugged. "I may have grabbed her arm and walked her to the door. But that was it. I didn't hit her or anything."

Izzy stayed quiet for a moment to see if Pedro would add anything else. This time Pedro managed to stay mum in the face of the silent treatment.

"You just really, really wanted her to leave you and Liz alone?" Izzy asked it in an accusatory way, like he was wondering aloud whether Pedro wanted that bad enough to kill her.

"Yeah," Pedro said, either missing or ignoring the inference. "But she was all hung up on me."

"He was totally hung up on her," Elizabeth Kowalski said. She finished drying a copper frying pan and hung it on a fancy rack above the kitchen island. "Maria had him wrapped around her little finger."

Mary Beth was admiring the kitchen's brown and beige backsplash and the oversized stainless steel refrigerator that looked like it could hold enough food to feed a rugby team. "What do you mean?" she asked.

Elizabeth dried her hands with a mauve Norwex towel, explaining how its silver-infused microfibers disinfected her kitchen without the use of any chemicals, then said, "Peter was like her little puppet. She'd dump him all the time. Run around with other guys. Make him look like a fool. But then whenever she'd call, he'd come running back."

"What about that weekend Maria went missing? Did Puh..." Mary Beth paused, wanting to call Elizabeth's husband, Pedro, but deciding she liked how this was going and not seeing a reason to provoke. "Your husband," she said. "Did he go running home to Maria that weekend?"

Mary Beth watched Elizabeth Kowalski closely for classic signs of deception––avoiding eye contact, fidgeting, flushed skin, pulsing jugular vein, nervous speech–– but the woman huffed, was all, like all these questions about Maria just made her feel annoyed.

"Nope. There was none of that. Lucky for him that was the first time he decided to actually put his foot down," she continued.

"What do you mean?" Mary Beth leaned forward.

"He was with me that weekend. I'd invited him to go home with me. My parents live in South Charleston. And he knew that if he broke the date to answer Maria's call, we'd have been done. She did try one of her ploys to get him to come home with her that weekend, though. Had said they needed to talk about something really important. You know, holding out the carrot of getting back together. But Peter called and told her he wasn't coming."

"What did he tell her he was doing, instead?"

Elizabeth shrugged. "I don't know what he told her. But I can tell you we spent the whole weekend together in Charleston. Went to the circus at the Convention Center—Ringling Brothers, I think it was—and also did a night at the dog track in Cross Lanes."

Mary Beth made a mental note that Pedro hadn't told his wife that his cover story with Maria, and the police, had been that he was spending it with his roommate, Denny Williams. Did that mean he was the type who habitually kept secrets from his wife? Big secrets? Or did he just want his wife to think he'd been a little more definitive in telling Maria about his new relationship than was actually the case?

"Anybody else see you two in Charleston that weekend?"

Again, Elizabeth Kowalski didn't bat an eye. "Sure," she said. "My parents. I'll write their number down for you."

Before Mary Beth even asked, Mrs. Kowalski was taking down a notepad clipped to a refrigerator magnet and started writing down the number. Mary Beth noted the loveliness of the pink, flowery stationery. "Here," she said, handing it over. "My dad's a retired principal at George Washington. Mom's a Sunday School teacher who spends her weekends organizing the soup kitchen at the mission. Are they good enough character references?"

"I'm sure they'll do just fine," Mary Beth said, folding the paper and slipping it in her pocket. "One more thing, though, Mrs. Kowalski."

"Yes?"

"You know anything about Maria coming to see Puh...Your husband, at Marshall the weekend before you and he did this trip to Charleston?"

Elizabeth squeezed her plump, fuchsia-colored lips into a pouty little beak. Her eyes went up and to the left, a sign she was accessing her memory. When a witness struggling for an answer looked up and to the right, it indicated they were accessing the creative part of their brain—a fancy, neuroscientific way of saying they were about to make some shit up.

"Not sure if it was the weekend right before or not but it was sometime around there. We were at a party at Peter's frat house and Maria showed up. Yeah, I remember that."

"What happened?"

Elizabeth shrugged. "Not much. Peter thought I didn't know about Maria, but his friends had told me all about her. When she showed up he thought he was real smooth trying to intercept her and keep us from meeting. But I just acted like I couldn't care less. Went on about my business. I wasn't going to fight over a guy. Peter could either choose her or me."

"Guess he made the right choice, then?" Mary Beth said, gesturing around their lovely, Pottery Barn-inspired home.

Before anything else could be said, the men re-appeared from the basement, Pedro asking was it okay to come up. When they got the all clear, Izzy announced, "We've got something important to tell you."

16

IT HAD BEEN A LONG DAY and Mary Beth needed a drink, bad. It was an urge she was trying mightily to avoid but it had her feeling tense and snappy.

Izzy meanwhile was pretty pleased with himself. He had his hands behind his head, leaning back in the passenger seat of Mary Beth's Camaro, saying, "No need to thank me or anything."

"Thank you? For what?"

"Are you kidding me? I got Pedro to cooperate. He's gonna give us his DNA, even after the way you threatened him."

"Big deal," Mary Beth said. "You got an offer of cooperation. I don't think the county commissioners are gonna pin a medal on you just yet."

Izzy huffed. "You can try and minimize it if you want. But at eight am tomorrow morning when we meet Dr. Kowalski at his office and get to watch while his nurse draws a full panel of blood, plus takes hair samples and cheek swabs, and any other damn thing we need—we'll have significantly advanced the ball in this investigation."

"We could have always got a warrant for all that."

"Maybe, maybe not."

"Whatever," Mary Beth said, not ready to give Izzy the praise he was looking for. "You want to grab something to eat?"

"Yeah, sure," Izzy said. "I'm starving."

Mary Beth sighed. "Guess we might as well spend the night somewhere. It's too far to head home and get back by morning."

"Yeah, guess you're right."

"Not sure the department can cover two rooms though. We might have to bunk in together. Princess gonna be okay with that?" Mary Beth asked, not being totally serious, but enjoying ribbing Izzy all the same.

"I'll spring for the extra room," Izzy said.

"Look at you. Living large."

It was well known throughout the station that Princess kept Izzy on a tight budget. He got two hundred dollars cash from each paycheck to do what he wanted with, which mostly consisted of meals or the occasional beer with the boys, and his wife controlled the rest.

"I think you're just jealous that I got more out of Pedro than you did," Izzy said. He was scanning the row of pylon signs down the main drag as he spoke and pointed at one. "Hey there's a pizza place. Wanna stop there?"

Mary Beth shook her head. "Nah, I'm not in the mood for pizza. Let's go somewhere I can get a good salad and you can get whatever you want."

"How about that Applebee's we passed on the way in?"

Mary Beth shrugged. "Sure. That'll work."

Izzy frowned at her. "What's your deal? We should be celebrating."

"Celebrating what?" Mary Beth was still thinking about how good a glass of whiskey would feel but was doing her best to abide that morning's vow to go at least a week without alcohol.

"This is big," Izzy said. "There's no way you can tell me it's a slam dunk we could have got a warrant for Pedro's DNA."

"Maybe."

"Maybe, nothing. Before I stepped in, all we'd done today—other than threaten Pedro in a way that was totally inappropriate—was help him fix his alibi. Upstanding physician, no criminal record, no clear motive, with an alibi and zero physical evidence tying him to the crime—we've got nothing on him. You really gonna tell me it's a foregone conclusion we could have got a judge to compel him to cooperate?"

Mary Beth tended to agree, but Izzy's celebratory attitude at this premature phase of the investigation was rubbing her the wrong way. "You're probably right," she said, agreeing just because she didn't feel like debating.

Izzy started to sulk. When Mary Beth signaled, waiting for traffic to clear so she could make the left turn into the Applebee's parking lot, the big baby flipped his back to her with a huff and made a show of staring out the window, looking as far away from her as he could manage. Mary Beth really was not in the mood to cater to anybody's hurt little feelings, but she decided to throw Izzy a bone nonetheless, so he wouldn't piss and moan the rest of the evening. "How'd you get him to go along with it, anyway?" she asked.

Izzy turned back to her, smiling now that he was finally getting some acknowledgement. "Like you said. I'm one hell of a male bonder."

Mary Beth looked at him like there had to be more to the story than that after all his gloating, and Izzy added, "Dr. K. asked me how he could get out from under this and I told him the fastest way would be to give us what we'd need to rule him out."

Traffic cleared and Mary Beth turned into the Applebee's parking lot. She noticed it was next to a roadside motel that looked cheap. She pointed it out to Izzy. "If that flea trap's okay with you, the department could probably swing two rooms and keep you in Princess's good graces."

"Fine with me." Izzy said without looking. He was focused on a dilapidated strip mall across the street where the only functioning business was a honky tonk called THE RODEO that had blacked out windows and a sagging bright yellow banner announcing BIKINI BULL RIDING TONIGHT. "Now, that's what I'm talking about," he said. "Let's go hit that shit up after dinner."

Mary Beth rolled her eyes. "No, thanks."

Not only was Mary Beth doing her best not to drink, but when she did imbibe, she preferred to do it alone. One reason was she had an image to uphold and was always mindful of avoiding the Jasper Creek rumor mill. But the other was that she'd really been turned off to seedy bars at a young age. When she was sixteen, right after her dad died, her mother used the life insurance money to purchase Mountain Flowers, a strip club/bar/brothel/drug den in what used to be McCray County. Mary Beth ended up waiting tables there for about six months before she'd finally had enough and left home to go live with her grandparents in Jasper Creek.

"Come on," Izzy said. "Live a little. We're out of town. You can let your hair down some."

Mary Beth parked the car. "No offense," she said, "but watching a bunch of bimbos straddling a mechanical bull doesn't sound like a whole lot of fun to me."

"Why you gotta slut shame?"

"Piss off," Mary Beth said. She cut the ignition. "If you want to get something to eat, let's go."

"Fine."

They went inside and got a booth by the window where Mary Beth could keep an eye on her car. When Izzy excused himself to use the bathroom, Mary Beth spent a few minutes on her phone, checking emails. She was pleasantly surprised to see she had a text message from Sam.

How'd it go? I'd love to help with the case if there's some-thing I can do.

Mary Beth texted back to let him know things were going well. She and Izzy were on top of it. Sam shot back a thumb's up emoji. Neither addressed the blow up they'd had that morning, nor would they. That was the Appalachian way. When you got angry you just avoided each other until the hurt subsided enough to suffer one another's company again.

Izzy returned as the waiter was getting there. He ordered a Bourbon Street Steak, medium well with a twenty-ounce Miller Lite. Mary Beth went with a grilled chicken salad and a water with lemon.

"Come on, get a beer," Izzy urged. "No voters around."

"Nah, I'm good," Mary Beth said.

The truth was, a beer did sound awfully tasty at the moment but Mary Beth knew if she drank one or two of those, the call of the whiskey would grow too loud to ignore, and she really needed to get off that train, riding the caffeine and stress up the hill all day and sliding back down with the liquor at night. She figured she'd had long enough to lick her wounds since Old Wengo and Sawyer's death–it was time to toughen up. Hopefully, the Ruiz case would give her the renewed sense of purpose she'd need to put it all behind her.

But Izzy kept pressing for some fun. "Come on," he said.

"Away from the wife for one night and wanting to cut loose, huh?" Mary Beth said. "Want me to just drop you off at a strip club somewhere and you can uber it back to the motel?"

Izzy laughed. "You know I'm not gonna do that. I just thought maybe we could both relax a little. I know you've always got to keep up appearances around Jasper Creek, but we're out of town, nobody knows you here. And I know you've had one hell of a year. Maybe it'd do you good to not...." Izzy let the sentence trail off.

"Not what?"

"I don't know. Not hold it all in."

Mary Beth rolled her eyes, sensing some arm-chair psychology coming her way.

"You've just been so on edge," he said. "Even for you. And I saw how you and Sam were staring daggers into each other back at the station."

She didn't like where this conversation was heading. Next thing you know, Izzy'd be suggesting they have themselves a little hug and maybe a good cry. "Thanks," she said, "but I'm doing just fine. Besides, honky-tonks aren't really my thing."

"You sure? We could ride the mechanical bull together. You can even sit in front if you want. It'd be fun."

"I'm sure."

The waiter returned with some waters and Izzy's beer. Mary Beth watched intently as the deputy took a long slurp of the frosty golden goodness. She twirled her straw, clicking the ice cubes against the glass.

"So Princess isn't gonna be mad you've got to stay out overnight on this one?"

Mary Beth knew the wife had been blowing up Izzy's phone. She'd heard the ding of at least ten text messages since leaving Pedro's.

"She'll be fine. It's cool. I should probably give her a call though." Izzy pulled his phone back out.

"Assure her we'll sleep head to toe," Mary Beth said with a wink.

"She's not worried about me. She knows I'm like a domesticated house cat at this point—can't survive in the wild anymore."

Mary Beth continued poking at her ice cubes. "She hates my guts, doesn't she?"

Izzy looked at her awkwardly. He sat the phone on the table and brought the tall beer glass to his mouth. "No. Nah. Uh-uh." After a long drink, he asked unconvincingly, "Why would you say that?"

"I get it," Mary Beth said. "If Bill had spent most his time with another woman, it would have gotten under my skin too."

Izzy took another drink. "She just doesn't get it, is all. Beautiful woman like Princess, every guy she's ever met her whole life has been trying to sleep with her. So, she doesn't believe a man and woman can ever truly be friends."

"Takes a big man to be married to a woman like that."

"You said it." Izzy picked up the phone again and started scoping for a private place to make the call. "I really probably should check in." He started to rise.

"Sit," Mary Beth said. "You stay here." She stood looking for her hat out of habit, hating like hell that she hadn't brought it with her.

"You sure?"

"Yeah," Mary Beth said. "I could use a stretch. I'll go check us in next door. Back in a few."

The neon VACANCY sign was flashing in the window of the little office to the roadside motel where a twenty-something guy was lounging behind a gray metal desk, reading a heavily dog-eared paperback. He had one of those thin, hipster beards and was wearing old gym shorts and a volleyball tee-shirt with cut off sleeves that showed off his taught ropey arms.

The glass door sounded a little bell when it scraped open. The guy looked up from his book, trying to nonchalantly flex as he scanned Mary Beth up and down. He raised his eyebrows, grinning before his gaze made it back up to her eyes. It kind of creeped Mary Beth out, given that the kid was close to her son's age.

"Well, how do ya do?" he asked with a strong accent that dripped deep south.

Mary Beth pointed to the vacancy sign. "Need two rooms. Just for tonight."

"Course." He turned to the back wall where a handful of numbered keys hung on hooks. "Won't be adjoining. That okay?"

"Yeah, sure."

Mary Beth glanced around, realizing just how old school the place was. Didn't even have a computer in the office.

As she was filling out the paper register, she asked, "What's the story with this Bikini Bull Riding place across the street?" Mary Beth knew Izzy was determined to head over there later and was apprehensive about what he might be getting himself into. She had an image of a bar full of racist rednecks where they needed chicken wire to protect the house band from brawls and flying beer bottles.

"Were you wanting to compete?"

Mary Beth looked at the guy like he was a wad of gum she'd just discovered on the bottom of her shoe. "Do I look like I'm wanting to compete?"

"You look like you could do anything you wanna do."

Oh, Jesus. Was that a line? Mary Beth couldn't tell if he was making fun of her.

"Are you hitting on me, little boy?"

"No, ma'am. That is—not unless you want me to."

Mary Beth rolled her eyes.

"I'm sorry. That was stupid," he said. "Bad joke."

"Can I just get the keys?"

"Yes, ma'am. Coming right up." He took a minute to mark his page in the paperback he'd been reading and then spent a few minutes shuffling some papers behind the counter as though that would somehow determine which keys he'd yank off the wall.

"What's that you're reading there?"

The guy had turned to retrieve the room keys. "It's John D. MacDonald. You read him?" He turned back with two brassy keys attached to red plastic diamonds.

"Nah," Mary Beth said. "Don't read much. What's it about?"

The guy's eyes lit up, causing her to see him a bit differently than she had up to that moment. "Oh, it's the best. Travis McGee. He's kind of a beach bum slash private eye. Lives on a houseboat, enjoying the good life down in Florida. Only takes jobs when his money runs out. Living free as a bird. Each book he's got a new mystery and a new woman."

"The love 'em and leave 'em type, huh?"

"No, no, no. Not at all. He's not like that. Trav's got character. He's not like some James Bond, Don Draper type. Would never take advantage of a woman. Cares about everyone of 'em. Won't even bone …uh," he paused, "hook up with them if they're too emotional, or whatever."

Something about the way he was looking at her, the youthful enthusiasm, reminded her of something—a happier time perhaps—that caused her to stare at him a moment and soak it in.

"Ma'am?"

"Right." Mary Beth scraped the keys up off the counter. "How much do I owe you?"

"Two rooms, one night. Be $169.60, with tax." He smiled at her. "Or just $160 if you're paying cash."

"It'll be a card," she said, whipping out her Visa.

"I was just foolin." He said, winking at her. "Hey, you're not with the IRS or anything are you?"

"No. Sheriff's department."

The guy laughed until he realized she wasn't smiling. Then she showed him her ID and his face went white. "Oh … okay. Well, yes, Ma'am—Sheriff. Um, let me ring you up here." The guy produced an old carbon copy swipe machine from behind the counter and made an imprint of her card.

"So, this bull-riding joint," Mary Beth asked, "is it the kind of place where they're sweeping up teeth at the end of the night?"

The guy shrugged and handed back her card. "I don't know. Never been in there. Don't remember ever seeing the police or an ambulance over there though. Guess that's a good sign."

That just meant nobody ever bothered to call them, Mary Beth thought, but she said, "Guess so."

When she turned to leave the guy called after her, "You need anything, ma'am. Anything at all. I'll be here all night."

17

IZZY WAS HALFWAY through his steak and on at least his second beer by the time Mary Beth got back to Applebee's and started pecking at her salad. She said, "What's this?" when the waitress brought her a tall Mic Ultra and Izzy said, "You weren't really gonna make me drink alone were you?"

Mary Beth sighed, saying, "guess not," and tipped her glass toward Izzy who cheered her before they each took a long sip. The beer was about as watered down as an alcoholic beverage could be but still hit Mary Beth like an oasis in the most arid of desserts.

"How's Princess?"

"Princess," Izzy said, "is pissed." He sawed another bite off his steak. "So, *we are* going to that bikini bar tonight. If I'm going to get in trouble, anyway, we might as well make it worth it."

Mary Beth speared a long strip of chicken and asked while chewing, "What do you want to go to some redneck bar for anyway?"

"Shoot, girl, you don't know 'bout Izzy Baker. I can boot scoot like nobody's business."

Mary Beth took another sip of beer, liking the taste of that one even more than the first.

"Come on," Izzy said. "As much trouble as I'm in. You owe me."

Mary Beth shrugged. Izzy was obviously a grown man who could more than handle himself, but she really didn't like the idea of him going over to that honky-tonk alone. "Fine," she said. "One drink."

Izzy smiled as he dug into his garlic mash.

"So, what's your read on Pedro?" she asked, changing the subject back to the investigation.

Izzy held up a finger until he could wash down his mouth full of taters. "Not much of a pool player. I can tell you that."

"I mean about Maria. You spent more time with him than I did. Is he our killer?"

Izzy considered the question for a moment, swishing his beer around like it was a fine wine. "Too soon to say for sure. I definitely think he's holding back on something. But if you put a gun to my head and made me answer right now, I'd have to say he doesn't have the balls to kill somebody."

"What about his wife? Think she has the balls?"

Izzy laughed. "I think she's got enough balls for both of 'em. But she's no killer either."

"No. No, she's not," Mary Beth agreed. "Still, if she's there tomorrow maybe we should get some DNA off her too. You never know."

"Guess it can't hurt to ask. See what she says. How she reacts. Might be interesting."

"I like it," Mary Beth said. "We'll tell her it's just routine—procedure."

She smiled at the thought of Elizabeth Kowalski submitting to an evidence extraction but not really thinking for a second the perfect little homemaker had anything to do with the crime. Her smile soon faded to a frown though as she thought about where they'd be if Pedro wasn't their guy—back to waiting around for a DNA Hail Mary from the Feds to solve a case with no good leads otherwise.

"You think this DNA draw with Pedro's gonna turn out to be a waste of time?" she asked.

Izzy spit a gristly bite of steak into a napkin. "Well, even if he's not our guy. We gotta do it anyway, right?"

Mary Beth agreed.

"Plus, his DNA can tell us if there's any kind of match to something the Feds might find. Even a distant one, like if it was one of his cousins. You see how defensive he got when we brought them up?"

"I did. Like he wasn't so sure himself."

"Exactly," Izzy said. "He told me something too when we were driving to his house about how all his cousins wanted to bang Maria."

"Oh, yeah?"

"What if one of them had a thing with her and that's what led to her getting killed?"

"Could explain this big blow-up Maria and Pedro had a week earlier," Mary Beth said.

She and Izzy spent a few minutes comparing notes on the different ways the Kowalski spouses had portrayed Pedro and Maria's relationship. Then Mary Beth asked, "So, how are you seeing this if we were to find DNA matching one of Pedro's cousins? A lover's spat?"

Izzy shrugged. "Could be. Maybe the guy gets rough and things go too far and he figures it'd be easier to just finish her off and hide the body than face the aftermath. Or it could be the cousin or whoever didn't want Pedro to find out about them. Could be anything at this point."

"Could even be that Pedro got sick of Maria cheating on him and got one of his cousins to go make sure it never happened again."

Izzy took another long drink and motioned the waitress for another round.

"I'm good," Mary Beth said. She looked back at the waitress, knifing her hand across her throat.

"No you're not. We're working here. Beer helps the creativity." Izzy beckoned the waitress again and Mary Beth decided not to fight it, nodding that she'd take another as well. She went ahead and took another long slurp of the beer sitting in front of her, half full, and finished it in one gulp.

"Pedro tell you anything else interesting?"

Izzy relayed the information about Pedro's lawyer—Mary Beth's long-time nemesis, Alexander Pomfried—having some kind of back channel to the cartel that he used to guarantee Pedro's brother, Raul, could rat with impunity.

"No shit?" Mary Beth said. "That dirty motherfucker."

Mary Beth had a ton of reasons to dislike Alexander Pomfried, not the least of which was the fancy-dressed southern gentleman's insistence upon calling her Sugar. As she finished her dinner, Mary Beth kept thinking about how if this case led to some dirt she could use to get Pomfried permanently disbarred, it would be the perfect *coup de gras* to his sanctimonious career.

After wondering awhile why the waitress was ignoring them, despite having cleared their plates twenty minutes earlier, Mary Beth and Izzy realized they were supposed to pay their bill using the video machine that had been sitting on the table the whole time. They settled up and then made their way across the street to THE RODEO. Mary Beth handed Izzy his room key on the way and swore she was only staying for one drink.

They weaved through a parking lot full of pickup trucks and waited in line before passing through a metal detector. Mary Beth wished her Glock was strapped to her hip instead of locked away in the trunk of her Camaro. Once inside they maneuvered around a crowd of high-heeled, bikini-wearing, silicone-enhanced, women waiting their turn atop the mechanical bull that was thrusting and swiveling on the main stage. The current contestant, a platinum blonde whose hands were too busy keeping her top from coming off to break her fall, was launched into the air and landed squarely on her forehead against the padded floor, causing rough looking men in cowboy hats to leap in the air, shouting their approval. Izzy joined in, shouting, "Ya-hoooo!"

The bouncers helped the dazed blonde walk it off as the D.J. called up the next rider, "Noelle," singing her name like the Christmas Carol, "No-el, No-el, the First No-el. You're the next contestant, come on down girl!"

Mary Beth and Izzy settled in at a small, round, high-top near enough to the action to satisfy Izzy. A buxom waitress in a plaid shirt tied off above her belly button stopped by to take their order.

"Bring me a Miller Lite," Izzy said.

"We've got a two-drink minimum," the waitress cautioned, looking at them like tenderfoots who just wanted to check out the spectacle and wouldn't last long.

"Okay," Izzy said, "then bring me two Miller Lites."

The waitress scribbled a note on a flip pad and looked to Mary Beth who, knowing she was making a mistake, said, "I'll take a whiskey, neat."

"What kind of whiskey?"

"Surprise me."

Noelle didn't last thirty seconds on the bull. She was followed by a brunette with Aquanet bangs and a skimpy red bikini that hung on for dear life, stretching to contain her perky ta-tas. The waitress returned with their drinks as Aquanet was gingerly mounting the bull.

Mary Beth had been wrong about one thing, there wasn't

any chicken wire, nor a band, but there were plenty of rednecks shooting them some side-eye. She spotted a table of some especially cocky ones who kept glancing their way like the sight of a white woman and black man sitting together was something to behold.

Izzy was too engrossed with ogling the ladies to notice, but it was burning Mary Beth up good and she said something after they'd each tasted their drinks. "Racist assholes."

Izzy turned to see what she was looking at and the three men all looked away.

Izzy turned back to Mary Beth, shaking his head. "They aren't staring at me."

"What?"

"They're checking you out."

"Whatever."

"It's true. Back in Jasper Creek, everybody just sees the badge. But here nobody knows you. You're a hot mama."

"Piss off."

"I'm serious," Izzy said. "Why don't you go talk to them?"

Mary Beth snorted, not sure herself if it was from laughter or disgust. She sipped her whiskey, thinking about how much those guys looked like the greasy types who used to patronize Mountain Flowers, skeezing up on the strippers who'd pretend to be interested. Mary Beth remembered watching all that play out, thinking that maybe the most she could expect from life was to let some half-evolved animal sweat all over her, holding her breath until it was done, to get whatever it was she'd thought she needed from a man.

What was it, anyway? Security? Stability? Love? Well, she didn't need any of those things now. She hadn't been able to count on her father or her husband for it, so she'd taken care of it herself. The world could keep its roughnecks, like those three over there. Mary Beth was doing just fine without them.

"No thanks," she said.

"You saving yourself for marriage?" Izzy'd been needling her for years that it was time to get out and start dating again.

"Already was married."

Izzy took a sip. "The way Bill used to tell it, you were saving yourself back then too."

Mary Beth nearly dropped her glass at that one. "Bill would never."

Izzy held up his hands, like Don't shoot the messenger. "Not to me," he said. "Bill knew we were tight. But it used to be the big joke around the station. Guys always calling him Officer Blue Balls."

"Bullshit." Mary Beth didn't want to believe that about Bill, but honestly, she could see how maybe he'd let something slip about their private life one time, a little indiscretion on a long stakeout perhaps, where he shared a marital frustration with a colleague and it made its way around the locker room.

Izzy leaned in like he had something serious to say. Mary Beth noticed his already glassy eyes.

"Plus, I knew who you were really saving yourself for."

"Fuck you." The words had fired out of Mary Beth without thinking and she felt bad for saying them. She looked away, not able to take Izzy's gaze. "Don't look at me like that." She tried to ignore him, drinking down the rest of her whiskey.

"You know he still calls me at least once a week," Izzy said. "Asking if I'll talk to you for him. If there's some way he can make amends."

"Well, there's not. If he calls again, hang up"

Izzy reached for Mary Beth's hand and she pulled it away like they were in the midst of a lover's spat, drawing some stares from the three cowboys who still made Mary Beth uneasy. She was afraid they might come over wanting to show how macho they were by kicking Izzy's ass.

"Quit being so damn stubborn and just admit that you still are, and have always been, in love with Patrick Connelly."

"I most certainly am not."

"Oh really. Then why is it—"

Mary Beth shot up from the table. "I'm not talking about this," she said.

Izzy surrendered. "Okay, okay, okay. Just sit back down."

Mary Beth eventually sat and they both stayed quiet for a few minutes, stewing as Honky-Tonk Badonkadonk thumped out the speakers, inspiring quite the dance moves from the line of would-be bull riders. Then Izzy said, "Just tell me one thing."

Mary Beth looked at him.

"When did you know?"

"Know what?"

"About Sam?"

Out of reflex, Mary Beth tried to look confused but it was no use. Izzy knew the truth about Sam's parentage. She'd confided in him amidst the trauma of the Old Wengo Mine Disaster, not long after revealing the truth to Patrick Connelly that he, not Bill, was really Sam's father. She, Izzy, and Patrick, were the only souls who knew, or would ever know. It was her deepest, darkest secret.

"What about him?" Mary Beth asked, playing dumb out of habit.

Izzy spelled it out. "Did you know the whole time you and Bill were together that Patrick was really the father?"

Mary Beth shook her head, thinking she must already be getting a little tipsy herself as a wave of something like nostalgia washed over her. It all seemed like the contrived plot of some bad romance novel looking back on it, how she'd really just been dating Bill to pass the time during her senior year of high school, waiting to graduate and go join Patrick, who was already a freshman in college. She was feeling stuck and left behind—and hurt by Patrick's insistence they see other people during their year apart; that it'd be good for them.

Is that how Maria felt about Pedro, she wondered. *What*

had that led her to do? And did it have anything to do with her being killed?

In Mary Beth's case it had been her jealous streak that pushed her into going all the way with Bill to begin with, after her cousin Raelynn told her—falsely, it would turn out—that she'd hooked up with Patrick while he was home for fall break, the night after he'd been with Mary Beth. Once she'd crossed that barrier with Bill, there was no going back and they slept together four or five times before she realized she was pregnant and just assumed he was the father.

The first thing she did was tell Patrick, but he didn't take the news well, hearing that the love of his life was in a family way with another guy—and a football player of all people. The word "whore" was used in what would turn out to be their last conversation for about twenty years. Bill, on the other hand, was nothing but noble upon hearing the news, dropping to one knee and cashing in his savings bonds to buy her a thin little ring.

"Sam looked so much like me," she said to Izzy. "I assumed he was Bill's. It wasn't until Sam started walking and talking that I started to get little inklings that I did my best to ignore at first. Little looks and things you know. Then he started reading when he was just three years old. Three years old, going through a *Dick and Jane* book like it was nothing. I didn't see how that could have come from me or Bill, but Bill was so proud. 'My boy, the prodigy,' that's what he'd say. So, I just told myself it couldn't be. I'd only been with Patrick one time when he was home for Fall break, and I just figured what are the odds?"

Mary Beth smiled wistfully. "Then when Sam was in second or third grade—I'd gone into his class for something—and the teacher had all the students going around the room, talking about the thing that scared them most. Everybody was saying normal things like snakes and spiders, the boogeyman–whatever–and when they got to little Sam, he said, 'mediocrity.' And it was like he said it in Patrick's voice–as clear as a bell. That's when I knew."

Izzy was looking at her, glassy eyed from alcohol but riveted. "You never told Bill?"

"I thought about it. Hundreds of times. But all I'd have been doing would have been trying to make myself feel better. Unburden things." She shook her head. "No. I figured if I really loved Bill, the best thing I could do was keep that secret to myself."

18

THE THREE COWBOYS Mary Beth was worried about had turned into Izzy's best friends by the time she decided to call it a night. One of them even let Izzy borrow his hat so the deputy could do his Eddie Murphy impression, busting them up by reciting the *48 Hours* speech about being the new sheriff in town and not liking rednecks.

Mary Beth interrupted the brewhaha long enough to tell Izzy to make sure he was ready to go by seven the following morning. He gave her the thumbs up and headed off to join in on the line dancing that started up once the bull-riding competition was over.

As Mary Beth left the bar, she realized she had a decent buzz going. She was already two whiskeys and three beers in, but when the fresh air hit her, she got the notion to go buy a little bottle she could take back to her room for a quiet night cap and a couple of cigarettes, away from all the people and racket. She crossed the street, thinking about where she might be able to score a pack of smokes and just a little airplane bottle or two of Jack Daniels when she spotted Mr. Sleeveless, the motel manager, leaned up against the wall by the office, puffing a cigarette.

"Mind if I bum one of those?" she asked.

The young man smiled as Mary Beth stepped into the light. He pulled a pack of Parliaments from his shorts pocket and offered it to her. "Anything for an officer of the law."

His drawl had her asking, "Where you from, anyway?" She took the cigarette and held her blouse to her chest as she leaned over to light it.

"South Carolina. Ever been there?"

"Been to Myrtle Beach about a hundred times."

"The Grand Strand. I grew up not too far from there."

Mary Beth took a long, savored drag. "What brought you up here?"

"This is my mom's place," he said, gesturing to the motel. "She married a guy who was from here. He died a couple years ago so I help her run it now."

Mary Beth eyed the two-story row of rooms that looked like they'd been built in the seventies without any renovations since. "Nice place," she said.

The guy smiled. "It's a shithole. But bless your heart for sayin' so."

Maybe it was the liquor, but he was really cute, Mary Beth thought. Young. But very, very cute. "I like how you talk," she said.

"I like how you talk, too."

"How's that?"

He dropped his cigarette and ground it out with his shoe. "Kind a twangy and sweet- sounding. Even when what you're sayin' isn't meant to be sweet at all."

Mary Beth smiled. She took another drag, already thinking about how she'd like another when that one was done.

"Hey," he said, "I finished that Travis McGee novel if you want it."

A novel was about the last thing Mary Beth was interested in. "Nah, that's okay," she said. "I don't want to take your book."

"I don't mind, really. I got a bunch more. I'm trying to finish the whole series by the end of the summer."

"You got a book report due or something?"

He shrugged, flexing his biceps when he did it, making sure she got a good look. "No. Just something to do."

Mary Beth was intrigued by this guy. Looking at him she would have guessed he was another perennial adolescent, floating through life like a leaf on the wind, living in his mom's basement, spending his nights playing Call of Duty or some other bullshit like that. But his eyes had depth to them. She recognized him as an old soul.

"So, you're really a sheriff?"

"I really am." Mary Beth could tell he was impressed.

"That dangerous?"

"Can be."

The guy pulled out another cigarette just as Mary Beth was finishing hers and she was glad when he offered her a second. "You ever have to shoot anybody?"

Mary Beth leaned forward to light her smoke. She didn't bother to cover herself this time and caught him sneaking a peek at the curves below her neckline.

She blew out a big puff of smoke, trying to look cool, saying, "Nobody who didn't have it coming."

"Jesus," he said, shaking his head. "You're something else."

"Some say it is so," Mary Beth said, going to one of her favorite lines, then asking, "Hey, what's your name, anyway?"

"Tom."

"Well, Tom," Mary Beth paused to take another long drag off her cigarette, sucking a third of it down. "Shouldn't a smart guy like you be off at college or something?"

He frowned. "Things just didn't work out that way. I was about half way through when my stepdad died and my mom needed my help. That was–God–six years ago. Been here ever since."

"Ever think about going back?"

He rocked his head back and forth in a compromise between a Yes and No. "Maybe someday. But we all gotta do what we gotta do, right?"

"Yes, we do."

Tom repositioned himself against the wall and she noticed him stagger a bit and realized she wasn't the only one who was a bit tipsy. *What did this guy do*, she wondered, *sit in his little office drinking all night?*

"Does eat at you though," he said.

"What's that?"

"That anxiety. The feeling like you should have done more, should have been more—like things aren't the way they're supposed to be."

Mary Beth watched him as she smoked, feeling like she knew exactly what he was talking about.

"My mom, she thinks we're all just biding our time here on earth. Like the whole point of this life, is to just wait around for the next one," he said.

"That what you believe?"

Tom sniffed loudly. "I don't know about all that. But it does feel like sometimes we're all just waiting around for something. Like something's gonna happen or something big is coming. You spend your whole life waiting on it and then one day you're down in room 218 changing a lightbulb and your heart just gives out."

"Your stepdad?"

Tom nodded. "Yeah."

Mary Beth thought on that as she smoked. She normally wasn't very philosophical but the moderate intoxication she was feeling had her indulging such contemplations more than she would, typically. "So, what's the point then?" she asked. "If we're all just sitting around waiting for something that's never gonna come?"

"Maybe there is no point." Tom smiled and gestured toward her. "Maybe life's just about passing the time with some good company."

Mary Beth smiled too. "Maybe," she said.

Tom stomped out his second cigarette and glanced toward the office like he needed to get back. "Hey, by any chance, do you like whiskey?"

Mary Beth didn't think about it for two seconds before saying, "Does the pope shit in the woods?"

Izzy's phone alarm went off for the first time that morning at six a.m. He snoozed it five times after, thinking for sure Mary Beth would be banging on his door like the gestapo any second.

The night had gone on longer than it should have, invading into the early morning hours, and Izzy felt like microwaved dog food. He didn't want to give up on sleep until absolutely necessary, figuring that since he didn't have a change of clothes or even a toothbrush on him, he'd just roll out of bed at the last minute and then rough it in the back of Mary Beth's car while she took care of business that morning. Then he could finish sleeping it off on the way back to Jasper Creek. Once they got there, he'd have Mary Beth run him by the station so he could shower and clean himself up before going home to Princess. Then all would be right with the world.

But when the phone alarm went off again at ten after seven with no word yet from Mary Beth, he started to get worried. Izzy blearily reached for the phone and shut off the alarm. He rolled over on his back and tried a couple of times to ring the sheriff but each time it went straight to voicemail.

"Shit." *She must have forgot to charge her phone.* Izzy smacked himself on the cheek a couple of times then slumped out of bed and struggled to put yesterday's clothes back on. He felt dizzy and had to sit back down for a minute, afraid he might be sick. He dropped to his back, arm across his forehead, and tried one more time to call Mary Beth.

"You've reached Sheriff Mary Beth Cain, of Jasper County. Please leave your name, number, and a short message after the beep."

"Goddammit," Izzy groaned. He'd have to go find her.

As he sat out into the parking lot, Izzy struggled to remember Mary Beth's room number. He knew it was on the first floor down near the office because she'd parked right in front of it. Couldn't remember exactly which one it was but as long as she hadn't moved her car, he figured he should be able to find her.

It was a muggy morning, overcast and threatening the kind of summer rain that would come on hard and fast then cook off minutes later. Izzy was walking briskly, worrying they'd be late for their meeting with Pedro, knowing the more time they gave him to think things over, the greater the likelihood he'd get cold feet about cooperating. He knew it was really important they be there on time.

Fortunately, Mary Beth's car was right where he'd last seen it, six rooms down from the office.

He plunked his forehead against the mustard-colored motel room door and started banging. "MB! Wake up! It's time to go!"

Then he waited.

No answer.

He pounded louder. "Yo! Mary Beth! We're gonna be late!"

He waited some more, putting his ear to the door this time.

Still no answer. Nothing. Not a sound.

Where in the hell is she?

Izzy did a once-around Mary Beth's car, cupping his hands to peer inside its tinted windows. No signs she'd been back in there since last night.

Looking at the room again he spied a small crease where

the curtains hadn't been completely pulled to. He did his best to scope through the window. It was dark inside but he could tell that the bed was made. The room appeared completely untouched.

Did Mary Beth even sleep here last night?

She seemed fine when Izzy last saw her. He tried to remember what time that was when she left the bar. It was still early, he thought. Probably around ten-thirty or eleven. And her car hadn't been moved so she couldn't have gone far.

Still, this wasn't like Mary Beth. She was extremely punctual. He tried her cell phone again as he did a three-sixty in the parking lot, looking for somewhere the sheriff might have walked to grab some breakfast or toiletries.

"You've reached Sheriff Mary Beth Cain, of Jasper Cou—"

"Dammit!" Just as Izzy was ending the call, he heard two gunshots fire off in quick succession. They echoed like cannon fire. Boom. Boom.

Instinctively, Izzy ducked but realized quickly that the shots had come from a distance, somewhere behind the motel. A sick feeling in the pit of his stomach told him that wherever they'd originated from was where he'd find Mary Beth.

Izzy started heading that direction, not quite running, more trotting at first, and reaching for his hip, forgetting he was unarmed.

He rounded the office, past some dumpsters, plunging through the smell of old garbage and cat piss, where he found a drainage stream that ran like a shallow moat behind the building. About fifty yards back down the rear of the motel was a ramshackle wooden bridge that spanned the stream, leading to an innkeeper's home set back in the woods, a three-story A-frame with a rusty metal roof.

Two more shots rang out, piercing the rattly buzz of the large air conditioning units. They were followed by unintelligible shouts in the distance, somewhere near the A-frame. Izzy couldn't make out what was said but detected at least two voices. One male, one female.

He ran in their direction.

19

IZZY DASHED ACROSS THE YARD, crouching low, looking all around for the active shooter. When he got to the A-frame house, he flattened himself against it, just as the rain began to pour. "Police!" he shouted amidst the sudden downpour. "Put down your weapon and identify yourself!"

No response.

The rain was really pelting. Izzy waited for a moment to see if it would lighten up. Thankfully, the A-frame provided an over-hang of about twelve inches along the front of the house. As the rain continued to pour, Izzy slid along the cedar planks, check-ing inside windows.

He tried calling out again, "Police! Who's back there?" He thought for a second he heard something like giggling but couldn't be sure with the sound of the wind and rain. "Put down your weapon, or you may get shot," Izzy ordered. He was unarmed, of course, but there was no reason that whoever was back there should know that.

The rain started to slow—one of those quick summer hitters. Izzy waited another minute, listening and not hearing anything before making a crouched run around the side of the house, past some old croquet mallets leaned against the slanted roof and an empty mesh rabbit pen.

Izzy froze at the corner and hazarded a quick peek into the backyard.

There was Mary Beth.

She was seated with her back to a picnic table that was littered with crumpled beer cans. The sheriff was holding her Glock to her nose like she was smelling the barrel. She was in her underwear, a pretty pink pair of cotton panties, with her long pale legs spread in a wide stance. Her curly hair was haphazardly tied into a top knot. The rain had slowed to a drizzle but she'd obviously been outside during the deluge as her drenched white tank top clung to her braless chest.

"Pssst. MB."

Mary Beth didn't respond. She looked like she was meditating, completely unphased by the elements, but swaying slightly, eyes closed, blowing softly on her pistol.

Izzy tried again, louder this time. "Pssst!"

Mary Beth opened her eyes slowly. She looked at him blankly at first then held her finger to her lips. "Shhhh."

Izzy didn't know what was going on. Why were they being quiet? Who else was out there? Was Mary Beth the one who'd been doing the shooting? Or was it someone else? Was she in danger?

Before Izzy could ask any of those questions a twenty-something man who was dingus-dangling naked, jumped out from behind an elderberry bush, crouched down like he was about to take a dump, yelled "Pull!" then leap-frogged into the air flinging two full beer cans high into the sky.

Mary Beth sprang into action, swiveling around in a one-eighty, losing her balance in the process and falling hard on her hip in the muddy grass but never taking her eyes off the cans. She had her arms extended with a two-handed grip, leaning sideways, and squeezed the trigger twice, blowing both Budweisers into a firework explosion of suds.

"Whooooo!" the naked man hooted. He bent backwards like he was howling at the moon, showing off his youthful abs and forcing Izzy to avert his eyes.

Mary Beth rolled onto her back where she wallowed in the muddy grass, laughing hysterically as she clutched the gun to her chest.

"Gaaaawd damnnnnn," the man said, slurring as badly as anything Izzy had ever heard. "You are ...without a doubt ...the sexiest damn thang ... I have ever seen ... in my en-ti-re life!"

Izzy couldn't believe what he was seeing. These two were completely shitfaced drunk. And one of them was armed.

Izzy approached Mary Beth, cautiously, saying, "MB, let's just put the gun down, okay?"

She rolled toward him, propping up on one elbow and pointed her Glock right at him. She waived it around playfully. "Izzzzyyyyy." Then she started laughing again. She flopped on her back, hitting her head this time, hard enough that it quieted her for a second and she set the gun down to rub the back of her noggin.

When she did, Izzy lunged for the pistol. He snatched it just before Mary Beth swatted him on the arm.

"Hey. What's the...What's the...What...What's the big idea, big man?"

Izzy stowed the gun in his waistband as the naked boy-toy noticed him for the first time, slicking back his hair and extending his hand. "Tom. Tom, uh ..." He searched in vain for his last name.

"Tom Cat!" Mary Beth shouted like it was the funniest joke she'd ever heard.

Tom pointed at her and slapped his knee. "Right. Tom ... the Cat. Damn nice to meet you."

Izzy let Tom's hand hang–seemed everything else was–then

the guy belched and swallowed hard like he might vomit. "You uh, you ... you wanna shoot?"

"No," Izzy said, forcefully.

Now that he had the gun his attitude about this scenario changed from one of caution to royally pissed. He felt like a father who just caught his teenage daughter making out with some scumbag. "You got some clothes somewhere you can put on?" he asked.

The guy turned in circles, stumbling as he looked aimlessly around the yard. "Shit. Where'd they—"

"Maybe a fig leaf or something? Anything?".

Tom Cat held up a finger. "Hang on." He disappeared inside the house.

Once he was gone, Izzy bent down over Mary Beth. "MB, what the hell?"

"Izzzzyyyyy," she said, caressing the back of his head with muddy fingers.

"We're supposed to be meeting Pedro right now. Remember? The big case?"

Mary Beth closed her eyes. "Pedro. Right. Pedro." She tried to sit up. "Don't worry. I'll–I'll shoot him."

Oh, God, what a nightmare, Izzy thought. "MB, we've gotta go. I've got to get you out of here."

He hooked his arms under hers and struggled to get Mary Beth to her feet.

"I'll shoot him, right in is chest." She was slumped over Izzy's shoulder and jammed a finger gun into his breastbone. "Shoot him right there."

"Come on."

Izzy did his best to walk her toward the house but she wasn't helping much.

With some considerable struggle they reached the sliding door that Tom Cat had left wide open. Inside, Izzy found Mary Beth's beau snoring, face down on a tweed couch. An empty gallon-sized bottle of Evan Williams sat on the coffee table along with an over-filled ashtray and a beige-colored bra that Izzy assumed belonged to his fearless leader.

He sat the sheriff down in a corner chair with a rounded back and started looking about for her pants.

"Just shoot him!" she yelled at the top of her lungs. "Bang! Bang! Boo-yah!"

There was no sign of the pants, but Izzy did manage to find Mary Beth's purse on the far side of the couch just as she was switching from laughter to tears, weeping as she said, "I'll shoot that baby boy right in his precious little heart."

Izzy checked inside the purse and said a prayer of thanks when he found her car keys. He checked his watch. Twenty til. If he really hurried, he could still get to Pedro's by eight. But there was no way he could take Mary Beth with him in her condition.

Maybe he could get her to sleep it off in that weird, triangular little house and then he'd come back and pick her up later.

He looked over and Mary Beth was head-in-hands sobbing, moaning, "shoot them all. Everyone of those sons of bitches."

Izzy groaned as he bent down, trying to get her to look at him. "Mary Beth. Listen. I've got to go. I need you to stay here. Okay?"

She looked up, not understanding. "Where?"

"I'm going to go see Pedro. You stay here and try to sleep. I'll come back for you."

Mary Beth wiped the tears from her bloodshot eyes, looking fierce all of a sudden. "No!" she said. "No! I'm coming."

God, what a fiasco that would be, showing up with Mary Beth drunk as a hoot owl in a trailer park. "You've got to trust me," he said. "I'll take care of this. I need you to stay here. Stay with–" Izzy looked disdainfully at the naked rump curled up on the couch and almost couldn't bring himself to say it: "Tom Cat."

"No. I've got to stay with you." Mary Beth said, pleading like a little girl now.

A version of this back and forth continued for minutes, Izzy trying to convince a drunk and bewildered Mary Beth to just go the fuck to sleep, and her proving painfully persistent, no matter what he said.

Izzy checked his watch again. He didn't have any more time to lose and Mary Beth clearly wasn't relenting so he tried a ruse. "Okay. You can come but I need you to find your pants first."

Mary Beth looked down, surprised by the sight of her bare legs and started looking around for her pants like they might have crept off somewhere by themselves.

"I've looked all around down here," Izzy told her. "I think they may be upstairs. Maybe in the bedroom?"

Mary Beth pointed to the stairs.

"Right," Izzy said. "Why don't you go look for them up there?"

Mary Beth stumbled in that direction then crawled up the steps.

As soon as she cleared the landing and was out of sight, Izzy made a run for it. He slid the door closed behind him, wishing there was some way he could lock it from the outside, and then took off in a dash.

Halfway across the field, approaching the rickety bridge that forded the stream separating the innkeeper's home from the motel, Izzy started having second thoughts about this plan. His head filled with images of Mary Beth, drunk out of her mind, injuring herself somehow. Maybe he should just forget about Pedro and tend to his friend. At least stay with her until she finally fell asleep.

Then, to his horror, he heard Mary Beth calling after him.

"Izzzzzzyyyyyyyyy!"

He looked back and couldn't believe what he saw. Moments ago, Mary Beth could barely walk. Now she'd caught some kind of second wind and was running at him–fast. Barefoot and pantless, but moving like a deer.

For a second, he was that little kid on the playground running from the girl who went around kissing the immature boys. He tried to escape her out of instinct, then realized that even if he could slip away, he couldn't just leave her like that—not out where she could mix with the public.

Izzy stopped at the little bridge, close enough to the motel to hear people milling around out front.

"MB, wait!"

He'd decided to just try to get her back inside the house, but she didn't slow down. Not at all. Instead, she leapt at him, tackling him onto the bridge with enough force that their combined weight cracked some of the wooden slats. Then Mary Beth snatched the car keys and kneed him in the stomach as she crawled over top of him.

The fall had knocked the wind out of Izzy and it took him a moment to get back to his feet. He managed it in time to catch the back of Mary Beth as she headed past the dumpsters toward the front of the hotel. *Jesus*, Izzy thought. *She's going to try and drive!*

He ran as fast as he could, catching up to Mary Beth as she was getting the driver-side car door open. He wasted no time trying to reason with her. Instead, he bear-hugged her from behind and lifted her up and away from the vehicle.

A woman exiting a nearby motel room mistook the intervention as an assault and screamed, "Leave her alone!"

Izzy became aware of other gawkers gathering on the scene while Mary Beth kicked and thrashed like a wild animal, trying to free herself from his grip. She screeched then dug her sharp fingernails into his arms. He briefly released her then grabbed Mary Beth by the elbow as she pulled away. Izzy spun her around and scooped her up on his shoulder in a fireman's carry.

Mary Beth dropped her car keys when he hoisted her. Izzy heard them jingle when they hit the ground and pivoted in that direction. He tried to reach for them and Mary Beth sank her teeth into his shoulder, deep enough to draw blood.

"Ahhh!" Izzy screamed and dropped to his knees, heaving Mary Beth away from him near a bystander who started backing away, yelling, "I'm calling the police!"

Now they really needed to get out of there. Izzy looked around at all white faces watching this little black man getting rough with a half-naked pale-skinned woman and knew that if the wrong kind of cops showed up he might end up getting shot before he could explain who he was and what was really going on. And even if he managed to relay the situation, the truth could ruin Mary Beth's career.

Izzy was holding his shoulder from where Mary Beth had bit him, while looking around desperately for the car keys. He spotted them lying halfway between him and Mary Beth, and they both lunged for them at the same time.

Izzy beat her by a millisecond. When he scooped up the keys, Mary Beth grabbed for her gun that was tucked in Izzy's waistband but he managed to get it away from her as he pinned her to the ground. There were more screams by bystanders and someone yelled, "Run!" at the sight of the gun.

Izzy looked down at Mary Beth whose mouth was agape, ready to bite into his arm.

"Wait! Wait! You can come!"

Mary Beth paused, looking at him cross-eyed.

Izzy struggled to catch his breath. "Just get in the car."

Mary Beth seemed confused at first. She looked at the car, then back at him to make sure this wasn't a trick.

"Let's go!" He commanded. He looked around the parking lot watching the bystanders scattering and expected to hear sirens any second.

Izzy ushered Mary Beth into the car, shoving her head down to get her inside and hastily belted her in place.

"Just stay put." he said.

By the time they got to Pedro's office, Mary Beth was thankfully starting to nod off. Izzy parked the car as gently as he could, watching Mary Beth's head begin to slump and debating what to do. On the one hand, if she did finally, by the grace of God, pass out, she wouldn't be getting up anytime soon. He could probably slip into Pedro's office, take care of business in ten minutes, and be back to drive Mary Beth home before anybody knew the difference. Just crack the windows and she should be fine.

But what if she did wake up while he was gone? There's no telling what she'd do. Or what if somebody walked by and recognized her? Even though they were out of town, Mary Beth had received a good bit of press in the last year. It was possible somebody would know who she was and might start taking pictures of her passed out in her skivvies.

Maybe getting her home and far from the public eye was more important than getting Pedro's DNA. It was possible Pedro would give them a rain check. Or if not, they could always go for a warrant.

As Izzy was making up his mind, there was a harsh knock on the window that made him jump and also jolted Mary Beth awake.

Izzy swiveled around. His heart skipped a beat when he saw who it was.

There, in one of his trademark seersuckers suits was Alexander Pomfried, a Mark Twain doppelgänger, only much heavier, with a smug grin spreading beneath his bushy mustache.

Izzy pivoted back toward Mary Beth, instinctively wanting to cover her in some way but she was already halfway out the door, stumbling down onto the pavement. She got stuck in a downward-facing dog position with her wet pink panties sagging low enough to expose the top of her butt crack.

Izzy raced around the car to Mary Beth but Pomfried had already seen all there was to see. His voice was brimming with sheer delight as he said, "Well, howdy, Sugar."

20

"**ALEXANDER POMFRIED?** He was there?" Mary Beth was still feeling foggy after waking up on Izzy's couch with no memory of the prior day. She'd been doing her best not to cry as Izzy recounted the drunken debacle.

"He was." Izzy was matter-of-fact, the unusual coolness in his voice revealing his deep disappointment.

"He saw me like that?"

"He did."

"In my underwear?"

"In your underwear."

Mary Beth shifted around on the soft leather sofa. She stuck her chin out, trying to project some air of dignity. She found it hard to face her friend and took her time examining all of Princess' fancy decorations—a lot of brushed nickel and reclaimed wood, and some expensive looking African masks. Mary Beth was really feeling like the turd in the kiddy pool but managed to hold back the tears until Izzy showed her the claw marks on his arm and the gash from where she'd bit his shoulder.

"Hey, hey, hey," he said, the warmth coming back to his

voice at the sight of tears. "Come on now. It's over. I'm fine. No harm done."

Mary Beth spent a few minutes crying and apologizing with Izzy hugging on her until she'd got enough of it out. Then she sniffed loudly and wiped her eyes with her sleeve, realizing for the first time she was wearing a WVU sweatshirt that must have belonged to Princess.

God, why had she let this happen? Izzy would forgive her–basically already had–and he wasn't the kind to gossip, but she'd still never get over the embarrassment, especially the thought of Alexander Pomfried seeing her half-naked and drunk out of her mind. She vaguely remembered going back to Tom's house and stopping to get her pistol just in case he turned out to be a creep. And there were some hazy flashes of the drinking and copulating, but nothing of the following morning.

Maybe that was a blessing. Something instinctual in Mary Beth's spongy brain told her the shame of it all was more than she could bear. Shame was a dangerous emotion for Mary Beth, the quick-tempered hillbilly girl who'd been quick to fight any kid–boy or girl–who said something about her drug-dealing daddy. She needed to block this out and fast.

Get back to the case, an inner voice of self-preservation whispered to her. *Focus on the work. That is what has always gotten you through. Maria. Focus on Maria. Maria, Maria, Maria. Maria and Pedro. Pedro and ... Pomfried?*

"What was Pomfried doing there?" she asked.

"Making sure we didn't extract any evidence from Pedro without a warrant. The good doctor must have called him after we left his house."

"Shit." Mary Beth picked at a clump of her matted hair, when a thought struck her. "Wait! But he's conflicted out. Pomfried can't represent criminal defendants in this county anymore. Not as long as I'm sheriff."

"He knew you'd say that. I told him he shouldn't be there

and he said that since he represented Pedro from way back, he had an obligation to protect his rights until he'd retained new counsel—who Pomfried brought with him. Some silk-stocking lawyer from Charleston."

"Who?"

Izzy shrugged. "Don't remember the name. I was too busy dealing with you to get his card. All I know is he had some real nice Italian leather shoes … until you puked all over them."

"You're serious?"

"Yep."

Mary Beth palmed her forehead. She tried to focus on her breathing, waiting for the tumultuous feeling erupting inside of her chest to pass.

"If you're interested, you can watch the video."

"Video?" Mary Beth almost choked on the bile bubbling up into her throat.

"The new lawyer took one with his phone. He said he was going to take it to a judge to get a restraining order against the department."

Mary Beth stood and paced, holding her stomach, trying to get her acid reflux to recede. She felt a wave of panic at the thought her behavior could prevent them from investigating Pedro, but as she let it wash over her, she was steeled by the belief that was impossible. "Wait," she said. "You can't get a restraining order against the police."

"Maybe not. But you can sue the shit out of the county for money it doesn't have."

"Sue, for what?"

"Violating Pedro's rights. Pomfried said we were trying to harass him into a false confession—threatening him with torture and prison rape." Izzy gave her his I-told-you-so stare. "Remember that sweet little story you told him about getting your teeth pried out?"

"Jesus." Mary Beth closed her eyes, trying to wish it all away. *Please God*, she prayed, *let it just be a dream*.

Then the doorbell rang.

"That's probably Sam," Izzy said. "He's been really worried about you."

The panic was back. "Sam? He—"

"Don't worry," Izzy said. "I told him you'd come down with a bad case of food poisoning and were staying here for a day or two so somebody could keep an eye on you. He asked if he could come over later."

"Food poisoning?"

"It's what I used to always tell my professors in college when I was too hungover to make it to class. It's technically true if you think about it."

The doorbell rang again.

"I'd better get that."

Mary Beth started scrambling for a cover story about food poisoning to use with her son. Her mind was so addled she couldn't think straight. She called to Izzy, "I don't want Sam to see me like this," but it was too late, he was already opening the door. She heard him say, "Oh, hey, Goforth. What's up?"

"Heard the Sheriff was here convalescing."

Mary Beth breathed a slight sigh of relief, realizing it wasn't her son, but only slightly. As much as she didn't want her son to see her so indisposed, the idea of one of her subordinates waltzing in right now wasn't much better. She'd spent so much time cultivating an aura of invincibility to win over her deputies, she didn't want Ben Goforth seeing her in her current condition even if he did think it was due to food poisoning.

Fortunately, Izzy understood that. "Yeah, he said. "She's still a bit under the weather. Princess and I are keeping an eye on her. She's not really up for visitors just yet. But I'll be sure to tell her you stopped by."

"Well, this fella here's with the Marshal's service," she heard

Goforth say. "Got some papers he's supposed to serve on her. ASAP."

Great. Now there was a federal marshal who could pile onto the embarrassment. There was a pause in the conversation at the door, then Izzy said, "You looked at this?"

"No. It's under seal." Must have been the Marshall who said that because Mary Beth didn't recognize the voice.

"Good," Izzy said, "consider it served."

"Judge Crowley insisted I serve it on her personally."

Please Izzy, just get rid of them, Mary Beth silently begged.

"Well, she's sleeping right now," Izzy said. "But as a sworn deputy of Jasper County I pledge to you that I will stick it under her nose the second she wakes up."

After a hesitation the voice said, "Okay, but she raises any issues about proper service, and I'm taking it up with you."

"Understood," Izzy said. "You won't have any problems."

The visitors left and Izzy re-entered the living room. He'd already torn into the sealed manilla envelope and was reading through a stack of papers.

"What is it?"

Izzy held up a finger so he could finish reading something. His face was glum. "Well," he said, "at least we know that lawyer's name now. Felix Lancaster, from Morgan and Powell, LLP."

"What's it say?"

Izzy dropped the stack of papers in Mary Beth's lap. "It says our department is temporarily enjoined from contacting Pedro or seeking any investigative warrants against him, without first giving his attorney notice and an opportunity to be heard."

Mary Beth bolted upright. "They can't do that!"

Izzy turned a couple pages and pointed to the good part, reading, "Injunctive relief is available pursuant to 42 U.S.C. section 1983 to remedy the Jasper County Sheriff Department's, and Sheriff Cain's, in particular, long-standing and well-documented history of violating the civil rights of criminal suspects, afforded them by the fourteenth amendment, including, but not limited to, the Sheriff's personal threats of violence and torture made to the Plaintiff." He shoved it in Mary Beth's face. "Read it yourself."

Mary Beth scanned through the documents, afraid she might find some screenshots of her in her underwear. The words were just as harsh, although the more she read, the more she realized the parade of horribles it contained were all conclusory statements. It alluded to prior media coverage and various evidentiary rulings and "threats" made to the Plaintiff, but never detailed anything specific.

"What the Court says constitutes good cause here is really vague. I bet we could get this overturned. I'll call Jeannie Boggs over at the DA's office. Royce Parker's retirement party is next week, but she's his top deputy. I'm sure she'd take this on. Or better yet, I'll buzz John Jacobs in the U.S. Attorney's office. I bet he can get this took care of with no trouble at all."

Izzy slapped his forehead in frustration. "Don't you see? They kept the basis vague for a reason. The same reason they filed it under seal. To keep this stuff out of the public record."

"Why would they do that?"

"Because you're probably right about the order. It probably won't hold up. Pedro's lawyer must have got a judge to do him a solid by granting this on an *ex parte* basis."

"So, let's fight it."

"No," Izzy said. "Don't you see? If you fight it, all the stuff does become public. If they'd put everything out there, you'd have been forced to defend yourself. But by doing it this way they can hold the juicy stuff, like that video we know is out there, over your head. Right now, nobody else knows about the little show you put on yesterday, but the second we try to challenge this order or get permission to serve Pedro with a warrant, the video of you in your granny panties puking your guts out will be all over the news, along with a detailed recounting of the sweet little prison rape stories you like to use to intimidate upstanding citizens. And it'll give the papers an excuse to re-run all those *Rough Justice* stories they did about you last year."

Izzy was right. Mary Beth didn't want to admit it—that her behavior had jeopardized the investigation—but she couldn't deny it. Now she'd have to choose between doing what the investigation required versus protecting her career.

"I told you this was going to happen, didn't I?" Izzy said.

"Told me what?"

"That if you kept holding all this stuff in, it was going to blow up in your face one day."

"Oh, here we go. Armchair psychology time. I just had a bad night that got out of hand. Okay? Nothing more than that."

Izzy crossed his arms. "You know you talk to them in your sleep, right?"

"Who?"

Izzy started ticking off the names one finger at a time. "Sawyer, Patrick, your Dad, Sam, Bill. Your whole Mount Rushmore of male demons."

Mary Beth wasn't buying that shit. She had never talked in her sleep. This was just Izzy's ploy to finally get her into therapy. Little Sigmond wouldn't be satisfied until she was meditating at some hippy commune, dressed in a smock and burning incense.

"It's true," Izzy pressed. "I should have recorded it."

"Bull butter."

Izzy huffed, looking at her like she was hopeless.

Mary Beth felt her stomach growl and realized she probably hadn't eaten in over twenty-four hours but was still kind of numb and off-kilter and not as hungry as she should have been. "Look," she said, trying to bring the temperature down. "You may be getting on my case for no reason. Until the Feds come back with their test results, we don't know if there's even a reason to investigate Pedro. You said yourself you didn't think he was our killer."

Izzy took a seat in his easy chair. "That was before."

"Before what?"

"Before Dr. Patel called this morning."

Mary Beth sat up straighter. "What'd he say? Did they find something?"

Izzy raised his hand for her to be patient. "He said it's all still preliminary but they've found at least one thing they think likely belonged to the killer."

"What?"

"A hair. A single black hair, that wasn't Maria's."

Mary Beth felt a charge of electricity surge up her spine. She knew that a hair could be an incredibly valuable piece of evidence, depending upon the condition it was in.

Something Dr. Patel had explained to her years ago, amidst a string of profanities and at least three cigarettes, was that a strand of hair potentially contained two types of DNA, nuclear DNA, which often could only be recovered if the hair root was still attached, and mitochondrial DNA, which was easier to find but was also less useful. Nuclear DNA was preferable because it is inherited from both parents and this could be used to make a complete DNA profile of the source. Mitochondrial DNA on the other hand, was inherited solely from the mother so the best the lab could do with it was to narrow the source down to someone who descended from a certain maternal line.

"Please tell me they found a hair root," Mary Beth said.

Izzy frowned. "Sorry. Dr. Patel says all we've got is mitochondrial DNA. Which means–"

"We can't narrow it down to a specific person."

"Right," Izzy said.

Mary Beth shrugged. Not what she hoped for, but being able to identify the killer's maternal line was a lot better than nothing. And if they could combine a hair match with some other evidence tying a suspect from that list to the crime, it could be enough to make a case.

Izzy was grimacing like she still hadn't gotten the point. "What?" she asked.

"We can't run mitochondrial DNA through the system," he said. "The CODIS database is based off of nuclear DNA. So are most of those genealogy databases out there. The only way we are matching that hair is by a direct comparison with a sample from the right suspect."

What Izzy was saying was that they'd need a warrant to get Pedro's hair to test, but couldn't do that now without risking Mary Beth's career.

"I see where you're going," Mary Beth said. "But what if we don't go directly after Pedro. We could get a warrant to test some of his family members."

Izzy rolled his eyes. "We go after anybody in his family and Pedro's attorneys will say it's just part of a scheme to harass him. Plus, who could we test? His mother's dead and the rest of his family's in Mexico."

"His dad still lives here."

Izzy slapped his forehead. "But all we've got is mitochondrial. It passes from the mother, remember? His father won't match."

"Right." Mary Beth knew that. Her brain just wasn't firing on all cylinders yet. "His brother would match, though," she said.

"Yeah," Izzy agreed. "But he's hiding out down in Mexico too. Good luck finding him. And even if you do, we've got no jurisdiction over him. You really think he's going to help us voluntarily?"

Mary Beth wasn't giving up. "Maybe Raul's already in the system," she suggested. "If they can match his record to the hair then that would tell us it was probably either his or Pedro's."

"I'm not sure they can run the match that way," Izzy said, shaking his head. "But regardless, Raul's not in the system. That was the first thing I checked. He was never convicted so no DNA was ever collected on him."

"What about their cousins?"

Izzy paused. "Hang on."

He pulled out his cell phone and started walking down the hall.

Mary Beth was going to call after him, but a wave of nausea prompted her to lie down instead. She was still flat on her back rubbing her temples when Izzy re-emerged minutes later.

"Testing the cousins won't work. I asked Vanessa. She said the cousins here descend from two of Pedro's uncles so they won't match. The uncles themselves could have the same mitochondrial DNA as Pedro, but according to Vanessa, one of them's dead and the other got deported three years ago."

Mary Beth sighed loudly. She was out of ideas. "Well, shit," she said. "So, basically we need a warrant for Pedro's hair?"

"Yeah. Or his DNA at least. Though, if we're going after him, we might as well get hair too so they can do a microscopic comparison for anything that might rule out other members of the maternal line."

Mary Beth stood and stretched her weary legs, feeling the pins and needles from prolonged inactivity. She was imagining the video of her on YouTube racking up views.

"There's something else," Izzy said. "Are you ready for this?"

"Honestly, I'm not sure I can take any more bombshells this morning."

Izzy arched an eyebrow. "Then you better sit back down."

21

"HO-LY DOG SHIT. MARIA WAS PREGNANT?"

"It appears so," Izzy told her. "Dr. P said they found fetal tissue—enough that they could possibly determine paternity if they had DNA from the father."

Mary needed another moment to process the shock. Once she had, she realized what a tremendous development this was in terms of trying to catch their killer. Izzy had really buried the lead. Fetal remains were a much bigger deal than hair. "Well, why didn't you say so earlier. Screw the hair. We can use the DNA from the fetal remains to do a CODIS search, right?"

Izzy nodded. "Yeah, but the fetal remains tell us who the father is. The hair tells us who the killer is. There's no guarantee they're the same person. And, Pedro isn't in the system. Never been arrested, so we've still got the same problem."

"Only, if Pedro's the father."

"He was her boyfriend at the time."

"Ish," Mary Beth said. "They were on again, off again, right?"

"Yeah," Izzy acknowledged. "But we know they had a big fight a week before Maria disappeared. And whatever it was about was so secret she didn't even tell her friends about it. Then Maria wanted him to come home the next weekend because they had '*important things to discuss*.'" Izzy looked up at her, emphasizing the point with his eyes. "I'm thinking, Pedro's finally moving on from Maria, moving up in the world, dating the nice girl he hoped to marry, when Maria traps him with a baby. She comes to see him at Marshall, tells him she's pregnant, and Pedro makes her disappear so she can't disrupt his plans."

"Except Pedro still has an alibi for the weekend she disappeared. It may have shifted from his roommate to his wife, but it's still an alibi."

"Unless his wife is lying for him—which wouldn't be any big stretch."

"Maybe," Mary Beth said.

"And even if Pedro's alibi's legit, then there's still the possibility he got somebody else to do the deed."

"Just looked up hitmen in the yellow pages?"

Izzy shrugged. "Like we theorized before, one of his cousins or maybe his brother, who—oh, by the way—disappeared south of the border right about the time Maria went missing."

Mary Beth flicked that supposition away. "Raul Kowalski just walked on serious federal drug charges and you're telling me he's going to turn around and do his baby bro a solid by offing his pregnant girlfriend?"

"I've seen crooks do stupider things for a lot less reason."

Isn't that the truth. Mary Beth's stomach grumbled again, aching from emotional upset as much as hunger. "I think a better possibility is that Maria was cheating on Pedro and got knocked up. Maybe that's what they were arguing about the last time they were seen together."

"That's possible. But Pedro's still got to be our number one suspect right now. And if it weren't for this," Izzy said, waving the restraining order like an evangelist's Bible, "we'd be going down to the courthouse this afternoon to get a warrant to test him. And you know it."

Mary Beth reclined back on the couch and stared up at the wood beams that crossed the living room ceiling. She knew Izzy was right. She just didn't want to think about the repercussions of doing what she knew she needed to.

"Whether Pedro ultimately turns out to be our guy or not, we should be trying to test his DNA and his hair, right now," Izzy said. "But doing so, means dragging the department through the mud and maybe ending yours and my career."

"Mine maybe," Mary Beth scoffed. "But how's it going to end your career?"

Izzy shook his head like the parent of an incorrigible kid. "You hadn't heard, either," he said.

"Heard what?"

"Got one last surprise for you, sleeping beauty. Hang on."

Izzy disappeared into his garage and came back carrying a flier. "You're not running uncontested after all," he said. "I found this in my mailbox when we got back." He handed it over.

RANDY LAW
FOR
JASPER COUNTY SHERIFF

ELECT A _REAL_ LAW MAN

"Son of a bitch," Mary Beth said.

Randy Law had been Bill's best friend on the force–a former high school football teammate, who'd even stood as best man at Mary Beth and Bill's impromptu wedding before a JP up in Pearisburg. But after Bill died and Mary Beth took over as sheriff, Randy let it be known in a number of not so indiscrete ways that he wasn't comfortable taking orders from a woman. So concerned was he that Mary Beth was infecting the department with a hormonal imbalance that might prevent them from ever solving another case that it got him served his walking papers. Mary Beth and Randy hadn't shared so much as a Christmas card since. And they were both quintessential Appalachians–spiritual heirs to epic feuds like the Hatfields and McCoys–so if there was one thing they knew how to do, it was how to hold a grudge. Randy would run purely for revenge and give it everything he had. Worst part was, Randy was extremely well-connected. A drinking buddy of most of the county's movers and shakers who was great at slapping backs and hobnobbing–the kind of stuff Mary Beth hated. By the time election activities really kicked up in September, Randy would be ready to outspend her ten to one.

"You screw up bad enough to let Randy Law get elected sheriff, and he'll fire me the second they finish counting the ballots," Izzy said.

"Jesus." Normally Mary Beth would never let a little embarrassment or bad press back her off a prime suspect, but the presence of Randy Law changed things. The guy was a deacon at King's Chapel Church, with a squeaky-clean reputation. The kind of bad press she'd be inviting by going after Pedro would practically roll out the red carpet for him to waltz right into her job.

Dammit, there has to be another way. Think, Mary Beth told herself. If only there was a way to get what she needed without Pedro knowing about it. Like Izzy said, it could still turn out he wasn't their guy and going after him through formal channels and bringing all the shit down on her head would be for nothing.

Mary Beth vowed to herself that if push came to shove, she'd do what she had to do, regardless of the consequences, but what her crafty spirit was angling for was a way to determine if going after Pedro would be worth that fallout. A smile spread across her face as the rough outlines of a plan began to form.

"Tell you what," she said. "Let's start working all other angles of the case and wait to see what the CODIS search comes back with on the fetal DNA. If it gets a hit, great."

"And if it doesn't?"

"Then, by that time, if another suspect hasn't materialized, I'll already know whether it's worth going after Pedro or not."

Izzy looked intrigued but also hesitant. "How do you plan to pull that off?"

Mary Beth patted her friend's knee. "Trust me," she said.

"God," Izzy replied, "I hate it when you say that."

22

MARY BETH WAS IN THE STATION house breakroom, sipping her coffee and watching the TV as Izzy's wife first broke the news about Maria.

This is Princess Baker, coming to you live from outside the abandoned Cierra Junior High, where Jasper County officials tell us human remains were discovered earlier this week in the school basement. Those remains have since been confirmed to be those of Maria Ruiz, the young Jasper Creek woman who seemingly disappeared without a trace, years ago.

The TV cut to some old news footage about the Ruiz disappearance. Mary Beth felt like she'd seen a ghost when they played a clip of Bill updating the public about the status of the investigation at that time. Then it was back to Princess.

Now that Maria Ruiz's fate has been discovered, many questions still remain about exactly what happened to her and how she ended up in that basement. We are told that the Jasper County Sheriff's Department is currently treating this case as a homicide.

Back to you, Carl.

Mary Beth was about to switch off the station-house TV when she heard the daytime anchor say:

We turn now to another breaking story related to law enforcement. Field Reporter, Ed Mullins, is downtown at the County Government Complex where a challenger for Jasper County Sheriff is officially kicking off his campaign today.

That's right Carl. Jasper County residents may know Randy Law from his local Harley Davidson dealership but what some may not know is that before becoming a successful businessman he was a decorated deputy here in Jasper County, serving under sheriffs Sid and Bill Cain. Now, after a break from law enforcement, he's looking to get back on the force as the county's top cop and promises to clean up what he calls an embarrassing pattern of corruption under the current Sheriff. Let's take a listen to part of his speech from just a few moments ago.

The camera cut to Randy Law behind a lectern, surrounded by serious looking men, a cadre that included two of the current county commissioners.

Jasper County, aren't you tired of the corruption? Aren't you tired of being a laughing stock?

A boisterous crowd responded with a resounding, "Yeah!"

We all know that just last year, federal prosecutors were conducting an investigation into our current sheriff for a sad history of corruption and civil rights abuses. Now, I know she's popular and got a lot of good press for the way she headed off disaster up at Old Wengo. But if it wasn't for her own family, that mess wouldn't have existed in the first place. And everybody knows her mother's one of the biggest crime bosses this state's ever seen.

"That's right," said a woman in the crowd.

I say, it's time we clean things up.

I say, it's time we show the world we're as serious about justice in Jasper County as anywhere.

I say, it's time we elect a **real** *law man. A straight arrow, who will always do right.*

That's why we've printed up stickers, signs, and magnets, all like this.

Randy pulled out a sign in the shape of an arrow, a not-so-subtle reminder of his maleness, which was re-emphasized by his dual slogans, "ELECT A STRAIGHT ARROW. RANDY LAW—A *REAL* LAW MAN."

"Randy Law, a real dildo," Mary Beth grumbled.

"Looks like he's fixing for a fight."

Mary Beth swiveled around to face Deputy Goforth, who was standing in the doorway of the station's breakroom, stroking his mustache.

"Yeah, it sure does, Benny," she said.

"Don't you worry though, Sheriff. Folks around here know all you've done to clean this place up. The sacrifices you've made. They won't forget you, come election time."

Mary Beth smiled. "Thanks. I figure we just keep doing our job and that will all take care of itself."

"Well, that's what I was coming to tell you, Sheriff. We've finished our job—done re-interviewing all the old witnesses on the Ruiz case and haven't come up with nothing new. Everybody other than that Denny fella are all sticking by their original statements. Not sure what we should do next."

Mary Beth wasn't sure either.

"Did Jenkins pull the reports on all the sexual assaults the last eight years?"

"Yep. Got 'em here." Goforth handed over a thin file. "Just twenty-five, which is less than I expected. All situational from the looks of it. Date Rapes, mostly. No serials. No unsolved. Still, Jenkins and Skipwith are running them all down to determine the perp's whereabouts when Ruiz disappeared."

"Good. How about crimes at the park?"

Goforth wiped his hands like a blackjack dealer. "Zip."

"Seriously? We haven't had a single arrest at the city park in the last eight years?"

"Not a one. It was all drug-related before and you done a real good job cleaning that up, hitting them at the source." Goforth winced like he'd said something he shouldn't. Then he tried to fix it, adding, "You know, busting up the meth dens and all."

Mary Beth knew what he'd been getting at, which was actually true. The main thing Mary Beth did when she took over as sheriff was strike a deal with her mother, Mamie, the head of the McCray County Mafia, to keep her junk out of Jasper County. In exchange, Mary Beth used tips from her mama to take out Mamie's competition, the meth manufacturers and crooked Jasper Creek doctors who were supplying the opioids.

That relationship, or "armistice" as Mary Beth liked to call it, had worked well enough as long as the McCray County Mafia operated outside of Mary Beth's jurisdiction. But then her jurisdiction expanded back in the fall, when the powers-that-be annexed dwindling McCray County into Jasper, putting the two formidable women on a collision course that ended with Mamie and the McCray County Mafia permanently exiled from West, *by God.* Mary Beth had heard but had yet to verify, that the old woman had since set up shop out of a high-priced whore house she was running in Dulcimer, Kentucky, just across the state line.

Yet the way the papers told it, Mary Beth, had been little

more than a stooge for her mama's criminal enterprise. Part of that perception was Mary Beth's fault. She'd done little to dispel such rumors because they'd made her job easier for a while, by giving her a kind of street cred. Perps were a lot quicker to confess when they figured the law was crooked anyway. Looked like all that might be coming back to bite her now, though, that Mr. "Straight Arrow" was aiming right for her heart.

"I'm still surprised," Mary Beth said. "There were so many drug busts there before." Something wasn't sitting right. "Benny, do me a favor and pull the report Bill put together in the Ruiz file about all the previous arrests at the park."

"Sure, Sheriff. You got it."

Goforth started to leave. "Benny?"

"Yeah, Sheriff?"

"See if you can also pull a report on all drug busts county-wide for the–oh, I don't know–let's say, three years prior to Maria's disappearance."

"Will do."

As Goforth was heading out, Izzy was heading in, looking worried as usual.

"Did you see it?" he asked.

"See what?"

"Randy Law. On the TV."

"Yeah, I saw it."

Izzy held up one of Randy's blue arrow signs. "These are already popping up all over town. I found this one down the block–not thirty yards from the damn station house. We've got to get serious, MB."

"I'm always serious."

"No, I mean about the election. We've got to start raising money and getting some folks to help who really know how to do this kind of thing."

Izzy's concern was well-founded. Mary Beth had never really had to run much of a campaign before. "Let's concentrate on solving the Ruiz case," she said. "We arrest the killer before November and we should be just fine."

Izzy made one of his frustration noises, part sigh, part groan. "How are we going to do that if we can't move on Pedro without dragging you through the mud?"

Mary Beth waved him off. "I told you not to worry about that. It's all took care of. Should have Pedro's hair and DNA in about a week or so."

Izzy gave her his disapproving look. "MB, what did you do?"

"Nothing. Nothing illegal anyway. At least I don't think it is."

Izzy closed the door to the break room. When he turned to face her, he said, "Spill it. I want to know exactly what kind of reckless scheme you've got going this time."

Mary Beth stood and arched her back. "Well, I just got to thinking about how we needed Pedro's hair, and how prissy he seemed, keeping his hair all dolled up with that goop, and it occurred to me, he's probably the kind of guy who goes to a particular barber. Not a walk-in kind of guy. Makes appointments."

"So?"

"So, I hired a PI up there to find out where he goes. And it turns out that he gets his hair cut once a month, like clockwork. The way medical practices fast-food their patients through these days, doctors are like high-priced time-clock punchers. Everything in their life is scheduled down to the minute. So, I know exactly the next time Pedro's going in for a cut."

"And what are you planning on doing with that information?"

"Already done it."

"Done what, exactly?"

"Had the PI bribe his barber to keep some of Pedro's hair, and the cup from the free coffee he always drinks, seal it up nice and tight in the evidence bag I gave him, and send it to us."

Izzy looked to the floor, shaking his head. "Let's say we get a hit. What are we supposed to do then? You know none of that would be admissible. The chain of custody is shit."

"We'll jump off that bridge, my friend, when we come to it."

There was a knock on the door. Goforth was back with the reports. Mary Beth snatched them up and started pouring over them, only realizing moments later that Goforth was still hovering, waiting for an attaboy. "Thanks, Benny," she said, not looking up.

"Just let me know, you need anything else, Sheriff."

After Goforth had gone, Izzy asked, "What are you looking at?"

Mary Beth didn't answer right away, trying to keep a count in her head.

"Fourteen drug arrests at the city park in the three years leading up to Maria's disappearance and not a single one in the eight years since."

Izzy was unimpressed. "Well, we did a good job clearing the drugs out of this county."

"Yeah, but for the first couple of years we were busting people left and right, all over the county, but never at the park, which everybody knew had been a hotbed."

"So, what do you make of that?"

Mary Beth scrunched her lips. "Not entirely sure yet, but check this. Out of those fourteen arrests, guess who personally collared twelve of them?"

"Who?"

"Mr. Straight Arrow, Randy Law."

Izzy shrugged. "He was a good cop. And he used to like to work the park."

"Yeah, but these aren't the kind of busts you hit on with a random patrol. If you're going to deal, you do it in the back of the park where you can see a squad car coming a mile off. You've got to go incognito to pull off a bust like this."

"Got to stake the place out."

"Or you've got to know when the action's going down."

Izzy smiled. "You're thinking Randy was the one with the

CI, the informant who assured Bill that Maria's disappearance wasn't retribution for Raul Kowalski ratting."

Mary Beth straightened the papers and tapped them on the table. "Actually, no, I wasn't, but now that you mention it, I bet you're right about that. For Bill to just accept that at face value and totally lay off that line of inquiry it would have had to come from somebody he trusted implicitly, and there was nobody he trusted more than Randy. They were bosom buddies."

"So what were you getting at?"

Mary Beth looked to make sure the door was closed. The station had ears, and Randy Law had a lot of friends. "Something Goforth said earlier, when we were talking about the lack of arrests at the park since I took over, he said something about hitting them at the source."

"And?"

"And, I think he's right. I think the reason we stopped seeing drugs at the park was because of the deal I struck with my mama to keep her junk out of Jasper. The park must have been explicitly her turf."

"Makes sense."

Mary Beth flipped to the next report. "That got me thinking, the other way we got the drugs out of here was from all the tips Mamie passed along about where we could hit her competition. So, I had Goforth pull another report of all drug busts county-wide in the three years before Maria's disappearance. Take a look at this."

Maria handed over the report where she'd made tic marks next to every place Randy Law's name appeared. Izzy whistled. "Impressive."

"More than impressive. He's got two thirds of the busts by himself. You'd think he was a vice cop instead of a sheriff's deputy. And look at this." Mary Beth pointed down the page.

Izzy read the name "Thomas Wiggins."

"That's my cousin Tommy. He's been one of my mom's closest

guys for as long as I can remember. High up. Not the kind who hangs out on corners slinging dime bags. The only way you get to him is with a sophisticated sting. And there's two or three other names on there I recognize too."

"So, what're you saying?"

Mary Beth hesitated, not sure it would make as much sense uttered out loud as it was making inside her head. "I think whoever was giving him his intel was targeting my Mama's operation."

Izzy leaned up against the vending machine, taking that in. "Could be. So, what's that mean to us? Nothing wrong with getting info from one drug dealer that you use to arrest their competition."

"No. Certainly not. Unless you're taking money, or turning a blind eye to your informants' drug dealing inside your jurisdiction."

"Whatever," Izzy said. "Randy may be a pompous ass. And you know I'm no fan of his, with all the shit he used to give me back in high school. But I got to say, he's no crook. You're stretching, MB."

Maybe, Mary Beth thought. Maybe she was wishcasting. Or maybe it was the sting of always being unfairly accused of abetting her mother's criminal enterprise when she'd actually gone to great lengths to contain it. But her gut told her there was something here. Randy Law popping up now, wanting to get back in the cop game right after Maria's body was discovered and likely being the one who was running the CI referenced in Bill's old reports, while also being the super sleuth who busted all those people at the same park where Maria was last seen. It felt like there was something there. One thing Mary Beth didn't believe in were coincidences. In her experience, things that seemed to go together usually did, it was just a matter of figuring out the connection. Just keep manipulating the pieces until they snapped together.

"Regardless," she said. "Randy Law seems like he may know about Bill's CI, and it sounds like he knew the city park at that time better than anybody."

Izzy took a deep breath. "Why do I get the feeling you are about to do something we're both going to regret."

Mary Beth stood and grasped Izzy's shoulder. "You said we needed to get serious about this campaign."

"I did."

"Well, I think it's time we pay my esteemed opponent a little visit."

Izzy sighed. "Okay. But promise me you won't make a scene."

Mary Beth gave him the two-fingered Scout's honor salute. She had an idea she was rolling over in her mind about this meeting and nearly called Goforth back in to run it by him but thought better of it, remembering how chummy he'd once been with Randy Law. She needed somebody she could trust.

"Seriously, MB. Promise me you'll be professional?" Izzy asked.

"Of course," Mary Beth said as she fired off a text message to Sam.

Still want to help with the investigation?

She got a thumb's up emoji response as she was opening the break room door. That's when she said to Izzy, "Grab that arrow sign and let's bring it with us. I've got a pretty good idea of where Randy Law can stick it."

23

RANDY LAW WAS A BIG OLD, crew-cutted, country boy, every bit the ex-jock, and already had the fake politician's smile down pat as he crossed the showroom of Law Harley Davidson to greet Mary Beth and Izzy. "I'd have invited the media if I'd a-known," he said. "Sheriff Mary Beth Cain, in the flesh. Did you come here to concede the race or just stop by to violate my civil rights?"

Mary Beth gave Randy her poisonously sweet smile. "You can forget about the former," she said, taking his hand with a firm grip and leaning in to whisper, "As for the latter, I haven't made my mind up just yet."

Randy laughed. "Same old, Mary Beth. Always a spitfire."

"Same old, Randy," Mary Beth said. "Always full of shit."

Randy looked around the showroom to see how many of his customers had overheard. He offered a little wave to a father and son who were admiring a Fat Boy Softail next to a circular rack of leather vests. "So, what can I do for y'all? Interest you in a bike? Maybe something with a sidecar?" he said, sneering down at Izzy.

Mary Beth put her hand on Izzy's chest to stop him from advancing on Randy.

"Actually, came to talk to you about a case," she said. "There somewhere private we can go and catch up on old times?"

"Sure," Randy said, looking glad to take the conversation away from his customers. "Come on back to my office."

Randy Law led them through the showroom past some pristine hogs, each one of which cost about as much as Randy's annual salary had been back when he was a deputy.

"Looks like you've done all right for yourself," Mary Beth commented, wondering exactly how he'd raised the money to buy into this kind of premium franchise. "Sure you want to go back to the slave wages this county pays its peace officers?"

Randy laughed. "Doing your duty always has a cost," he said.

They followed Randy into a back office full of half-walled cubicles with papers strewn everywhere, contracts and leasing information and product specs. A freshly-minted stack of Randy Law for Sheriff signs were piled up in a corner. Randy's office was the only one in that back area that had four walls going all the way to the ceiling. The door was thin pine with an opaque window made of rippled glass.

"Have a seat," Randy said.

Mary Beth and Izzy pulled some frayed roller chairs to attention on the far side of Randy's cluttered desk.

"What can I do you for?" he asked.

"Came to test your memory," Mary Beth said. "See what you can recall about the Maria Ruiz case that might be helpful."

Randy nodded like he'd been expecting the question. "Just saw Princess's report about that on the TV," He whistled. "Your wife sure is a good-looking woman, Izzy."

Izzy didn't say anything but Mary Beth could tell he was smoldering. Randy was one of the guys who'd really given Iz a hard time in high school and had often been overheard wondering aloud in the police station how a runt like him had landed a knockout like Princess.

"You were smart not to let anything out about the hair you found," Randy said.

Mary Beth felt her stomach drop. *How in the hell does he know about that?* She knew her pale complexion was giving away her surprise because Law's eyes gleamed with delight..

"Oh," he said, answering a question that hadn't been asked. "I think you'll find I've got friends all over this town. A lot of who want to make sure the next sheriff has all the information he'll need to hit the ground running in January."

"You son of a–" Izzy started, rising from his chair.

Mary Beth held out a hand to restrain him. After all his admonishments about proper decorum, here she was calming him down.

"Well, maybe you wouldn't mind helping us out until then," she said.

Randy had a short-sleeve dress shirt on that was unbuttoned at the neck with a loosely knotted red tie—his hard-working businessman look. He reached up and loosened the tie some more, then decided to just whip the thing off and dropped it between stacks of papers on his desk. His voice dropped an octave when he said, "And just why in the hell would I want to help *you* do anything?"

"Because," Mary Beth said. "This isn't about me. And it's not about you?"

"Oh, yeah? What's it about then?"

"It's about Bill–the man we both loved–and the case that haunted him more than any other. We both owe it to Bill to put aside our differences and do whatever we can to solve it."

Randy's face softened at the invocation of Bill's name. "What is it you think I'd have to offer, anyway?" he asked. "That was a long time ago. And it wasn't my case."

"One of the things Bill was looking at is whether there was

a drug angle to Maria's disappearance. She was dating a guy named Pedro Kowalski at the time. Not too long before she disappeared, Pedro's brother, Raul, rolled on a fairly significant capo in Arizona who was connected to the Solares Cartel."

Mary Beth paused to see if Randy wanted to jump in but he stayed mum. If any of this was ringing a bell with him his face didn't show it.

"Anyway, Bill's reports said he checked with a reliable CI who assured them that Maria's disappearance wasn't retribution for ratting on their guy in Arizona."

She paused again. Still nothing but poker face from Law.

"Any of this sounding familiar to you?" she asked.

"A little," Law responded. "But like I said, it was a long time ago. And that was Bill's case. We'd talk about it some but I never worked it."

"What about the CI, though?" Izzy asked. "You were the big drug busting man back then. You know who this CI was?"

Law looked around his desk a minute while he thought. "Not really, no."

"No idea at all?" Mary Beth asked.

Law held out his palms. "We'd have informants back then, sure, but nobody I can recall who was super high up. At least not that I knew of. But Bill had his sources too. The only way to know would be if we could ask him."

That was the one thing they obviously couldn't do. It was also a convenient way Law could claim ignorance and no one could really call him on it.

"What about the park?" Izzy asked.

"What about it?"

"You used to work out there a lot. We've checked the record about how many guys you busted there."

"Was that a question?" Law asked.

"No," Izzy said. "The question is: You ever see anything out there you think could help us with the Ruiz case?"

"Like what?"

"Like, anything. Like a guy who was harassing female joggers. Or maybe you might have seen that brown conversion van out there before."

Law looked him square in the eyes. No signs of avoidance or deception. "Nothing I can think of."

"Come on now," Mary Beth said, getting back to the informant thing. "Just between us old friends. I've been through the records. The number of busts you were pulling down. You must have had some intel from somebody."

Law turned and gave her the same unflinching stare. "I worked them the way we always did. You bust somebody, flip 'em, and keep climbing the food chain. But it was all local boys. Nothing that went beyond that."

Mary Beth gave him her lie detector stare and got nothing back. She had to remind herself that lie detectors only worked on people capable of feeling guilt or doubt. She knew from experience that Randy Law was often wrong but he was rarely, if ever, in doubt. And if he had anything to feel guilty about, he was doing a great job of hiding it.

"You sure, there's nothing else you can tell us?" she asked.

"Afraid not."

Mary Beth tried her sweet, sly little smile. "You're not holding back just so you can come in and crack the case after the election, are you?"

Randy smiled like he could understand her thinking that. "Look," he said. "All ball-busting aside. I know we've had our differences, but you were right about one thing: I did love Bill like a brother. There's nothing I wouldn't have done for him."

"He felt the same about you," Mary Beth said.

Randy looked legitimately touched by that. "Thank you for saying so."

They shared a moment that under the right amount of intoxication might have included a tear or two. Neither one would piss on the other if they were on fire but they did share a common loss, and in that instant, Mary Beth felt a tiny comradery with Randy as they both basked in Bill's memory.

"Election aside," Randy said. "If there was anything I could do to help you solve this case, I would."

Ten minutes after Mary Beth and Izzy left, Randy Law let his secretary know he was headed out to take care of a few things. She reminded him about a fundraising dinner he had later that evening and then he slipped into the back lot where he got into his charcoal-colored Dodge Ram truck and headed downtown.

When he got to the traffic circle at the town center, he circled the courthouse three times before parking. Then he got out and looked around a couple of times before crossing the street, never noticing the little silver Honda Civic that had tailed him there.

Sam Cain was in that car, snapping a couple of photos with his iphone of Randy Law as he entered the Law Offices of Alexander Pomfried. Once Randy was out of sight, Sam texted the pictures to his mother.

The receptionist tried telling Law that Pomfried was in a meeting and couldn't be disturbed.

"Just tell Alex it's Randy Law and it's important," he said.

A couple minutes later she was leading him back to where Pomfried greeted him like a long-lost friend.

"Is that the next sheriff of Jasper County, I spy?"

"From your mouth to God's ears," Randy said, admiring Pomfried's monogrammed dress shirt and gaudy cufflinks.

"Thanks, Dottie," Pomfried said to his assistant and motioned for Randy to take a seat. He turned to a credenza with a crystal decanter of brandy and poured two snifters. "So, you decided to run after all," he said, placing a glass in front of Randy. "Last time we talked–what was it? At the Haskell's Christmas party, I think. You were saying she was too popular to beat after the Old Wengo affair. What changed your mind?"

Law did his best to look non-committal. "I'd already put the money together and a lot of the apparatus before the Old Wengo thing. The gun was cocked, as they say. So, I figured I might as well shoot."

Pomfried took a generous sip of his brandy, then rocked back in his chair and ran his thumbs up and down the insides of his suspenders. "Well, what I told you still stands. Anything you've told me in the past remains privileged. You'll have no problems from me. I'm not really even doing criminal law anymore."

"Yeah, I heard. That's actually what I came to talk to you about."

"What's that?"

Randy picked up his snifter, smelled it without drinking, and gave Pomfried his newly-practiced politician's smile, asking him, "How'd you like to get back in the game?"

Randy looked around a minute after pushing out of Pomfried's office, then crossed the street briskly at a diagonal from the crosswalk, where his truck was parked over at the visitor's center. He'd climbed in the driver's seat before he noticed it–one of his straight arrow signs on the windshield, held beneath the wiper blade.

Randy got out and removed it, looked around again but didn't see anyone suspicious. Whoever left it was long gone.

He turned the arrow over a couple of times, examining it. There was nothing written on it. No calling cards to speak of. But then again, there didn't need to be. He knew who was sending him a message.

She was always smart, Randy admitted to himself. Probably

twice as smart as Bill ever was, if the truth be told. But Mary Beth Cain still wasn't half as smart as she thought she was.

Randy wasn't entirely sure what the sheriff thought she knew about him, but he was pretty certain it was less than the truth. And regardless, he still had a few surprises up his sleeve.

Pomfried was right. He had decided not to run last Fall, but recent events changed his mind. Running had become a matter of self-preservation. Mary Beth would be a tough competitor, no doubt, but he had the money on his side, and no matter whether he won or not, any allegations she might throw at him now would sound like something she'd cooked up to slander a political opponent. With her reputation for rule-breaking, that would be an easy sale that might just keep him out of jail. Of course, if he did manage to win in November, anything she might dig up wouldn't matter anymore because he'd be the law then.

Randy Law. The Real Law Man.

24

SOMETIMES WHEN GOD closes a door, He opens a window. Mary Beth was reminded of that pithy little saying a couple weeks later during what passed for a family dinner in her house. Sam was home and Izzy had come by as well since Princess was out of town covering a story about wildfires in Kentucky. Mary Beth had made one of her signature dishes she liked to call Pizza Hut delivery, along with a bag of salad and bottle of Yellow Tail merlot she picked up at Kroger's.

She knew she was backsliding on her vow to never drink again but it had been a real pisser of a week. First the CODIS search for DNA matching the fetal remains turned up bupkis. Then all of Pedro's cousins produced airtight alibis for the weekend Maria disappeared, all seven of them having been out of town on a construction job in Maryland at the time. But the kicker came while Mary Beth was enjoying some thin-n-crispy pepperoni lovers and got the call from Dr. Patel that just about put the final nail in the case's coffin.

"No fucking match," he said without so much as a Hello.

"What's that?" Mary Beth stepped into the living room, leaving the others in the kitchen so she could hear him better.

"That hair you sent me–doesn't fucking match."

Mary Beth groaned. "Are you sure?"

"Yes, I'm sure. Who's the goddamn doctor here? We ran all the tests. Put it under the microscope, too. All we got is mtDNA again," he said, using a common abbreviation for mitochondrial DNA. The translation was that the hairs Mary Beth garnered from Pedro's barber didn't match the one found on Maria's body in either the microscopic examination or the mitochondrial DNA tests. Mary Beth knew that the lack of an mtDNA match also ruled out Pedro's brother, Raul, as the source of the hair since he descended from the same maternal line.

"What about the cup he drank from?"

"Nothing," Dr. Patel said. "No goddamn DNA at all."

"Shit."

That was a real kick in the fanny because it meant there was no way to link Pedro to the fetal remains. The mtDNA couldn't be used to establish a link to the fetal remains either because it is passed by the mother and therefore the fetus would have different mtDNA than the father. So now, not only was the case circling the drain, the only thing left to do would be to try to obtain a warrant to get Pedro's nuclear DNA through official channels, which would mean fighting the federal injunction and facing a public pig roast when Pedro's attorney released the video of Mary Beth at her worst.

"Well, that's just fucking great," she said.

"Don't you use that language with me. It's not my goddamn fault. You're the one who–"

Mary Beth ended the call without another word and re-entered the kitchen in a sour mood. Sam noticed. "What's up?" he asked.

"Nothing. Let's talk about it after dinner." Mary Beth sat back down at the table where Izzy was on his phone too, peppering

THE MOUNTAIN MYSTIC

the call with enough "babies" for her to safely presume he was talking to Princess. "Yeah, sure," he said. "Hang on." He handed the phone to Mary Beth with a concerned expression. "Princess would like to speak to you."

"Oh-kay." This was a first. Mary Beth was pretty sure she'd never talked to Princess on the phone before. She wasn't entirely sure what to say. "This is Sheriff Cain," would be too formal, yet "Mary Beth" felt too familiar. So, she settled on, "Hey."

"Hey, Sheriff. You still interested in that psychic? The one from old McCray?"

Geeze. Mary Beth had almost forgotten about her, she'd been missing for so long. "Hell, yes," she said.

"Then I've got a proposition for you."

This was interesting. "Okay," Mary Beth said, "shoot."

"I'm looking to trade information. I've got some people at the network interested in the Ruiz case. They're talking about giving me a segment that would run nationwide but I need to break something new. Some information that hasn't already been reported on a million times."

"So, if I can give you a previously unreported detail about Maria's case, you can tell me where to find the psychic."

"That's it. What have you got?"

"What do you already know?"

Princess laughed. "You know my husband doesn't tell me anything. All I know are the details that are already out there."

Mary Beth looked over at Izzy with amazement. Here was his wife, the prettiest woman in the county, a news reporter who slept next to him every night and could probably get just about any man in Jasper Creek to do whatever she wanted, and he hadn't let a single detail slip.

"We don't talk shop at home," Princess added. "I don't want to put Izzy in that position."

"I understand," Mary Beth said. She was weighing what she could give Princess without jeopardizing the investigation. The

189

case might be going cold but it was important to hold something back that could be used later to trip up a suspect, if they ever found one, or confirm whether they were telling the truth. There were really just two things she had to deal: the hair and the fetal remains. Deciding which to give Princess was easy. Mary Beth hadn't even told Guadalupe about the fetal remains yet, knowing the old lady would never be able to keep it a secret. She'd have insisted on having a separate funeral with a tiny coffin and might even put a picture of the remains on her *ofrenda* during *Dia De Muertos*. There was no way Mary Beth wanted the pregnancy broadcast on the news. But the hair she could live with.

"Unfortunately, there's not a whole lot I can offer you," Mary Beth said. "But there is one piece of evidence that hasn't been reported on yet."

"Great. What is it?"

"A hair. Forensics found a hair on Maria's body that we know is not hers."

"It belonged to the killer?"

"We think so. Given where the body was found, walled off in the basement like that, the odds of the hair showing up there coincidentally seem pretty remote."

"That's good," Princess said. "So can't you run it through your databases or whatever to find whose hair it is?"

"Unfortunately, no. Hair doesn't always work like that," Mary Beth said, not wanting to get into a full-blown explanation of nuclear and mitochondrial DNA. Princess could do her own research on that subject.

"Seriously?"

"Seriously. If we find our suspect, the hair can help confirm whether it's our guy, but it'll still take old fashioned police work to get us to that point."

"Okay," Princess said. "I got you. Well, maybe this broadcast can help bring in some tips."

"Maybe," Mary Beth said. "So, now it's your turn. Where can I find my psychic."

Princess chuckled. "I'm looking right at her."

"What?"

"Yeah. I'm over here in Dulcimer, doing a story on the wild-fires. Stopped in for dinner with the crew at this little inn, and your psychic's over in the corner reading tarot cards." Princess texted her a picture.

"That's her," Mary Beth said. She looked at her watch. It was six-thirty. It would take at least an hour to get to Dulcimer. "Princess whatever you do, just don't let her out of your sight."

25

SAM HAD INSISTED on coming along with Mary Beth and Izzy. He was there when they picked the psychic up, arresting her under the pretense of fraud charges, and bringing her back to the station where they left her in an interrogation room to stew a bit. It was a technique designed to break the subject down but seemed to be having a greater effect on Sam who was about as fidgety as Mary Beth had ever seen him, sitting on a hard metal bench outside the interrogation room, making his little noises.

She didn't ask but was pretty sure Sam had stopped taking his Intuniv, the ADHD medication he'd been prescribed as a kid. Most people with ADHD benefitted from stimulants, like Ritalin or caffeine, so they'd tried that on Sam when he was first diagnosed back in grade school, but his brain was so turbo-charged it set him off like a Tasmanian devil. The usually quiet kid talked, non-stop for thirty-six hours, after taking the lowest therapeutic dose. Mary Beth wasn't Catholic but she was about to take him to a priest to ask for an exorcism before he finally settled down. After that they found Intuniv which helped him control his mannerisms and achieve better focus on things he found uninteresting, like most activities of daily living, but it also had a sedating effect that Sam hated. She could always tell when he was off the meds because the little tics gradually intensified.

"I don't know what you're so nervous about," she told him.

"This just doesn't feel right. Why do you have to keep her in there so long?"

Sam nodded to the interrogation room where Mary Beth had the Mountain Mystic handcuffed to a metal chair.

"Trust me, Sammy. I do this for a living."

"But she's been in there almost two hours."

Mary Beth looked at her watch. "Not quite. She's got ten more minutes."

Twenty minutes later, Mary Beth entered the interrogation room alone.

"This is outrageous!" the old woman bellowed. Gone was all of her subdued, mysterious little aura. Now she looked more like a frazzled alley cat than a medium. Her hands were cuffed behind her back and her thin, wispy hair was flailing about as she yanked and twisted, rocking her metal chair against the hard floor. "What am I even doing here?"

"You're the psychic," Mary Beth said. "You tell me."

The old woman hawked a golf ball-sized loogie onto the table. "You have no right to keep me here like this. I haven't done anything."

"I've been worried about you," Mary Beth said. "The way you just picked up and left in the middle of the night like that. Thought maybe you were afraid somebody was coming for you."

"I was! You!"

Mary Beth had brought a big bottle of Dasani with her into the interrogation room where she had the heat jacked up to eighty-five. She took a good long drink, watching the old lady watch the bottle. When she finished, she said, "Now see, that's concerning to me. Why would you be worried that the law might be coming for you?"

"Let's just say, I had a feeling I might get harassed."

"A premonition?"

"No. Common sense."

Mary Beth tipped her bottle to the old lady and took another long drink. "How 'bout we just get to it then?" she said.

"How 'bout it?"

Mary Beth sat a legal pad and a pen on the desk and came around and uncuffed the old lady who immediately started massaging her bony wrists.

Mary Beth pointed to the pad. "I want a full confession. You tell me how you knew where we'd find that body and how in the hell you knew about that dream I had as a kid. Oh, and the goddamn pregnant bullfrog. I especially want to know how you knew that'd lead me to the Cierra Junior High."

The old woman kept rubbing her wrists. "I've told you. I don't know how I know these things. They just come to me."

Mary Beth slapped the table hard with both hands. She stared the old woman down. "Bull. Shit."

The woman turned up her palms. "I can't explain it to you any other way."

"Try," Mary Beth said. She dropped a pen on the legal pad. "Fastest way for you to get out of here is to tell me what I want to know."

The old woman stared at her for a moment and Mary Beth could tell she'd already made her mind up to cave but pride compelled her to wait a few beats before officially conceding. Then she snatched the pen.

"Just give me a minute," she said.

"A minute for what?"

"Shhhh!" the woman scolded. "I'm trying to concentrate."

Mary Beth watched as she closed her cloudy eyes, and took three deep breaths, long and slow. The old woman felt around for the pad, found it, and began drawing. Then she opened her eyes and pushed the pad across the table. "There," she said.

Mary Beth looked down at a scribbled heart with what appeared to be a date written inside: 10-22-11.

"What in the hell is this?"

The old woman shrugged. "I have no idea. It's just what I saw."

Mary Beth had lost all patience for the psychic schtick. She had a case to solve. And if the initial polling held up, she only had a few months left to clear it before she'd lose her badge to that asshat, Randy Law.

"Listen, lady. I'm not kidding with you."

"I know that," the woman said, regaining some of her eerie calm. "I'm not kidding with you either. You needed to know who killed that girl you found. That's my answer."

Mary Beth held up the pad. "A heart, with a date in it? That's who killed her?"

The woman frowned. "Now you're just being ridiculous."

"I'm being ridiculous?"

"Just try to suspend your cynicism for a minute. Take a look at that image and tell me what you see."

Mary Beth rolled her eyes and flipped the pad around. "I guess it kind of looks like a tattoo."

"Well," the woman said, "do the police keep track of that kind of thing?"

Actually, they did. The FBI had a Tattoo Recognition Database that could be easily accessed.

"Wait here," Mary Beth said.

"Doesn't appear that I have a choice."

Mary Beth let the old lady get the last word as she hurried from the interrogation room.

Izzy, who'd been watching on a closed-circuit TV, met her in the hall.

"Let me see the pad," he said.

She handed it to him. Izzy took out his phone and snapped a picture of the drawing then said, "We should know soon."

Mary Beth went and sat with Sam, while she waited. She did her best to stay cool, trying not to expect anything but her heart was pounding with anticipation.

Izzy re-entered the room about thirty minutes later carrying the pad and a computer printout. He had a big smile on his face. "We got a hit."

"No way. You're shitting me?"

"I'm not," Izzy said. "Look at this."

Mary Beth raced to his side. The printout had a photo of a tan arm with a tattoo that was an exact match, a heart with the date 10-22-11 written in the middle. She read the name at the top. "Octavio Condor Silva."

"Doing twenty-five to life at ADX Florence in Colorado for drug trafficking and murder. He's a cartel hitman," Izzy said.

Mary Beth continued reading the criminal record. Izzy was right. Multiple murder charges that had previously been dropped due to uncooperative witnesses. Affiliations included the Arizona outfit connected to the Solares Cartel. Then there it was, under Known Associates. A name that sent a chill through Mary Beth's body like she'd just plopped down on a missing bicycle seat: Raul Kowalski.

This was their guy. It had to be.

She pointed to Raul's name and Izzy nodded. He'd already seen it.

"It gets better," he said.

"How?"

"I went ahead and pulled Arizona DMV records for Octavio Silva. Guess what kind of vehicle he was driving eight years ago."

Mary Beth didn't have to guess. "A brown conversion van with the digits SXL in the license plate."

"Close," Izzy said. "A brown conversion van with the digits 8XL in the license plate."

Mary Beth snapped her fingers. "That's why Bill never tracked it down. The witness was off by a digit."

"8 and S are easy to mistake," Izzy agreed.

Sam looked at them both eagerly. "Does this mean you've found him?"

Mary Beth didn't want to say Yes. She didn't want to jinx it somehow but she could feel in her bones that this was the guy. She told Sam, "We're gonna find out for sure, honey." Then she switched from mom mode back to sheriff as she said to Izzy, "Go cut the psychic loose but tell her not to leave town again. We're headed to Colorado."

26

IZZY'S LOYALTIES were really being tested. It had taken some time to arrange the Colorado trip. They needed to obtain the necessary warrant and get it issued in Colorado and then coordinate with the prison staff, and by the time everything was set, the day Mary Beth was wanting to go was the same night Princess' segment about the Ruiz case was set to air on national news.

As much as he loved his friend, Izzy knew missing Princess's broadcast could mean divorce so he convinced his boss to delay the trip by two days. One day so he could watch Princess' segment, and then one more day to celebrate. The Bakers had decided to make an event out of the broadcast and invited Princess' mama and Izzy's brother Bobby as well as Mary Beth over to their house to watch.

The sheriff had come with a whole dossier she'd put together on Octavio Silva. She'd kept it secret while Princess was on the big screen talking about how authorities had found a hair they were hoping to match to a suspect in order to crack the cold case. Izzy's wife had clearly done her homework. Mary Beth was impressed with the scientific accuracy of her reporting.

Initial reports are that FBI criminalists were able to extract mitochondrial DNA from the hair. This is different from nuclear DNA which is typically used by police to identify suspects. What that means is that police are not able to create a complete DNA profile that could be used to match the hair to anyone in law enforcement databases from a prior conviction. But if police are able to narrow in on a suspect, that person's hair could then be compared to the evidence to establish a link.

At commercial, Princess left the room and Mary Beth flipped open her file and showed Izzy Octavio's mugshot, complete with a nice long ponytail and bushy, unkempt, Jihaddy-looking prison beard. She started making a scissoring motion with her fingers, saying, "Oh, we've got our suspect and we're coming for you big boy."

Two days later she was doing the same thing on the flight over, pulling out the mug shot and pointing a finger gun at it, saying, "boom." It had been a while since Izzy had seen Mary Beth so happy. You'd never guess that the polls were showing Randy Law holding a ten-point lead because Mary Beth seemed like she was on cloud nine. Even she and Sam were getting along, so much so that Sam drove Mary Beth and Izzy to Charlotte, which was the closest place they could get a flight to Colorado Springs. In the past, you would have had to seriously bribe Sam to get him to willingly spend three hours in a car with his over-bearing mother pecking all over him, but now he was so excited about the break in the case, he volunteered.

Mary Beth hadn't come right out and said it, but Izzy knew that in her mind, solving this case would in turn solve all her problems. She figured making an arrest in something so high-profile would allow her to squeak past Randy Law in the election, despite his money and connections, and bringing Maria's killer to justice would also get Sam to finally appreciate her. Perhaps most importantly, it'd make Mary Beth feel like she'd repaid whatever debt it was she always believed she owed to Bill. That was an awful lot of weight to put on one investigation, but Izzy had to admit that the prospects were looking good. He would have laid down serious money on the odds that the hairs they were going to pluck off Octavio Silva would be a positive match for the one they found on Maria's remains.

The trip out there was exciting for Izzy, too. He'd always wanted to check out a Supermax prison, and the one in Colorado was supposed to be the best. It was created for prisoners deemed too dangerous, too high profile, or too big a national security risk to house anywhere else. In addition to organized crime members, ADX Florence was home to the cons who kept committing violent crimes behind bars, as well as spies, escape artists, and terrorists of both the foreign and domestic variety. Along with pieces of shit like Zacarius Moussaoui, one of the 9/11 co-conspirators, and the Shoe Bomber, Richard Reid, it had housed homegrown vermin like the Unabomber, Terry Nichols, Eric Rudolph, and that little twerp Dzhokar Tsarnaev who'd helped his brother set pressure cooker bombs near the finish line of the Boston Marathon.

Last but not least of the inmates there was Jasper County's very own domestic terrorist, Clementine Stenson, who'd received a lot of notoriety in recent months, becoming something of a Tex Watson to Sawyer's Manson in celebrity criminal culture. "We should stop in on Quiet Clem," Mary Beth suggested during the flight over. "For old time's sake." But Izzy, who'd nearly been executed on Clem's order, wasn't interested, saying, "I think we've got plenty to do while we're there."

From the outside, the prison looked a lot like the way Izzy imagined Area 51 would, minus the flying saucers. It was a massive, heavily fortified compound out in the middle of nowhere with guard towers like air traffic control stations. The prison guard who led them around gave them the lowdown on the place, welcoming them to the "Alcatraz of the Rockies," and boasting about the prison's controversies.

"There are some who say we're violating the Eighth Amendment's proscription against 'cruel and unusual' punishment or that life here qualifies as 'torture' under international law. But I submit to you that the lily-livered sons-a-bitches who say that have never had one of their brothers shanked by the Aryan Brotherhood or Gangster Disciples. Know what I mean?"

"I hear that," Mary Beth said.

She was enjoying this. Meanwhile, Izzy was wondering why he'd ever wanted to see the place. Two minutes in and he could already feel the claustrophobia setting in, staring around at all the hard, bare, walls. The windows throughout were just four inches wide and only gave you a view of the sky—no landmarks at all—which was really disorienting. But the worst part was how suffocatingly quiet the prison was. Izzy had been to the Jasper County Detention Center plenty of times and it always sounded like showing up to a fish fry over there. "Yo, Izzy. What up dawg? What's up, big man?" or even "Piggy, piggy, piggy, eat shit, motherfucker." Something, anything, every time he'd been there. But ADX was like a library overdosed on Xanax.

The guard showed them the prisoner's exercise area he referred to as "the pit," which was basically an empty swimming pool where inmates could "take ten steps in a straight line or thirty-one steps in a circle" but could never get the slightest peek at the outside world. No external information at all to use for planning any kind of escape.

"The worst of the worst are kept in permanent solitary confinement," the guard said. "Twenty-three hours a day, in a seven-by-twelve-foot cell with a concrete bed and a steel shitter bolted to the floor. We got one guy so nasty he's been without human contact since 1983—other than when the guards bring him his meals."

Mary Beth whistled.

"And if anybody gets especially ornery," the guard said, "we move them to the black hole."

"What's that?" Izzy asked.

"A special area of lockdown near the center of the prison that can hold up to 148 prisoners segregated in complete darkness inside totally soundproofed rooms." The description made Izzy shudder, thinking back on the time he'd been held for nearly two days in the total darkness of an underground mine. He'd decided he was on the side of those who considered such treatment an unconscionable form of torture.

"What about our boy?" Mary Beth asked. "Octavio Silva. Where's he at?"

"Oh, Octavio? He's been a model prisoner. Has more privileges than most. We keep him in what passes for Gen Pop around here. You shouldn't get any problems out of him."

"Good," Mary Beth said.

The guard set them up in a private room where attorneys came to meet with their clients. Izzy and Mary Beth were sitting there in silence so thick it felt like it had hold of Izzy's throat until he picked up the distant rattle of chains scraping across the prison floor.

The metallic sound grew steadily louder, then the six-inch thick steel door swung open and three guards led Octavio in. Izzy panned up from Octavio's feet, shackled by heavy leg irons, up the orange jumpsuit to where his hands were cuffed in front, noticing the little cross tattoo on the third knuckle of his right hand. Moving up, Izzy noticed Octavio had shaved the swarthy beard he had in his mugshots.

"Son of a bitch," he heard Mary Beth say a second before he realized Octavio hadn't just shaved his beard—he'd shaved everything. He was as bald as Telly Savalas on chemo. Even his eyebrows were shaved, clean as a whistle.

Octavio started laughing, smiling wide, showing off a silver tooth.

Mary Beth demanded the guards tell her, "What in the hell was going on."

"What do you mean, ma'am?"

"I mean, we came here with a warrant to extract a sample of his hair and he waltzes in here sheared like a damn sheep."

Octavio cackled.

"I'm sorry, ma'am," the guard said. "No one told us."

"I didn't tell you so no dirty screws could tip him off."

The guard started getting a little huffy. "Well, ma'am, I don't know what to say."

Mary Beth was dangerously angry, her face was turnip red. Izzy rated her current mental state as Mount Vesuvius on his scale or her moods that ranged from mild irritation to nuclear holocaust.

Any second, Izzy was expecting Mary Beth to start spewing her lava on him because the con must have caught wind of Princess' broadcast two nights earlier where she described the discovery of a hair on Maria Ruiz's remains that authorities were hoping to match up with the killer. Thus, Izzy's requested delay in heading to Colorado had given Octavio time to try and thwart their efforts.

"He's got to have hair somewhere," Izzy said.

Mary Beth looked at him sharply. He did his best not to wince.

"You're right," she said.

"Guards!" She placed her warrant down on the consultation table that was bolted to the floor. "There's my warrant should any of you care to read it." None seemed interested. "We've got a hair found on a murder victim that we're dead certain will match this man if we can find a hair to test."

The three guards stared at her like they were all feeling froggy, just waiting for somebody to tell them what to do.

"Get his shirt off," Mary Beth said.

The guard standing behind Octavio yanked his shirt from behind, lifting it up over his head like a hockey player trying to get an advantage in one of the sport's awkward slugfests.

"Get off me!" Octavio yelled.

"He's resisting," the guard by the door shouted, which gave the first guard all the justification he needed to slam Octavio' head down on the table.

"Jesus!" Octavio yelled.

Mary Beth moved in close, running her fingers over his scalp, inspecting it like a phrenologist.

"Turn him over," she commanded.

Another guard moved in, seizing Octavio by the shoulder and helping to flip him on his back.

"Izzy, get out the tweezers." Mary Beth used her finger tips, going gently over Octavio's shaved chest, even his nipples, looking for just one single remaining hair.

"Ooh. You giving me chills," Octavio said. "I could do this all day."

After a minute or two, Mary Beth gave up. She backed away, hands on hips. The guards stood Octavio back up.

"That was fun." Octavio started shaking his hips like Elvis. "You want to check down here next? I'm clean as a porn star."

"You think you're real smart, don't you?" Mary Beth, said.

The con licked his lips. "I'm gonna think about you when I go to bed tonight."

"Quiet, convict!" One of the guards commanded.

Mary Beth watched Octavio for another moment, burning holes in him with her eyes. "Izzy," she said.

"Yeah, Sheriff?"

"Go stand over there."

Izzy did as he was told, taking his place next to the three guards in their slate gray uniforms. He watched Mary Beth give Octavio one of her sickly- sweet smiles—the kiss of death if you ever had the misfortune to see it. Then she uttered three words that would crack the case wide open: "Bend him over."

27

CHUCK WOOLERY couldn't have made a better match. The hair they plucked from between Octavio's butt cheeks contained mitochondrial DNA that matched the one they found on Maria's body. Therefore, it either belonged to Octavio, or someone in the same maternal line, which was a pretty small list. Most of his family had never even been to the United States. That, combined with the fact that Octavio had a record as a Solares hitman and a witness had seen a van matching his near the scene of the crime, Mary Beth felt extremely confident they had more than enough to convict. A conclusion she cheerily shared with Octavio's attorney during a return visit she and Izzy made to Colorado weeks later.

The lawyer did his best to project confidence. "The hair matches, but the fetal remains don't. So, what's that tell you?" he asked, referencing the fact that a subsequent test of Octavio's DNA with the fetal remains had come back negative.

"Tells me your boy's headed to the electric chair," Mary Beth said.

The defense attorney, God bless him, continued to advocate.

"Come on, Sheriff. We both know Octavio's a button man. Nothing more. Don't you want to know who pushed the button?"

Mary Beth wanted to know the answer to that so bad it made her palms itch. But she didn't want to seem overeager. Especially not with this attorney, who looked so young Mary Beth couldn't believe he was old enough to have a law degree. *They're getting younger all the time*, she thought, *and more confident—blissfully unaware of their ignorance.* This guy pretty much took the cake though, in Mary Beth's opinion, with his little rimless glasses, wearing what looked like it might have been his father's suit, it hung so loose.

"Is that what you're offering?" Mary Beth asked. "To finger the person who commissioned the hit?"

"It is."

"In exchange for what?" Izzy asked.

"Taking the death penalty off the table. I realize West Virginia doesn't execute people, but if you take the case Federal, in light of the interstate nature, then that could be in play."

"That's not our call," Mary Beth told him. "The Feds would have to decide that."

The kid waved his hand like he negotiated death cases every day of the week. "Yeah, but they'll go along with whatever you recommend. It's your case."

Just like that. No equivocation, whatsoever. Going to serve his client up on a silver platter without even talking directly to the prosecutor. This kid had a whole closet full of participation trophies at home—Mary Beth would have bet her life on it.

She and Izzy looked at each other. Nothing was said but at the same time a unanimous decision was made.

"Let me make some calls," she said.

Jasper County's long-time district attorney, Royce Parker, had recently retired in the middle of his term and everybody was waiting for the county commissioners to make their rec- ommendation to the governor about appointing an interim replacement. Until then, Jeannie Boggs, who'd been the Senior Deputy District Attorney, was the county's top lawyer. That was good because she and Mary Beth had always got on well.

After chatting for a couple of minutes, Boggs agreed to reach out to the Feds. After some discussion with the U.S. Attorney's office, she was given their consent to conduct a 'Queen for a Day' interview with Octavio where he could tell them anything he wanted with impunity—meaning it could never be used against him—and if they liked what they heard the Feds would likely go along with a joint plea agreement that would take the death penalty off the table. Octavio would have to cooperate in any subsequent prosecution, and plead guilty to murder, but in exchange, he'd avoid execution.

The interview was conducted as soon as Boggs was able to get to Colorado, arriving with a draft proffer agreement. After Octavio and his attorney signed off, he started to sing.

"It was Raul."

Mary Beth was shocked. Maybe she shouldn't have been. But she was. She'd been expecting to either hear that Pedro had hired out this hit or that it was some kind of revenge killing for Raul turning informant. But the idea that Raul, himself, was the one who wanted Maria killed hadn't really crossed her mind.

"Why?" she asked.

"What he had to do. To skate."

Mary Beth didn't understand at first, but Izzy got it. "You're saying that killing Maria was what Raul had to do to avoid retribution from testifying against the cartel?"

Octavio gave a half-hearted shrug as though his life didn't literally depend upon providing satisfactory answers.

"Si—yes. He wanted to skate. They told him that's what he had to do. Kill the girl and make sure her body was never found."

"Who told him that?" Mary Beth asked.

Octavio shrugged again. "That, I don't know. The man his

lawyer got him in touch with. Someone high up. We never met no one real high up. We were just street guys."

"So why were you involved?" Izzy asked.

Octavio furrowed his brow like he was just realizing he shouldn't have been. "Raul was my boy. I was the one who got him hooked up. Got him in the jam he was in. So, I owed him. Plus, I...."

Octavio turned and looked to his attorney like he wasn't sure he should say anything else.

"Immunity for past, unrelated crimes?" the attorney asked.

Jeannie Boggs said, "We can't promise that until we know what we're talking about."

"But," Mary Beth interjected, "nothing he says here can be used against him and if it happened outside of West Virginia—" she let the sentence trail off but the implication was obvious. Outside of their jurisdiction was somebody else's problem. They were interested in the Ruiz case.

"No specifics," the attorney instructed.

Octavio said, "Like the Italians say, I'd already made my bones. Raul—he was still a virgin."

This wasn't adding up for Mary Beth at all. It made no sense to her why the cartel would have wanted Maria dead. What was she to them? If it weren't for the hair and the van license plate confirming Octavio was the killer, Mary Beth might have suspected this was a false confession by some kook. But given that evidence and Octavio' rap sheet he had to be the Who. Mary Beth just wasn't buying the Why.

"Had you ever met Maria before?" she asked. Mary Beth was starting to wonder if maybe there'd been a personal angle to this murder and this story linking it to Raul was just load of crap he'd come up with so he'd have something to deal. Raul was reportedly hiding down in Mexico somewhere. Thus, they might never find him and he was, therefore, a convenient person for Octavio to pin it on.

"Never laid eyes on her before that day," Octavio said.

Izzy asked him to tell them how he did it.

"Met her in the park. We took my van 'cause nobody round there knew it. Plus, it was getting dark, already cold out. There was hardly nobody there and we met her way in the back where it's pretty private."

"She came there to meet you?" Mary Beth interrupted.

Octavio said," Nah. But Raul knew she was gonna be there."

"How?" she asked.

Octavio looked deep in thought for a moment, then said, "She was supposed to be meeting somebody."

"Who? Raul?"

"I don't think so. But he knew her though. We pulled up and he acted real frantic like something was wrong, asked her if she'd come over real quick and help him. She sticks her head in the side of the van to see what's the matter and I snatched her. We duct-taped her mouth and her arms and legs and drove off."

Mary Beth felt her blood boil at the image but did her best to keep her voice calm and steady. "Where'd you take her?" she asked.

"That old school where you found her. Drove like what seemed like forever. Twistiest roads I ever saw. Raul had to drive 'cause it was making me sick."

"Why there?" Izzy asked.

"Raul said he knew it. He'd cut grass out there with his cousins one summer or something but said that nobody wanted to pay to keep it up no more, so they were just gonna let it rot. Figured nobody'd ever go out there."

"You do it down in the basement?" Mary Beth asked.

"Yeah. We even wore gloves. Guess I should have worn a hairnet." Octavio smiled like he'd said something funny but nobody was laughing. He continued, "Raul already had the drywall and stuff we needed. He put her rosary beads in her hand so she could say a prayer before we did it."

"How'd you get in the door?" Izzy asked. "It was chained."

"Raul had the key to the lock. I guess he was the one who'd chained it."

That wasn't very smart, Mary Beth thought. It was a detail that could lead back to him. But, of course his whole purpose in putting her down there and walling her in was based on the assumption she'd never be found.

Mary Beth asked, "Who pulled the trigger?"

Octavio answered quickly. "Raul. He needed to be the one to do it. I gave him the gun. He pulled the trigger. Cried like a little bitch, too. Afterwards we cut off all the duct tape in case it had fingerprints on it and walled her in."

Mary Beth felt the fury rising up in her, making her neck hot and itchy as little beads of sweat started to form. The image of Maria being shot in the back of the head flashed through her mind. She couldn't imagine how terrified Maria must have been not knowing what was happening or why. Mary Beth had to remind herself to try and stay calm and objective, to treat this like it was any other case. If she didn't, she knew she might miss something.

"What kind of gun was it?" she asked.

"Nine-millimeter."

That squared with what Dr. Patel had predicted. "What'd you do with it?" she asked.

Octavio smiled like he was really proud of this part. I dug the slug out of the floor and picked up the casing. Dropped them in the Mississippi River on the drive back to Arizona."

There was a silence until Octavio's attorney said, "You've heard our proffer. So do we have a deal?"

Mary Beth pushed her hat back and scratched at her forehead. It seemed like a pretty complete accounting. Still, Mary Beth wasn't satisfied. "I don't think so," she said.

"What?" The baby attorney's voice cracked a little, the first indication he grasped the magnitude of what he was involved in.

"The deal was, we had to be convinced that Octavio was telling the truth," Mary Beth explained.

"I told you what I know!" Octavio said, pounding his cuffed hands against the table. He looked at his little lawyer expecting him to do something.

But there was little the attorney could do other than say, "I don't understand. My client just told you Raul Kowalski was the one who commissioned the killing. And the one who pulled the trigger."

"Raul, who conveniently disappeared somewhere in Mexico years ago and had no reason to want Maria dead," Mary Beth responded.

The attorney tried to speak but Mary Beth cut him off. "Don't give me the line about the mystical, boogeyman, cartel wanting her dead. Why in the hell would they care about Maria Ruiz?"

"Man, this is bullshit!" Octavio said. "Can't you do something?"

Mary Beth actually felt sorry for the little attorney now. He gave her a panicked look that reminded her a bit of Sam when he'd been inside his head so long that upon resurfacing into reality, he realized he'd done something extremely negligent like leaving the house with the stove on.

"You want to make a deal," she said to Octavio, "then I need to know who really got you to kill Maria."

Octavio looked at her like she was stupid. "I already told you," he said, extra slow, "it was Raul."

"And exactly who was it that told Raul killing Maria was his ticket to getting out from under any payback from the cartel?" Izzy asked, sounding like he was giving Octavio a little more benefit of the doubt than Mary Beth was.

"I don't know. I wasn't there for that. All I know is it was the guy his lawyer hooked him up with."

"So, for all you know, Raul could have just made that up," Mary Beth said.

"No. No way. He was scared. Scared to death. He begged me to help him." Octavio seemed convinced but Mary Beth wasn't. Now she was thinking if Raul had played a hand in this, maybe he'd just concocted this cartel story to get Octavio's help.

"You ever meet Raul's brother, Pedro?" she asked.

Octavio shook his head. "Never met him. Raul talked about him, but I never met him."

Izzy jumped in. "Did he tell you Maria was Pedro's girlfriend?"

Octavio looked surprised by that. "No. No, I think I would have remembered that."

Izzy followed up, "Did Pedro have anything at all to do with this?"

Octavio seemed a little less certain of himself now, like maybe he was just realizing he might have been played. "Not as far as I know."

Mary Beth took her hat off and sat it in her lap. She clasped her hands together in the middle of the table. "So, you're telling me that you drove all the way from Arizona to West Virginia to whack some girl you never met because Raul said that's what the cartel wanted to happen, and you never even bothered to ask why they wanted her dead?"

Octavio leaned forward too, looking at her like he might be stupid, but he wasn't a liar. "It's not my business to know why."

"Unbelievable." Mary Beth pushed back from the table, making a horrendous screeching sound as her metal chair scraped across the floor.

She and Izzy stood and started to leave when Octavio yelled after them, "All I know is it had something to do with the baby!"

Mary Beth froze. Shockwaves coursed throughout her body. Then she felt a sudden sense of *deja vu*. It was a feeling she sometimes got working cases and it always meant she was on the right track.

"Say that again," she said.

"All I know," Octavio said, "is the lady getting whacked had something to do with her being knocked up. I don't know by who. Maybe it was Pedro, and Raul bullshitted me about the whole cartel thing. I don't know. But I'm telling you the truth."

Mary Beth stared at him, engaging her personal lie detector test. Octavio never took his eyes off of hers and she realized that she believed him. Or, more accurately, she believed that Octavio believed what he was saying.

"So, do we have a deal?" the attorney asked.

Mary Beth put her hand on the doorknob and opened it half way. "We'll let you know," she said.

"When?" he asked.

"When we find Raul."

28

FINDING RAUL was going to be a problem.

John Jacobson did his part. By August, the U.S. Attorney had worked out an agreement with Mexican authorities to extradite Raul Kowalski to the United States, if apprehended. But Mexico had no records of Raul since his initial entry eight years earlier. For all they knew he could be dead or living under an assumed name somewhere, including one of the many rural parts of the country that existed entirely off the grid.

Meanwhile, Princess had scored some serious ratings reporting on the arrest of Octavio Silva and the resulting publicity bump had pulled Mary Beth into a statistical tie with Randy Law in an election that was less than three months away. Izzy'd been doing his best to get Mary Beth to lay off the Ruiz case and focus on campaigning but she wasn't trying to hear that. "This is how I campaign," she told him. Truth was though, there wasn't much left to do on Maria's case other than wait and hope the Mexican police could find their guy.

Mary Beth eventually got so desperate she and Izzy paid the Mountain Mystic another visit. When they showed her a picture of Raul the old woman jumped back like they'd just dropped a rattle snake on the table.

"What?" Mary Beth asked.

The mystic crooked a bony finger at the photo. "That's him, dear. He's your killer. I can feel it."

"You're certain?"

"Absolutely. I can see death all around him. And I feel Maria's terror. Her anguish. Her-"

"Okay, I get the point," Mary Beth said. "Now, how do I find him?"

The old woman gave them one of her stoic looks. "I have no idea."

"Come on, lady. I don't have time for this game. You led us to Octavio. I don't know how in God's name you did, and at this point, I don't really care. I just need to know how to find Raul." *And finding him before the damn election would be nice too*, Mary Beth thought.

"I'm sorry dear." The old lady had nothing else for them.

"Great," Mary Beth said. She and Izzy stood to leave.

"The only thing I can tell you is-"

"Yes? What?"

"When I think about your question, I get a strong maternal feeling. The way I did when your son was here the first time. Like his mother could provide the solution to the inquiry. Perhaps your mother could—"

Mary Beth gave her the hand. "Stop right there."

"What's the matter dear?"

"Your psychic antenna must be going haywire."

"Why is that?"

"Because if you're talking about my mom, the last thing you'd feel is anything maternal."

Mary Beth and Izzy barely spoke on the way back to the station, both dejected from the lack of any additional leads. Once they got there Mary Beth climbed down from Izzy's Blazer and opened the door to her Camaro. Izzy rolled down his window to call after her. "Don't feel bad, MB. You've done everything you can. If the Mexican police can't find Raul, how are we supposed to?"

That's when the lightbulb went off. "You know what?" she said.

"What?"

"The police may not be able to find Raul. But I bet the cartel can."

Izzy laughed. "What are you gonna do, go see El Chapo?"

Mary Beth shook her head. "Nah. That would be a lot more pleasant than what I'm thinking."

She got in her Camaro and closed the door.

Izzy honked his horn and she rolled down her window.

"Where are you going?"

Mary Beth frowned. She didn't feel good about this, but she knew she was going to go through with it. "I'm going to go make a deal with devil," she said, then tore ass out of the parking lot, afraid that if she said more Izzy might try to talk her out of it.

When Mary Beth got on Route 52, even though there wasn't much traffic, she went ahead and flipped on the party lights then gunned the engine pretty much the whole way until she reached Dulcimer, Kentucky.

Mary Beth had often described her mother, Mamie, as having the appearance of Paula Deen and the personality of Attila the Hun. The place Mamie was living in now would have fit right in down in South Beach, Miami, or perhaps Beverly Hills. It was an 18,000-square-foot mansion with a white stucco facade and a portico entrance supported by Greek-inspired columns. Less than a mile away, Mary Beth had passed a trailer park and a handful of hovels where folks lived hand-to-mouth, yet here was this palatial estate in the middle of Dulcimer.

Rows of cars lined both sides of the street leading up to the enormous home and an adjacent field was being used as a parking lot for hundreds of vehicles. Mary Beth bypassed all that and pulled up to the house around a circular cobblestone driveway surrounding a large marble fountain. When she opened the door, a valet offered to park her car for twenty bucks until Mary Beth showed him her badge.

She approached the oversized oak front door manned by a large black man in a SECURITY t-shirt who was wearing an earpiece and a backwards hat. He was checking IDs and collecting an entrance fee, then strapping plastic bracelets on people as they entered. Mary Beth showed him her badge too which got less of a reaction than when she explained that she was Mamie's daughter.

"Oh shit. Come on." The security guard left his post to personally lead Mary Beth through the chaos of a wild house party, the likes of which Mary Beth had only seen in movies. There were multiple cash bars, a bowling alley, pool tables, a "hookah room"–whatever that was–and a casino. People were drinking and doing drugs everywhere, and Mary Beth spied a couple of lovely ladies in skimpy bathing suits leading intoxicated men to upstairs bedrooms.

They finally found Mamie outback of the house, poolside, beneath a cabana. She was wearing an old-fashioned bathing suit that could have been ripped from the wardrobe rack for one of those 1960s TV shows, like *Gidget* or *Beach Blanket Bingo*, with a frilly white robe, and a thick, gold rapper's chain around her neck that looked as out of place on Mamie as an escalator in a dog house. Mary Beth was thankful the robe covered her mother's flabby arms that sagged like bat wings.

To Mamie's left, a film crew was recording some kind of rap video. A shirtless, heavily- muscled black man with cornrow hair and a Mr. T-esque collection of gold chains was standing on the swim-up bar, surrounded by bikini-thong wearing women who were all shaking their money-makers at the camera while he busted his rhymes.

"Hey, Mama," Mary Beth said.

Mamie sat her margarita down on a side table and raised her bug-eye sunglasses. "Well, as I live and breathe."

"What's the story with Tupac over there?"

"Oh, that is Geoffrey, dear," she said. Mamie was born and raised in McCray County, West Virginia but she idolized Scarlett O'Hara and had spent a lifetime patterning her speech after the southern belle, insisting upon talking with a ridiculously overdone accent that never failed to grate on Mary Beth's nerves. "They call him G Money," Mamie explained. "I have half a mind to make him your next stepdaddy."

"What would that make?" Mary Beth asked. "Four? Five? I've lost count."

Mamie frowned and lowered her sunglasses. "I'm sure you didn't come here to discuss my love life." Her voice had lost some of its syrupy sweetness. "Why don't we dispense with the pleasantries and just skip to the part where you apologize."

"Apologize!" Mary Beth, snapped. "Me? Apologize to you?"

"Well, you do want something don't you?"

"Who said I wanted anything?"

Mamie smiled and slowly stirred her margarita. "Come on dear. Why else would you be here?"

The whole way there Mary Beth had thought about how much this meeting was going to hurt. She knew her mother would insist she pay some insufferable price before offering any assistance–something illegal most likely, or at least highly immoral–but there was no way in hell Mary Beth was going to apologize.

"You of all people should know that a mother is only ever appreciated when her child needs something," Mamie said.

The old bat had a point there, but Mary Beth didn't want to acknowledge it. Her only weapon now was deflection, while she gathered her wits. "Seriously, Mama, what in the hell is all this? When did you start living at the Playboy Mansion?"

Mamie lounged back in her chair. "The rap video shoot is just today's party, dear. Tomorrow it will be a Latin theme. Our most popular events though are Mystery Mansion parties. We get some real high rollers there. People of influence who occasionally get themselves in some compromising situations." Mamie started fanning herself daintily. "That's where the blackmail money comes in," she said with pride.

Mary Beth didn't want to hear any more about her mother's latest criminal enterprise. "Well, speaking of blackmail," she said. "You're right. I actually do need something from you." Mary Beth explained her situation. She needed to find somebody who'd gone underground in Mexico and wanted to know if Mamie's cartel connections could help her out.

"*Alleged* cartel connections," Mamie corrected.

"Whatever. Can you help me or not?"

Mamie sat up, ready to get down to brass tacks. "Possibly. But we haven't discussed the price."

Here we go, Mary Beth thought. She'd been expecting this. The last time these two women met, Mary Beth had banned her mother from West Virginia, giving her a week to get out of Dodge if she wanted to avoid prosecution. She expected her mom would want to worm her way back in now. Try to take over her old turf or even expand it. There was no way Mary Beth was going to let that happen. Solving one case wasn't worth that— even if solving it helped her win the election and keep her job. But she was ready to negotiate. There had to be something she could come up with to persuade the old lady.

"What do you want?" Mary Beth asked and then braced herself for the answer.

Mamie cleared her throat. "I would like for you and Sam to join me here for Thanksgiving dinner this year."

Mary Beth hesitated waiting for the other shoe to drop but Mamie stayed quiet.

"That's it?"

"That's it. I'll have everything catered. No need to bring anything."

"That's all you want?"

Mamie smiled. "That's all."

Few things in her life had ever stunned Mary Beth quite like the banality of this request. "Whyyyyy?" she asked, suspiciously.

Mamie acted confused by the question. "Because I would like to share the holiday with my daughter and my grandson."

"No, I mean why aren't you asking for more. Like for something illegal and horrendous?"

Mamie patted the end of her lounge chair. "Have a seat, dear."

"I'd rather stand."

Mamie looked put off, her upper lip tensing, giving just the tiniest flash of the sadistic cruelty that lurked behind her candy-coated exterior. Then she steadied herself and said, "It has occurred to me since the loss of your brother that perhaps I've been too hard on you."

"Mama–"

"Let me finish."

Mary Beth quieted, though her mouth was hanging open from shock at this seemingly genuine expression of almost human emotion–from *her* mother.

"Now, I know you blame yourself for Sawyer."

"No, I don't," Mary Beth shot back. There was a tearing in Mary Beth's guts at the mention of her brother.

"Well, good. You shouldn't. Sawyer was a grown man who made his own choices. And you? You've always had to be strong, haven't you? Lost your father when you were still a girl. Then your husband. I know what it's like to have to be strong. Have to make it in a man's world. You have to sometimes do things that are unpleasant to protect the ones you love."

Mary Beth's lower lip began to quiver. *Son of a bitch*, she thought. What kind of tragic irony would it be if her mother, the person she loathed most in the world, was the only one who really got her.

"Oh, there, there, dear. Let's not go all sissy over it. We women do what we have to do, don't we?"

Mary Beth sniffed loudly, stifling the tears. She had never been so stunned in her entire life. Mamie Logan-Thompson-Newton-Turner had just done something loving-ish toward her without asking for anything incriminating in return. All Mary Beth could do was offer an ambiguous nod of thanks.

By that time, G Money had finished his shoot and was trying to get Mamie's attention. He was holding a bottle of Grey Goose while settling into the hot tub and motioning for Mamie to come join him.

Mamie squeezed Mary Beth's shoulder. "Now if you excuse me," she said, "I have guests to attend to."

29

RAUL KOWALSKI always met his clients at the marina.

He'd discovered it on his first night in Puerto Vallarta after going to a bull fight at the Plaza Del Toros about a quarter mile down the street. It was the first and only time Raul had ever been to a bullfight. He'd thought going to one would somehow make him feel more in touch with his roots–like a real Mexican–but he ended up leaving before it was over because the whole thing just made him feel bad for the bull. It wasn't that he was some mamby-pamby animal rights guy. Far from it. It's just that the event didn't seem sporting at all. The bull had no chance from the start. Long before the matador ever entered the ring the animal had been so worked over by picadors on their horses, sticking the beast like a pin-cushion full of lances, that the bull was already half dead.

There was this one part that was still imprinted on Raul's mind years later. The picador horses were padded with some kind of armor and had blinders on that kept them from being able to see the bull–otherwise, they'd freak the hell out. The bull, after being stuck a gazillion times, got hold of one of those horses, and jacked it up against the wall of the arena, holding him there while the horse frantically neighed in distress. Just before the other picadors circled around to help, Raul locked eyes with the bull and saw something there he recognized. It was like the fearsome toro was resigned to his fate–that he'd known his whole life he was born and bred to be ritualistically slaughtered for others' amusement, but he was determined to make sure somebody else felt some of his pain on the way out.

That's exactly the way Raul felt the whole time he was running drugs for the cartel. Like the game had always been rigged against him, growing up in the shadow of a younger brother who'd gotten all the brains and the looks and the parents' adulation. It had left Raul figuring he might as well get a little satisfaction anyway he could, even if it was through illegal means.

On that first night in PV, after leaving the bullfight, Raul had crossed the busy highway to the marina, nearly getting run over by one of those late-model, air-condition-less taxis that flew around everywhere, never slowing, always beeping their horns, while driving on the wrong side of the road. Docked there, he found the yachts and the schooners and the rich tourists living it up, and decided that was where he was going to get his little bit of satisfaction in this new chapter of his life. The ex-pat community he eventually fell in with all said he was crazy. He didn't know anything about boats or snorkeling, but Raul told them that was where they were wrong. "I don't have to know," he said. "I just need to buy the boat, then hire people who do."

Years later he had a thriving business operated under his new name, Mauricio Dela Cruz. He was working six days a week but in paradise, every day felt like a vacation. Raul just had to make the deals, then sit back and enjoy the sun while the people he hired did the work.

There were eight people signed up for that day's excursion. Six Canadians and a black couple from the States whose accents reminded him a little bit of home. Raul was glad they were there because the Canadians were always loud and drunk and never tipped. Meanwhile, the Americans were throwing money around and seemed like they might even be game for his after-hours services–the private land tours he only offered at night to special customers who wanted to see the real Puerto Vallarta from someone who looked Mexican enough to provide an air of authenticity, but was also American enough for them to feel safe checking out the seedier side of PV's nightlife.

"Everyone's got to wear a life jacket at all times," Raul said. "That's my one rule because I'm too fat and hungover to go diving in to save anybody."

That always got a laugh. Especially from the Canadians who'd brought a big cooler full of Corona and Pacifico and were already half in the bag by ten am. Raul's captain steered them out past the luxurious hillside villas of Gringo Gulch and around Mismaloya Beach to the Los Arcos, three huge rocks like tiny islands with underwater caves where the clients could snorkel for an hour or so until they got tired.

Along the way, Raul pointed out the place where John Huston filmed *The Night of the Iguana*, the movie that had turned Puerto Vallarta from a little-known fishing village to an international tourist destination thanks to a scandalous affair between Elizabeth Taylor and the movie's star, Richard Burton. The women always loved it when he recounted that story. For the men, Raul would point out the nearby jungle where they filmed the Arnold Schwarzenegger movie, *Predator*.

Once the snorkeling was through, they went to a hidden beach and ate lunch at a seaside restaurant where the tables and chairs were set up in the sand, just feet from the lapping, crystal clear water. Raul never had to pay for his meals or drinks. It was part of his consideration for bringing tourists to such establishments that could only be reached by boat, or arduous treks through untamed jungles. The restaurant was staffed by indigenous locals who lived in a nearby village that lacked electricity and running water.

Raul had two *al pastor* tacos and nursed a Negro Modelo, mildly annoyed at how drunk and loud the Canadians were getting. When the men came by with the giant iguanas, he was glad that the Canadians went off to have their pictures taken with them and were then sold on some parasailing that would keep them out of his hair for a bit. It gave him a chance to focus on the Americans who were enjoying some coco locos.

Raul was intrigued by them, especially the woman. She was a stunner. Looked like that model who used to be with David Bowie. *What was her name?* Raul tried to remember as he watched her rub some more lotion on her rich brown skin. The rum in the hot sun must be starting to hit her, he thought, because she was laughing hysterically at her husband's jokes.

That was the part of the equation that didn't add up: the husband. Raul wasn't a tall guy by American standards but this guy was short. Like, really short. Much shorter than his wife. There could only be one explanation, Raul figured: this little man was rich.

When his wife stepped away to look at some trinkets the traveling vendors were peddling, the little man leaned over and tapped bottles with Raul, saying, "So, Mauricio. If a man wanted to really impress a lady, where would you recommend he take her tonight?"

Raul smiled. This was exactly the conversation he was hoping to have. But he didn't want to push too soon. The Americans hated how pushy the salespeople there could be. When they walked up and down Puerto Vallarta's famous boardwalk, the Malecon, he'd often see them crossing the street when they spotted the tequila shop cappers coming their way.

"Where have you been so far?" Raul asked.

"We did dinner down in the Romantic district last night. Been around the Marina. And, of course, the Malecon."

"All the regular tourist spots." Raul said it with an air of condescension.

"Yeah," the man agreed. "I'd like to take her to something more authentic. You know? Something the locals do."

"I know just what you need. If you're up for it, that is."

"I'm up for anything."

Just like that. Raul had laid down the challenge and the man had accepted. He knew guys like this–short guys who always had something to prove, needing to make sure you knew they were just as much of a man as everybody else.

"There's a mountain-top restaurant only the high rollers go to. You have to know somebody to get in. Beautiful views of the harbor. And they've got some gaming, some entertainment. It's the real deal. If you think you can handle it, I can get you in there tonight."

"Seriously? You can do that?"

"For you? Yeah. I do these private tours after hours for special clients. What hotel you staying at?"

The man told him he was staying at the Wyndham.

"Great," Raul said. "That's right by the marina. When we get back, you and your wife can go freshen up and rest for a bit, and then I can have my driver come pick you up around seven."

"I love it," the man said, never once asking about the price. This was the kind of client Raul loved. It didn't matter to him what it cost.

"Oh wait," the man said, snapping his fingers.

"What?" Raul was afraid he was about to change his mind.

"It's kind of stupid, but I promised my wife I'd take her to one of those pedicure places where the fish suck on your toes. There's one down near the end of the Malecon that she heard was really good."

"No problem," Raul said. "That's not far from where we're headed. We can go there first. The pedicure only takes–what–thirty minutes or so? Then we'll head to the club."

"Perfect," the man said.

Perfect, Raul thought. *Absolutely, perfect.*

Later that evening they were sitting at a sports bar, sipping some beers and watching Liga MX, while the man's wife got her toes sucked at the spa next door. It was taking longer than expected and Raul was getting a little annoyed. He kept checking his watch, thinking the Garra Rufa fish must be especially hungry, when the little man said, "I hear there's a cigar shop a couple of blocks from here where they sell Cubans–wanna take a walk?"

Raul had nothing better to do while they waited, so he downed the rest of his beer. They walked around an alley behind the Malecon, away from the crowds where they were alone on the darkening street, except for some little girls in their Catholic school uniforms who were doing double-Dutch.

"Hang on a second," the man said. "I just have to."

Before Raul could ask him what he was doing the man had jumped in on the double- Dutch and was doing it really well, on one foot and then the other, motioning for the girls to pick up the pace. They didn't speak any English but were delighted by this little American showing off.

Raul found himself mesmerized by the little guy who out of nowhere did a backflip–an actual backflip–in perfect rhythm with the circling ropes, not missing a beat when he landed.

He started to clap for the American when he felt the cloth cover his mouth.

There was an overwhelming chemical smell that burned Raul's eyes. A strong bony hand was holding it tight against his face. He tried to turn but whoever had come up from behind him had grabbed hold of his left arm and chicken winged it behind his back. The next thing he knew he was being driven down onto the cobblestone street face first.

The only thing Raul remembered after that was just barely

getting his right arm underneath him, trying to break his fall, and the pain in his elbow before everything faded to black.

When Raul woke up he was lying on a dusty concrete floor with three police officers standing over him in their baby-blue short-sleeve shirts and black *Policia* caps.

"*Hola, Raul. Como esta?*" one of them said.

He hadn't entirely regained his senses yet or he'd have been cagier, but as Raul was coming to, he said, in English, "How'd you know my name?"

The officer motioned for his friend, the third officer, a thin, light-skinned man who was holding a manila envelope, and pulled out some papers.

"It wasn't hard," he said, switching to English.

"What?" Raul asked.

"This is a first."

"A first for what?"

The officers all laughed before one explained. "It's the first time we found someone handcuffed outside the station with a package like this." The man fanned out the papers. "I mean look at it. We got a rap sheet, a birth certificate, an expired driver's license–and this." He held up an official looking document. Before Raul could make out any of the words the officer explained, it was, "an extradition order from *Los Estados Unidos*."

30

STRESS LINES CREASED Deputy District Attorney Jeannie Bogg's furrowed brow, framed by her long limp brown hair that she parted in the middle, making her look like a frazzled Mona Lisa. "We've got a serious issue," she said.

Mary Beth was still feeling relaxed from the weeks she'd spent down in Mexico and wasn't immediately concerned. She also knew Jeannie was a worrier. In practically every case she'd tried there'd been a conversation like this at some point where the grizzled ADA would convince herself they were going to lose. Mary Beth gave Izzy a knowing wink–like Here we go again–as they took a seat opposite Jeannie in the attorney conference room, down the hall from the Jasper County DA's office

"The DNA doesn't match," Jeannie said.

Mary Beth was slightly disappointed to hear that. Part of her thought they might discover that Raul had knocked Maria up and killed her to keep Pedro from finding out. But it wasn't essential to the case against him. Didn't affect Octavio's account at all.

"Okay, so?" she asked.

"That's not all." Jeannie palmed her forehead. "Octavio recanted."

Now she had Mary Beth's attention. "What?"

"Yeah," Jeannie said. "His attorney said Octavio wants to take the rap for the whole thing. I guess he never thought you'd actually find Raul and now that he's been extradited to the U.S., Octavio is trying to fall on his sword for him."

Izzy asked, "Can't we still use Octavio's statement against Raul?"

Jeannie shook her head, No. She showed them the agreement they signed. "Queen for a day, remember. We told him nothing he said could be used against him."

"But we aren't using it against him," Mary Beth argued. "We're using it against Raul. Confession by a co-conspirator, right?"

Jeannie looked like she was considering the possibility for a second, then winced, shaking off the idea. "Honestly, I don't think so. I seriously doubt a judge would let it in. And that Charleston lawyer who's representing Raul has already filed a motion to exclude it, along with a motion to dismiss."

That Charleston lawyer was Felix Lancaster, who Pedro was now paying to represent his brother, and who was also in possession of a very embarrassing video of Mary Beth half-naked, drunk, and throwing up. They were just a month from election day. If that video were to surface now it would be disastrous. Mary Beth and Izzy exchanged worried glances.

"Octavio's saying he was coerced," Jeannie said. "He's claiming he was threatened into making a false confession, implicating Raul."

Mary Beth rolled her eyes. This coercion line was getting old. "I never did any such thing."

"Not you." Jeannie flipped through her legal pad looking for a name she'd scribbled down. "He said it was another inmate. A Clementine Stenson."

"Quiet Clem?" Mary Beth said. Clem had been Sawyer's

right-hand man and one of her mother's henchmen, too, who would have made a good Bond villain at seven feet tall. Mary Beth knew he was an inmate at the same prison as Octavio but didn't know why he would have a dog in this fight. "That doesn't make any sense," she said.

"I'm just telling you what he's claiming." Jeannie went on to say that it didn't matter if it was true or not. If Octavio refused to testify then his prior statement would likely be inadmissible on hearsay grounds, regardless of whether or not it was coerced. "Which leaves us with no admissible evidence tying Raul to the crime."

Mary Beth needed a moment to think. She took her hat off, brushed back her hair and put it back on again. "That's not true," she said. "We've got Octavio dead to rights, and his only connection to Maria, or Jasper Creek for that matter, is Raul, right?"

"Yeah."

"And we can show that Raul knew about the school out there. Even had a key to get in."

Jeannie was shaking her head, negatively. "Way too circumstantial. We need Octavio's statement to tie it all together–provide a narrative. Remember we've got the burden of proving everything beyond a reasonable doubt. We can't just go in there and say maybe Raul was involved. The judge would never let the case you just described even get to a jury."

Mary Beth had an idea about that too though she was a little loathe to say it out loud. After hesitating she finally decided to spit it out. "What about the psychic?"

"You're joking," Jeannie said.

Mary Beth responded defensively. "I've heard of police using psychics before."

"In investigations maybe. But never at trial."

There was an open statute book on the desk in front of Jeannie that was about six inches thick. Mary Beth flipped it shut with a thud. "Well, we've got to do something, dammit! We can't just let him walk."

Jeannie had that defeated look again. "I guess that'll be up to the new DA. A weak case like this, in something so high profile. It's above my paygrade."

Mary Beth wasn't sure she'd heard her right. "What new DA?"

Now Jeannie looked really concerned, like maybe she feared being the messenger of bad tidings. "I just assumed you heard," she mumbled.

"Heard what?"

"While you were away the commissioners made a recommendation for replacing Royce as interim DA and the governor's office approved it."

"Approved who?"

On cue there was a throat clearing behind Mary Beth and Jeannie motioned in that direction with her eyes.

Before Mary Beth could turn to see who Jeannie was gesturing to, her ears were assaulted by a pompous voice she loathed. "Well, howdy, Sugar."

Mary Beth felt her sphincter muscles tighten like a Chinese finger trap. "Pomfried?"

"Yours truly."

Alexander Pomfried, the round mound of legal renown, was positively beaming, running his thumbs up and down the insides of his suspenders, pushing his rotund stomach out with pride. This was Mary Beth's absolute worst nightmare. Pomfried, the most prominent defense attorney of his generation and Mary Beth's biggest critic, who she'd gone to great lengths to conflict out of defending any more criminal cases in Jasper County, was the new DA—the one who'd make every prosecutorial decision on every bust Mary Beth made.

"I hope this is some kind of sick joke," she said.

"It's not a joke," Jeannie whispered.

Mary Beth stared menacingly at her nemesis. "What the hell,

Pomfriedl? You're a piece of shit defense lawyer. Why would you want to be the district attorney?"

Pomfried cleared his throat like he was about to address the Rotary Club. "There are many reasons. One, it's a great honor. Two, it gives me a chance to serve my community. And three—" Pomfried glared down over his half-lens glasses. "It was the best way I could think of to … piss … you … off."

Mary Beth felt the heat rise on her cheeks. "You can't do this!" she bellowed.

"Sugar, it's already done."

Mary Beth's head started to spin. She was speechless–an unfamiliar feeling that had only happened a handful of times in her entire life, but this was one of them.

Pomfried said, "I imagine Ms. Boggs, here, has explained to you that we can't be moving forward on the Raul Kowalski prosecution. Do appreciate your efforts there though."

Jeannie cleared her throat. "I–uh–was just getting to that."

Mary Beth realized she'd been set up here. She knew nothing would please Pomfried more than to put the kibosh on this case she'd worked so hard on. "Wait a second," Mary Beth said. "You can't decide that!" She stood and poked Pomfried hard in the chest. "You represented Raul before. And you represented his brother, Pedro, in regards to this very case. You're as conflicted as a priest in a whorehouse."

Pomfried hiked up his pants, rolling his sizable girth around in a threatening way. "Of course I am, Sugar. And I am quite aware of my ethical responsibilities—thank you very much. That's why I have recused myself from this matter. It was Ms. Boggs, here, who determined that we can't proceed."

Mary Beth turned on Jeannie the way the other eleven disciples must have looked at Judas.

"We can't win without Octavio's testimony," she said nervously. "And I'm as concerned about the appearance of a conflict as you are. If we bring the highest profile case in the history of this county and lose, people might think we threw the case on purpose."

Mary Beth could shake Jeannie, she was so angry. Izzy sensed it and grabbed hold of her arm but Mary Beth brushed him aside. There was no way she was giving up on this case. She'd gone too far to bring Raul to justice–traveling all the way to Mexico, like some kind of Nazi hunter to subdue the fugitive. There was no way she was going to let him slip away now. Mary Beth launched a verbal assault onto Jeannie. "Boss Hogg here just said he's recused. So, what's the problem? You're too scared to do your job?"

"I most certainly am not!" Jeannie snapped. "I'm just a responsible prosecutor. And I have a duty not only to this one case, but to maintaining the public's confidence in this office. Which, I may add, has become quite difficult to do, given some of the publicity law enforcement has received in the last year."

Ouch. Touche, Mary Beth thought.

"The point is," Jeannie continued, "no matter how much we were to wall the district attorney off from the case, there will still be the appearance of impropriety in the public's mind. They'll assume that either there was undue influence, or the prosecutor didn't give it their best shot because they were worried about what the boss would think. Nobody in this office can touch this case now. It's too toxic."

The two women stared each other down, both seething but neither speaking, until a calm quiet voice broke the tension in the room. "What if somebody from outside the office did it?"

They both wheeled around to look at Izzy.

"What are you suggesting?" Jeannie asked.

Izzy said, "If nobody from this office can prosecute, why not bring in somebody independent–like a special prosecutor? There seems to be a lot of those these days."

Pomfried forced a belly laugh of undulating rolls beneath his pinstriped Oxford. "Now you just tell me who in the hell is gonna come in here and throw their career away on this unwinnable, high-profile case, trying to convict somebody with nothing other than the most tangential of circumstantial evidence and the word of a damn psychic?"

Mary Beth thought that was a pretty good point but Izzy didn't seem fazed by it. "I think I may know somebody."

"Who?" Mary Beth asked.

He looked at her with that smirk he sometimes got when he'd caught her in a fib. "Somebody who'd do *anything* to help you, sheriff."

"No," Mary Beth said. "Not him. Anybody but him."

"Who else would do it?" Izzy asked.

Mary Beth didn't have an answer.

"Tell me who it is you have in mind," Pomfried said.

Jeannie, who looked like a weight had suddenly been lifted off her, said, "I don't care who it is." She turned to Pomfried. "This is my call, right?"

"Absolutely and unequivocally," Pomfried said.

"Then, I don't care who you've got in mind, Izzy. You find a licensed attorney who is willing to go to bat on this case the way it is now, and I'll appoint him special prosecutor with *carte blanche* to handle it however he or she sees fit."

"Oh, he's licensed," Izzy said. "And highly respected. A decorated Assistant U.S. Attorney."

"Sounds perfect," Jeannie said.

Izzy turned to Mary Beth who'd slouched down in her seat trying to decide what was worse, letting Raul go or going along with the idea Izzy was now pushing. The deputy squeezed Mary Beth's shoulder. "I'll just have to make sure he's able to get into the state," he said.

Pomfried and Jeannie both looked confused. "You make it sound like he needs a visa or something," Pomfried said.

There was a pause during which Mary Beth could feel Izzy

watching her. When she finally looked up and met his eyes, he said, "Something like that."

31

SIMILAR TO HER MOTHER, Mary Beth had also banned Patrick Connelly from ever returning to West Virginia. He was no career criminal, like Mamie, but he had made the mistake of conspiring with the old lady in an effort to win back Mary Beth's heart.

"It was all done out of love," Patrick had assured Izzy countless times. His sole motivation was to try and get back into Mary Beth's good graces at a time when she found herself in a tough spot, under investigation by the U.S. Attorney's office. Patrick, a U.S. Attorney himself, but in a different division–the civil land use section out of D.C.–came up with the brilliant idea that maybe he could clear Mary Beth's slate by brokering a deal with the criminal prosecutors to let her go, in exchange for her assistance in arresting Mary Beth's brother, Sawyer. There were several outstanding warrants against Sawyer at the time that federal marshals had been afraid to serve while Sawyer stayed holed up in the militia compound he'd built at the Old Wengo mine.

It was a good idea, but there were two problems. One, Mary

Beth would never go for any idea that resulted in her baby brother going to prison. Second, despite Sawyer's wildly popular anti-government rants, weapons stockpiling, and militia building, he'd not yet become a big enough thorn in the government's side for them to be willing to make the trade for Mary Beth.

So, Patrick engaged in some three-dimensional chess by reaching out to the Bobby Fischer of criminal conspiracies, Mary Beth's mother, Mamie. The deal they struck was for Patrick to give Mamie the inside intel on a massive public works project that could make her millions, and, in exchange, she used her considerable influence over Sawyer to get him to crank things up a notch. When Sawyer's guys blew up a mostly empty federal courthouse in McCray County, everything seemed to be falling into place. Sawyer quickly became public enemy number one, such that the Feds were more than willing to wipe Mary Beth's slate clean if she could bring him in. And Mary Beth was forced to help herself by accepting the deal because arresting Sawyer became the only way she'd be able to avoid a bloody confrontation when the Feds converged on the Old Wengo Mine.

It really should have worked. Patrick just underestimated Sawyer's blood lust and Mary Beth's powers of perception. It turned out Sawyer was so determined to blow the Feds to hell he was willing to sacrifice his followers in the process. Mary Beth was forced to shoot him before he could detonate explosives that would have killed hundreds. And of course, once the smoke cleared, she put the pieces together. The last time he and Mary Beth spoke, Mary Beth not only made it abundantly clear she never wanted to see Patrick again, but told him if he ever set foot inside the state of West Virginia she'd reveal his plan to the authorities.

Patrick was, therefore, pretty surprised when he saw the 304-area code pop up on his cell phone. He recognized the number, having called it so many times over the last few months, but this was the first time Izzy Baker had ever called him.

"Izzy? What's wrong? Is Mary Beth okay?"

"Yeah, yeah. She's fine. But, listen, did you really mean it when you said you'd do anything to get Mary Beth to forgive you?"

"Of course, I did. Did she say something? Is she willing to talk?"

"Not exactly. But I think there is something you could do that might smooth things out. It would at least buy you safe passage back into West Virginia. Temporarily, anyway."

Patrick was all ears. "What can I do?"

It took Izzy half an hour to tell Patrick the whole story. When he finished, Patrick said, "So let me make sure I've got this straight. You have a convicted felon-a *bona fide* cartel hitman-who's already confessed to this old murder and now says he did it alone. And his vehicle more or less matches the eyewitness account, and there is physical evidence-a hair-that ties him to the murder scene?"

"That's right."

"But you want me to convict somebody else for the murder who has no criminal record-other than an old drug charge that was dismissed-without any clear motive or physical evidence or witness testimony connecting him to the crime other than the word of some hillbilly psychic?"

Izzy cleared his throat. "More or less."

Patrick started looking around the Georgetown Starbucks he was sitting in for hidden cameras like he might be on one of those prank TV shows. "Is there anything else I should know?"

"Actually, there is."

"I'm almost afraid to ask," Patrick said, "but go ahead."

"They've been holding Raul Kowalski without bail since he was extradited, due to the flight risk. So, his lawyer has pushed for an expedited hearing on his motions to exclude evidence and have the case dismissed."

"How expedited?"

There was a pregnant pause on the other end of the line. "A week from Monday."

"A week from Monday! That's like ten days from now. I couldn't possibly be ready by then. I'm not even a West Virginia lawyer. I don't even ...." Patrick trailed off, not sure he wanted to admit to the level of his ignorance when it came to criminal law. Most people assumed lawyers knew everything about the law but the truth was the majority of them were so highly specialized they knew little more than lay people about the areas they didn't work in. Patrick hadn't studied criminal law since he'd taken the bar exam. For his entire career he'd exclusively been a civil attorney working in the land use division where the closest he ever got to crime and punishment were penalties for environmental polluters.

"The DA's down here said they could take care of getting you admitted *pro hac vice*," Izzy explained. "Could just walk you down to the judge as soon as you get here and get it signed off on. No big deal. As for the rest of it? Well, you're the lawyer."

"A civil lawyer," Patrick admitted. "You do know I've never even had a jury trial before, right?"

Izzy sounded surprised. "Actually no, I didn't know that. But believe me, if there was anybody else we could get to do this I wouldn't be calling. You said you wanted to try and make things right with Mary Beth, didn't you?"

"Yeah." He did. But Patrick wasn't sure how embarrassing himself in a courtroom would do that.

"Well, she cares more about this case than any she's ever worked on. Maria Ruiz was a close family friend. She used to babysit Sam, for Pete's sake. And Bill worked himself to death trying to solve this thing. She's desperate to see the person who pulled the trigger brought to justice. And we know Raul did it. If you can find a way to save the day and convict him, I'm sure her feelings toward you are going to soften quite a bit."

"How's she going to feel when I end up getting her case dismissed?"

The other end of the line fell ominously silent. "You may not want to unpack, while you're here. Because if that happens, you should probably high-tail it, pretty quick."

"Great." This proposal was sounding worse and worse.

"So?" Izzy asked. "Will you do it?"

Patrick held the phone from his ear, knowing he was going to regret this decision, but knowing he'd regret it even more if he said, No. For twenty years the thing his heart had wanted most was to be reunited with Mary Beth. Fate had always seemed to conspire to keep them apart but now that he knew Sam was actually his son, he was more desperate than ever for them to be together. He'd walk over hot coals, eat glass, swim through shark-infested waters, to make it happen.

"Yeah, sure," he said. "Why not."

"Excellent! I'll send over some information about the case so you can start reviewing it. But I'd recommend you get down here as soon as possible so they can get you admitted."

"Can't wait," Patrick said.

Though the people he cared most about were located in Jasper Creek, Patrick hated that place with a passion. He'd been forced to move there as a teenager after growing up in the Philly suburbs and endured a culture shock he likened to a cross between *Deliverance* and that torture scene in *A Clockwork Orange* where they put Alex in a straight-jacket and pried his eyes open so he couldn't look away from images that made him violently ill. Since graduating high school Patrick had only returned to West Virginia a handful of times for weddings and funerals. Now he'd be going back for the second time in less than a year.

He spent the rest of the afternoon trying to clear his calendar, but Patrick wasn't even sure how long he'd need to be there. If by some miracle he was able to keep the case from getting dismissed, would they go straight into the trial or would that be sometime later? How long would it take to prepare for a jury trial, anyway? Weeks? Months? A year? He really had no idea what he was getting himself into and started feeling more and more anxious as that reality sat in.

The uneasiness only intensified when he got Izzy's email and started reading through the voluminous motion and brief that had been filed. It was full of constitutional arguments about the Sixth Amendment and "Confrontation Clause," things Patrick only vaguely remembered from law school–and case cites and statutory references that were thrown around like they must be household names amongst the criminal bar but meant absolutely nothing to him. Then it went on and on about hearsay, which was an objection Patrick had heard so rarely he had to strain to remember the rule's exceptions. The land use cases he dealt with were almost always handled informally–resolved over the telephone or in a board room somewhere–so he hadn't really argued evidence law since his mock trial class during his second year of law school.

What was worse than Patrick's rustiness was the fact that the motion's logic seemed unassailable. The only evidence of Raul Kowalski's guilt was a prior statement by Octavio Silva made during a proffer to the prosecutor. Octavio had since recanted, claiming that he was coerced into making a false statement by a fellow inmate–the infamous Quiet Clem–and would refuse to testify. Therefore, the only evidence the state could offer against Raul would be testimony by those present during the proffer about what Octavio had said. That was textbook hearsay–an out of court statement offered for the truth of the matter asserted–and thus inadmissible unless it fell within an exception to the hearsay rule.

According to the motion, the only potential hearsay exception would be if Octavio's confession was considered an admission by a co-conspirator. But that exception could not apply because–as the motion aptly pointed out–the co-conspirator exception only applied to admissions made during the commission of a crime or in furtherance of the conspiracy. That was where the *Crawford v. Washington* case came in that the motion kept citing as something everybody should know. It apparently made it clear that statements made during police interrogations or once the person was in custody were considered "testimonial" and thus not admissions by a co-conspirator.

Patrick read the next portion aloud. "In addition to the hearsay rule, prior 'testimonial' statements cannot be admitted against a criminal defendant, unless the defendant has the ability to confront and cross-examine that witness as required by the Confrontation Clause of the Sixth Amendment to the United States Constitution."

Patrick had to google the Sixth Amendment to remember what it said, but sure enough it was right there in the Constitution. A defendant has the right to "be confronted with the witnesses against him." Then he looked up the *Crawford v. Washington* case, and it was on point. Unless Raul had a prior opportunity to cross-examine Octavio–which he hadn't–any prior statements Octavio made about Raul were inadmissible. And without it, there was no case. Period. Ball game. End of story.

The motion to dismiss seemed like a slam dunk.

To make himself feel even worse, Patrick then googled the defense attorney who'd drafted the motion and found the webpage for Felix Lancaster, who was not only a seasoned trial lawyer but also a published author and leading authority on evidence law.

"God," Patrick said. This was going to be ridiculous. He dropped his smart phone onto his desk like it had burned his hand. Patrick's mind filled with images of Joe Pesci in *My Cousin Vinny* wearing a red tuxedo with tails and a ruffled shirt, the epitome of a fish-out-of-water-attorney in a country courtroom ruled over by an angry judge. Patrick would be lucky not to get himself thrown in jail for unwittingly committing some unforgivable courtroom sin or violating some local idiosyncrasy.

Patrick groaned as he stared up at the water-stained ceiling tiles in his little government office, realizing his chances of success in this endeavor were about the same as the odds of the Washington Generals beating the Harlem Globetrotters. The question wasn't who would win, but just how embarrassing the blowout would be.

"Well," Patrick said to himself, "at least I won't have to be in Jasper Creek for very long."

32

MARY BETH HAD AVOIDED Patrick since his return to Jasper Creek by insisting that he deal exclusively with Izzy for anything he needed from the sheriff's office. She'd decided that if Patrick managed to keep the case against Raul from being dismissed, Izzy could handle the testimony about the investigation since he'd been there for all of it, which would keep her from having to interact with him at all. She was still way too angry to speak to him and had every intention of staying that way until they put her into the ground. But when it came time for the motion hearing she couldn't not go. Mary Beth decided she'd show up right at the scheduled ten a.m. start time and slip in the back to try and avoid any awkward interactions with her old high school boyfriend.

Until then, she killed time by indulging one of her favorite new pastimes, driving around town rounding up Randy Law yard signs she determined were in violation of West Virginia's outdoor advertising statute. She'd found seventeen such offenders that morning that would stay nice and secure in the trunk of her car until she got home that evening, at which point she'd make a bonfire out of them and roast some marshmallows for the neighborhood kids. The latest poll had come out the day before, showing Randy pulling back out to a three-point lead off the negative press she was getting about how Raul Kowalski was expected to walk. Randy had even scraped enough money together to run a TV commercial about the high-profile case, spinning it as another instance of police corruption and incompetence threatening to allow a criminal to walk free.

When Mary Beth got to the courthouse, she had to fight through a crowd of interested spectators huddled in the back of the courtroom. The seats were all filled and Mary Beth nearly bumped into Randy Law as she pushed her way inside. The son of a bitch was leaning by the doorway and as she brushed past him and she couldn't avoid making eye contact. Though she moved quickly to the corner of the room, Randy still gave her a finger point like she'd just assisted him on a layup. Mary Beth felt the press and the public watching. She forced herself to grant him a courteous head nod before turning her attention up front.

All she could see of Patrick was the back of his perfectly-coiffed brown hair. Izzy was seated behind him, along with Sam and Guadalupe, which made her feel a little guilty she wasn't with them, showing support. She thought about going to let them know she was there but just as she was considering it, Patrick turned to say something to Izzy and, in spite of herself, she felt the thunderbolts in her chest.

Damn, he looked good in that crisp navy suit with the red power tie. *Looks the way a U.S. Attorney should look*, she thought, *like truth, justice and the American way*. It took Mary Beth a moment to conjure up the image of her dead brother and to remind herself of the handful of other people who'd been killed in the confrontation at Old Wengo–which she held Patrick personally responsible for–before a white film of hatred coated her heart again.

She looked over at the defense attorney, Felix Lancaster, who was a sharp dresser too, wearing a charcoal pinstripe–conservative and respectful, but expensive looking enough to communicate his prominence as the highest-priced lawyer in this situation. Felix was handing something to Patrick, a black binder, and Mary Beth felt a moment of panic remembering that Felix was also in possession of an extremely embarrassing video of her. She didn't know how that could have anything to do with the current hearing, but the paranoid side of her started imagining him playing it for the judge and all the assembled onlookers to gawk at.

God, she thought, *Randy Law sure would love that.* Imagine the TV commercials he'd run then.

Mary Beth's thoughts were interrupted by a steel door like a bank vault near the front of the courtroom that swung open with a boom. Deputy Goforth appeared there ushering in a shackled Raul Kowalski to a seat next to his attorney. Mary Beth noticed just then that Pedro and Elizabeth Kowalski were seated over there in the front row behind the defense table.

The bailiff commanded everyone to rise. "Oyez! Oyez! Oyez! All persons having business before this court are admonished to draw near and give their attention, for we are now in session, the Honorable Judge Markley presiding. God save this state and this Honorable Court."

Judge Markley was a tall, solidly built man with dark, slicked back hair that stood in stark contrast to his short white beard. He told everyone to be seated.

All things being equal, Mary Beth would normally have thought Judge Markley was a good draw in a murder case. He had a reputation as a hanging judge who liked to convict and hand down harsh sentences. But he was also a stickler for the rules and, like all judges, hated to be reversed on appeal. Jeannie Boggs had handicapped their odds of winning this hearing as somewhere around a hundred to one.

Felix Lancaster stood to begin arguing his motion when Judge Markley raised a hand to stop him. "I have already read the defense's motion and accompanying brief, Mr. Lancaster," he said, holding up the thick stack of papers so everyone could see just how much reading the jurist had been forced to endure. "I understand the primary thing we need to decide here is your motion to exclude any evidence of prior statements of one--," Judge Markley peered down through his reading glasses--"Octavio Silva, regarding the accused."

"That's right, Your Honor," Lancaster said. "And it is our position that it is clearly inadmissible hearsay prohibited by the Rules of Evidence and the United States Constitution. In addition to the fact that it was made during a protected proffer, and, as is set out in the affidavit attached to our motion, Mr. Silva claims that it was a false statement he was coerced into making under duress, due to threats of physical violence made by a fellow prisoner named Clementine Stenson–who, I should point out, is a childhood friend of the current sheriff of Jasper County, Sheriff Cain."

Mary Beth felt the entire courtroom turn in unison and stare at her standing there in the corner. She wanted to melt into a puddle of goo but did her best to keep a stiff upper lip, knowing her pale skin must be flashing like a stop light.

Then a strong voice came thundering to her defense. "Sheriff Cain may have known Mr. Stenson as a child but she is also the one who arrested him for murder and is the reason he's sitting in federal prison right now."

Patrick was standing with arms crossed, emanating righteous indignation that anyone would dare impugn the sheriff's integrity by suggesting she had put Quiet Clem up to coercing a false confession. Mary Beth wanted to applaud, but the judge was less impressed.

"Mr. Connelly, you will have your turn to speak, sir."

"Yes, Your Honor." Patrick looked slightly cowled by the judge's rebuke as he took his seat.

"Please continue, Mr. Lancaster," the judge said.

For the next twenty minutes, Felix Lancaster waxed eloquent about the long and proud history of the rules of evidence, the underlying reasons why hearsay should not be admitted–its inherent unreliability and the undue weight jurors were likely to give it–and how those same concerns motivated the nation's wise old founders to incorporate such vital safeguards as the Confrontation Clause into the Constitution. When he was finished the judge and everyone else in the courtroom turned to Patrick as though no one could believe there was anything he could possibly say in response.

"Well, Mr. Connelly?" the judge asked. "Tell me how you think you can get around the Confrontation Clause and the hearsay rule."

Patrick stood, facing the judge at an angle that allowed Mary Beth to note his strong jawline. "That's simple, Your Honor. We will call Mr. Silva to testify."

There was an audible reaction in the crowd at the boldness of the pronouncement, followed by a confused silence. "I don't understand, Mr. Connelly," the judge said. "Mr. Silva has made it clear that if called, he would say he committed this crime alone."

"At which point, Your Honor, we could use his prior statement to impeach him. That way he would still be present during the trial and the defendant would still have an opportunity to cross-examine him, so there'd be no Confrontation Clause issue. Mr. Silva could tell his current story about claiming to be pressured to make the prior statement–which I believe Quiet Clem Stenson will vehemently deny–and the jury can decide what to believe."

"Objection! Your Honor, this is clearly–"

The judge turned his scowl on the defense attorney. "Just a moment, Mr. Lancaster." But he wasn't so much concerned with keeping order as saving time because the judge obviously knew what Lancaster was about to say. "What you are proposing, Mr. Connelly, is a blatant attempt at bootstrapping. You are going to call a witness for the sole purpose of impeaching him with a prior statement as a way of trying to backdoor this hearsay into evidence."

That was true. Mary Beth had seen lawyers try this sort of thing in court before, and it had never gone well. The judges always saw right through it and put a quick stop to it.

"What I am proposing, Your Honor, is not letting a murderer go free because the witness who fingered him got cold feet," Patrick said.

Boom, Mary Beth thought. If Patrick had a microphone, he could have dropped it right there because he evoked an outburst of cheers from the sizable contingent of Maria's family and friends who were gathered in the courtroom. Mary Beth did a little fist pump. "Go ahead with your bad self, Patrick," she said under her breath. "Don't take no shit."

Judge Markley rapped his gavel to quiet the audience, but looked a bit conflicted. He was well aware of the courtroom's feelings. Most who'd followed the case were of the opinion that Octavio Silva had initially told the truth when he implicated Raul, assuming his buddy would never be caught, and had only changed his story out of loyalty once that occurred. The Judge appeared to share that analysis, saying, "I understand your feelings Mr. Connelly. And I share your skepticism about any suggestion that Mr. Silva's prior account was coerced. But, the law on this matter is clear. I have no choice but to exclude those statements. And without them, I do not see how you can make out a *prima facie* case against this defendant," the judge said, pointing his gavel at Raul.

Judge Markley was getting ready to drop that wooden hammer on a ruling that would set Raul free, and at the same time, drive a stake through Mary Beth's heart. After all she had been through to try and finally get justice for Maria after so many years—pinning all her hopes for a reconciliation with her semi-estranged son and dead husband's ghost on the outcome—to get so close just to watch it slip away, tore at her heart.

"So, unless the State has any other evidence," the judge said, "I have no choice but to–"

"Wait!"

Everyone turned to Patrick who was standing with both hands in the air like superman trying to stop a runaway train. "Please, Judge," he said. "Please wait. There is more."

33

"YES, MR. CONNELLY?"

Patrick ran a finger around his collar, uncomfortable about whatever he was about to say. "We do have another witness who can make out a case against Mr. Kowalski."

Felix Lancaster jumped to his feet. "Objection, Your Honor! There's been no such witnesses disclosed to the defense."

Patrick responded quickly. "That's because she wasn't considered a witness until I got involved in the case a little over a week ago. Prior to that she'd been kind of an informal consultant to the sheriff department's investigation."

"Who is this witness?' the judge demanded.

"Mabel Honaker."

Everyone looked around confused, not recognizing the name.

Patrick's voice dropped to a near whisper, adding, "Also known as the Mountain Mystic."

Gasps and a few laughs filled the courtroom. Mary Beth cringed.

"The who?" the judge asked.

"The Mountain Mystic," Patrick said, managing to sound

slightly more confident this time. "She is a psychic who has aided the police in their investigation."

"Your Honor–" Lancaster started to protest but the judge cut him off.

"Hang on just a minute Mr. Lancaster. I want to hear this." The judge took his reading glasses off, folded them, and sat them down in front of him.

Patrick took that as his cue to keep speaking. "Well, you see, Judge, it was actually this psychic whose visions led the police to discover the victim's body in the first place. As you know the remains were found walled in, down in the basement of an abandoned school. A place where only someone with direct knowledge, or true psychic ability could discover."

There were some oohs in the audience that made Mary Beth feel slightly less embarrassed about disclosing her department's use of a psychic.

"Then, Your Honor, this same woman had another vision that led the authorities to Octavio Silva, a convicted cartel hitman from Arizona, who has no other ties to West Virginia other than this crime. A completely random person who could never have been found through traditional police means."

"And exactly how did she lead them to Mr. Silva?" the judge asked.

"A vision, judge. She had a vision of a very specific tattoo Mr. Silva has. A heart with his daughter's birth date inside it. When she saw this tattoo in her vision she was able to draw it and then police matched it to Mr. Silva by using the FBI's database."

The judge nodded, impressed. People throughout the audience were as well, turning to each other and whispering, "Did you hear that?"

"And we know she was right, Judge, for three reasons: (1) analysis of Mr. Silva's hair was a positive match for a hair found on the deceased's remains; (2) the vehicle Mr. Silva drove at the time matched witness accounts of a van seen in the city park from where the deceased is believed to have been abducted; and (3) as the defense motion points out, Mr. Silva admitted to participating in the abduction and murder."

A lady seated in the back row said loud enough for all in the courtroom to hear, "Oh, my God."

Then Patrick fired a vicious point at Raul that would have made a seasoned prosecutor proud. "Mr. Silva initially stated to authorities that he carried out this killing with, and at the behest of, the defendant, Raul Kowalski, who was the one who actually pulled the trigger."

The room shifted toward Raul. All eyes glared at the presumed murderer.

"It is also before the court," Patrick continued, "that Mr. Kowalski had recently been granted immunity for drug charges in exchange for his testimony against a cartel operative in Arizona."

The judge looked confused. Patrick explained, "This is important, Judge, because Octavio Silva's original statement to authorities, the one the defense has excluded, is that the reason Maria Ruiz was killed was in order to assure that Mr. Kowalski did not suffer any reprisals from the cartel. We don't know why that's what the cartel required, but Mr. Silva previously stated that someone connected with the cartel approached Mr. Kowalski and told him if he wanted to avoid repercussions, the price was to murder Ms. Ruiz and make sure her body was never found."

Mary Beth saw more heads shaking around the courtroom, almost in unison, as if the pieces were falling in place. She was struck with two thoughts. One was that people were eating this psychic stuff up. If, by some chance, the judge actually let that evidence in, she could really see a jury deciding to convict based on that alone. The other thought was less positive. It was something that had been eating at her for a while now—a piece of this puzzle that still didn't fit: Why in the world would the cartel have wanted Maria dead? Mary Beth was personally convinced of Raul's guilt but she still didn't know why he'd done it.

She was wondering if they'd ever get an answer to that question, as Patrick continued his argument. "What's really compelling here, Judge, is that we know that Raul Kowalski and Octavio Silva knew each other from Arizona. And we know that Raul Kowalski and Maria Ruiz knew each other here in West Virginia. So, you see Judge, Raul Kowalski--" Patrick fired another vicious point at the defendant that made Mary Beth smile--"is the only thing that connects Octavio Silva to Ms. Ruiz. And he connects them to the place where the body was discovered. The prosecution is prepared to put on evidence that Raul Kowalski had done landscaping work at that abandoned school and may have even had a key to the chains on the front door. This is an isolated, obscure location, Judge, that Octavio Silva could not have known about, but for his connection with Raul Kowalski."

The judge interjected a question. "And this psychic, she didn't know Silva or Kowalski?"

Patrick shook his head. "She's an old woman who's lived her whole life in McCray County–or what used to be McCray County. As far as we can tell, she'd never met or even heard of anybody involved in this case."

Felix Lancaster sputtered, "Your Honor, this is preposterous. In the entire history of American jurisprudence, no court has ever admitted testimony of so-called psychic phenomena. It is completely unprecedented."

"Not true," Patrick said. "It is unusual, certainly, but not unprecedented." Patrick picked up a stack of papers. "Judge, may I approach?"

The judge waved him up. "I'd like to hand you a few cases that are relevant to this issue." Patrick delivered a stack of neatly clipped papers to opposing counsel and a matching set for the judge. As he was walking back to the prosecution table, he caught Mary Beth's eye and winked at her before she could look away.

"The first case there is *Stambovsky v. Ackley*, a New York real estate case from 1991 where the buyer of a home was able to rescind the purchase because the home was haunted."

The judge raised his eyebrows, staring down at the case.

"That's right, Judge. In that case the seller had previously claimed that the home was haunted, but concealed that fact from the buyer. Since there was indisputable evidence that the seller had previously admitted to paranormal activity in the house, the court found, as a matter of law, that the home was indeed haunted."

The judge ran his finger along the page, looking for the holding and nodding with disbelief when he found it.

"I also have there several probate cases where the testator–the person making the will–not only believed in but was guided by a psychic advisor, and the courts found that such belief did not invalidate the will or suggest that the testator was not of sound mind when the will was made."

The judge continued nodding as he paged through the cases with interest.

Patrick turned to the back of his stack of materials. "This last exhibit contained in your packet there is not a reported decision but a newspaper account from 1897 about a landmark case that took place right here in West Virginia regarding a woman named Zona Heaster Shue."

The judge repeated the name. "Zona Heaster Shue. Why does that sound familiar?"

Mary Beth was thinking the same thing. It was an unusual name that she felt like she'd heard somewhere before.

"You may know her as the Greenbrier Ghost," Patrick said.

Mary Beth covered her mouth to keep from making a sound. She wanted to shout, "Ah, hah!" She knew the story of the

Greenbrier Ghost. She used to tell it to Sam when he was a kid. And it was perfect for the argument Patrick was making.

Zona Heaster Shue had died under mysterious circumstances–discovered at home by an errand boy who'd been sent there by the woman's husband. When the doctor was called to examine the body, he was unable to complete a thorough examination due to the husband's overwhelming grief, so the cause of death was chalked up to an undetermined natural cause. Zona Shue's body was then buried but her spirit wouldn't rest. According to Zona's mother, she was visited on multiple occasions by her daughter's ghost who reported how she had been strangled by her husband.

That's where Patrick picked up the story, explaining to the court, "What was significant, judge, is there was confirming physical evidence–just like we have in this case. Zona Shue's body was exhumed, and it was determined that she had been killed exactly the way the ghost said she was. Additional investigation also found that the husband had a prior wife who'd died under similar circumstances. Then, as you can see in your newspaper reports there, the mother testified at trial and during cross-examination her account of being visited by the ghost was elicited and received by the jury."

Patrick waved the article in the air. "This is precedent, judge. A West Virginia trial court, admitting testimony of a paranormal vision, to convict a murderer."

Wild and wonderful, Mary Beth thought. *Only in West Virginia.*

"Judge!" Lancaster protested.

"I know, Mr. Lancaster, I know."

"We'd be the laughing-stock of the country," Lancaster said.

"Just a minute," the judge said. "I need a moment to think." He closed and rubbed his eyes as the courtroom remained deathly silent.

Mary Beth had a feeling the judge might just go for it. He

looked riveted as Patrick laid out the impressive details of all that the psychic knew. Plus, he was, at the end of the day, an elected official. As much as the judge's legal instincts would tell him that admitting testimony of a psychic was ludicrous, his political instincts were no doubt telling him that the fastest way to get voted off the bench was to let a presumed murderer go free in the highest profile case the county had seen in generations.

Finally, the judge spoke. "Okay, here's what I am going to do. I am going to reserve ruling on the evidence about this psychic until such time as it can be presented at trial and tested by cross-examination."

"Judge!" Lancaster protested.

"I know what you are going to say, Mr. Lancaster. And all of your arguments about the unreliability and unproven nature of psychic phenomena are matters which I have no doubt you will do an excellent job of pointing out to the jury at trial. And, in fairness, I will also grant you wide latitude to present your own scientific evidence debunking any such alleged phenomena. Finally, after all that has been considered, I will entertain any motions to dismiss made at the close of the evidence, either before or after the case goes to the jury."

Mary Beth saw what the judge was doing, and it was kind of brilliant. The perfect hedge. She'd seen judges do this before when they thought a case should be dismissed but didn't want to take the heat for kicking it. Instead, they'd let the case go to the jury and hope there was an acquittal. If so, then the judge was off the hook because the right result occurred without the judge having to be the one to dismiss the case and appear soft on crime. If not, and the jury convicted, and the judge still felt it was wrong, he could always set the verdict aside after the fact.

"Therefore," the judge said, "Mr. Connelly, I am going to deny the current motion to dismiss, provided you can commit to me that you intend to proffer this psychic at trial along with evidence of how she has aided the sheriff department's investigation."

Patrick turned and locked eyes with Mary Beth from across the room. She wanted to turn away, but knew he was asking her a question. Was she really willing to go through with this? He'd put his neck on the chopping block. He needed a commitment from her that the sheriff's department would back him by testifying to the full chapter and verse about the psychic's involvement in the case.

Mary Beth gave him a thumbs up. Patrick gave her that cocky little smile that she used to both hate and adore. Then he turned back to the judge and said, "Absolutely."

34

IZZY BROUGHT A BOTTLE of champagne into the DA's conference room where Jeannie Boggs, Sam, and Guadalupe had all gathered with Patrick to celebrate his victory.

"To the best new prosecutor in Jasper County!" Izzy said.

Patrick raised his paper cup full of the bubbly and said, "To getting justice for Maria Ruiz."

They all toasted and were sipping their champagne when Patrick noticed Sam staring uneasily at the door. He turned in that direction and saw Mary Beth armed with her typical weaponry, not the least of which was the scowl on her face.

The room drew quiet as she entered, her footfalls echoing like an old west gunslinger taking position for a showdown. The entire time, her eyes never left Patrick's. He felt his testicles shrivel.

"What. In. The. Hell …" she said in a cold killer's voice, then smiled slightly, "Was that judge thinking?" A smile slowly spread across her face and everyone breathed a sigh of relief. Mary Beth took a step closer and extended a hand to Patrick.

He took it, thinking for a moment about kissing it but deciding a shake would be more appropriate.

"Congratulations," she said.

"Thank you, Sheriff."

Izzy started to pour Mary Beth a cup of champagne but she waved him off. "No thanks. I can't stay. I just wanted to come by to say that I appreciate what you did in there today. And I just needed to know one thing."

"What?" Patrick asked.

"How in the hell did you ever pull the Greenbrier Ghost out of your ass?"

Patrick smiled. "I have my new research assistant to thank for that one. It was all his idea." Patrick pointed to Sam and watched Mary Beth's smile turn back into a scowl. "He … volunteered," Patrick added. He also wanted to assure Mary Beth he'd done nothing to clue Sam in to the fact that he was his biological father, but that wasn't something he could easily do in front of everyone else.

Sam helped a little though. "Isn't it great, Mom?" he said. "I asked Mr. Connelly if he could use any free research, and he told me he could use all the help he could get. When he told me about the kinds of cases he was looking for, I remembered the stories you used to tell me about the Greenbrier Ghost."

"Is that right?" Mary Beth looked at Patrick with a forced smile that sent a shiver down his spine.

The awkward exchange was interrupted by someone else at the door. "Excuse me."

They all looked over to see Dr. Pedro Kowalski and his wife standing there, the wife nudging Pedro, who said, "Sheriff Cain, can I speak with you?"

Mary Beth took a step toward them and Patrick interceded to put on the brakes. "Wait. You can't talk to him. Pedro's represented by counsel. You shouldn't talk to him without his lawyer present."

"It's okay," Pedro said. "I'm not represented anymore. Not since Raul got arrested. Felix and I both wanted to make sure he didn't have any conflicts and could do whatever he needed to represent Raul."

"Oh," Mary Beth said.

Jeannie Boggs stood. She put one hand on Sam's shoulder and the other on Guadalupe's. "Why don't we give them the room?" she said. The three of them started to leave and Patrick started to as well, but Jeannie said to him, "You better stay. This is your case."

That was a good point, but Patrick still looked to Mary Beth for permission and was both relieved and surprised when she nodded her consent.

Once the others had left, Elizabeth Kowalski nudged her husband again. He reached in his pocket and pulled out a flash drive that he handed to Mary Beth. "Here," he said, "This is for you."

Mary Beth took it, turning it over in her hand. "Is this what I think it is?"

"It is. And it's the only copy. No one will ever see the video Felix took."

"Video of what?" Patrick asked, but Izzy quickly shut him down. "It's not important," he said. "Has nothing to do with the case."

Mary Beth thanked the Kowalskis. Then Pedro said, "There was something I was hoping you could do for me."

"What's that?" Mary Beth asked.

"The baby. Maria's baby. I–" Pedro looked at his wife then back to Mary Beth. "I'd like to be tested. I just have to know."

Patrick assumed that Pedro had learned about the fetal remains from Felix Lancaster because it still had not been reported publicly, but was required to be disclosed to the defense.

"That won't be necessary," Mary Beth said. "We tested Raul

and he didn't match at all. If you were the father, the test would have shown that he was a close relative."

Pedro took a deep breath, and his wife covered her mouth to try and steady her emotions over hearing the news.

After a moment of absorbing the information, Pedro looked to the door like he was about to leave, then said, "That's what we argued about. That night. The last time I saw Maria, when she came to Marshall and surprised me–surprised us–at that fraternity party."

Everyone else remained quiet. Pedro continued, "She told me she was pregnant, and she didn't know whether I was the father or not." Pedro shook his head with disgust and confusion. "I'm not even sure what I was more mad about, the idea that I could have been the father just as I was finally ready to move on, or that somebody else could have been."

"Did she tell you who the other guy was?" Mary Beth asked.

Pedro shook his head, No. "She never would say. But she called me later that week and asked me to come home to take a paternity test. I think the other guy was supposed to take one, too. I just couldn't bring myself to do it. That was the weekend I went to Charleston with Elizabeth, instead. The weekend she disappeared."

Mary Beth took a seat. Patrick watched as she mulled things over. It certainly sounded to him like whoever the father was, if they could ever figure that out, was the missing chapter in this story. "What about Raul?" she asked. "Do you have any idea why he would have done this to Maria?"

Pedro looked completely bewildered. He gestured toward Patrick. "Only what I've heard in court about the hitman's confession."

"Have you talked to Raul?" she asked.

Patrick started feeling a little uncomfortable here. Raul was a criminal defendant and a represented party. They couldn't inter-rogate him either directly, or indirectly, by sending someone else in to ask him questions. Something in Patrick's gut told him that was where Mary Beth was headed.

Pedro said, "I'm paying for his lawyer. And I want him defended. But if he did what he's accused of. If he--" Pedro's voice broke. He had to gather himself before continuing. "If he killed Maria, then he should pay for it."

Patrick felt a little relieved that Mary Beth didn't push the issue any further. He thought for a second she'd try to send Pedro in to elicit an admission from his brother.

Whether that same idea occurred just then to Pedro or not, Patrick couldn't know for sure, but it seemed like a distinct possibility when he said, "Maybe it is time I talk to him, though. Would that be okay?"

Three hours after Pedro met with Raul, both brothers were in Mary Beth's interrogation room, along with Felix Lancaster, for a meeting the defense attorney had requested. Lancaster looked like he really didn't want to be there but had no choice. He kicked things off by saying, "I want to initially state that the judge's ruling this morning was clearly erroneous. No way it will hold up on appeal. Even if you got some crazy jury to convict off the word of a psychic, it'll never stand. We'd just get a new trial."

Patrick shrugged. "Then what are we doing here?"

"I'll tell you what we're doing here," Mary Beth said. "We're here so Raul can beg for his life because Felix is puffing. He knows his boy is about to go down. Psychic or no psychic, juries and judges in this state, even appellate judges, don't take too kindly to letting cold-blooded murderers walk free on technicalities."

Lancaster leaned across the table, trying to exert some control over the situation. "Nothing could be further from the truth," he said. "The only reason we're here is because my client has insisted, over my strong objection, that we discuss a deal."

Mary Beth started to speak but Patrick gently placed his hand on her elbow to quiet her. She let him leave it there for a moment before gently pulling her arm away.

"Let's hear your proposal," he said. Patrick wasn't nearly as confident as Mary Beth about the potential outcome of a trial—in part, because he had no idea how to try a case.

"We off the record?" Lancaster asked.

"Of course," Patrick said. "This is all hypothetical."

"Okay, well then, hypothetically, if Raul knew the identity of the person who commissioned Maria Ruiz's murder, he would give that to you in exchange for reducing the charge to manslaughter."

"In your dreams," Mary Beth said before Patrick could respond. "He kidnapped a woman, put a gun to her head, and pulled the trigger. Manslaughter, my ass."

Patrick gripped Mary Beth's elbow again but she yanked it away this time. "Murder one," she said, even though it was technically Patrick's decision.

Lancaster looked at the Kowalski brothers. Pedro was covering his ears like he couldn't stand to listen to any of this. Raul shrugged like he didn't really care what happened to him at this point.

"Murder two," Lancaster said. "That's the final offer. Otherwise, whether you're able to convict my client or not, you'll never know the truth."

Patrick looked at Mary Beth and Izzy. Izzy stood and started pacing, wanting no part in this decision. Mary Beth obviously didn't like the sound of a second-degree murder conviction, but Patrick knew she desperately wanted to get to the bottom of the mystery behind Maria's death.

"Suppose we agree," she said, "and all you do is give us the name of some other link in the cartel chain who's just a messenger. Then we still don't have the truth."

Lancaster shook his head. "No, this is *the* guy."

"How can you be so sure?" she asked.

Lancaster looked at Raul. He said, "Because of the baby."

With that he had everyone's undivided attention. Lancaster gestured for him to continue. Raul said, "The guy told me to make sure no one ever found her or the baby. And I said, what baby? And he said, never mind what baby. Just make sure nobody ever finds her and then there won't never be no baby."

Lancaster added. "Just so you know. It is my belief–hypothetically–that the cartel never had anything to do with this at all. For one thing, from what I've gathered about the Diaz prosecution in Arizona, it sounds very likely to me that he'd been caught skimming and the cartel wanted him to take a fall."

"I don't understand," Patrick said.

"I'm saying that I think Raul's prior attorney reached out to a former client who he believed had some connections with the cartel, and that former client took advantage of the situation. He then–hypothetically–used Raul, by telling him this cartel story to take care of a personal problem he had."

"Knocking up Maria," Mary Beth said.

"Precisely," Lancaster said.

Mary Beth bit at her bottom lip. Patrick watched her processing things, waiting for her cue as to what to do next.

"So, we know we're dealing with a married man," she said.

"Would stand to reason," Lancaster responded. "But there's a whole lot of those in Jasper County. If you want to know which one had Maria killed, then we need a commitment to murder two."

Patrick turned to Mary Beth. "What do you want to do?"

She thought for another moment. He could tell the idea of letting Raul plead down to second degree murder was really eating at her, but she just needed to know.

"Tell me something," she said. "The information your client can provide, could it implicate our current district attorney at all, Alexander Pomfried?"

It was obvious from the gleam in her eye that Mary Beth liked that idea, but Lancaster quickly shot it down. "No. We have no reason to think that. My client would testify that Pomfried told him he was going to reach out to a former client for information, and then this man contacted him separately. We have no reason to think Pomfried knew anything about what happened after that."

Mary Beth crossed her arms. "Okay," she said, "you'll get your murder two in exchange for the name and cooperation, if–" she paused like she was still thinking through whatever condition she was about to lay down. "If we can confirm with DNA that whoever you name was indeed the father."

Lancaster said, "I don't think that will be a problem. I suspect you've already got his DNA on file."

Izzy, who'd been hanging back, leaning against the wall, chimed in. "We've already run a DNA search through the database."

"I'm not talking about the criminal database," Lancaster said. "I'm talking about the control database you keep on your officers."

"What?" Mary Beth and Patrick asked in unison. They both looked to Raul.

"He was a cop," Raul said.

"Who?" Mary Beth demanded.

"It was him!" Raul pointed angrily across the room. Patrick and Mary Beth both wheeled around in disbelief, following the invisible line from Raul's accusatory index finger that was aimed directly at Izzy.

35

"IZZY?"

Mary Beth couldn't believe what she was seeing. Raul was fingering Izzy? This had to be a joke. A really bad one.

Izzy looked even more shocked than her–and angry. "What the hell?" he said.

"Nah, man," Raul said. "Not him. Him!"

Mary Beth panned back and forth from Izzy to Raul and back to Izzy again, finally realizing that what Raul was actually pointing at was the wall Izzy was leaning against, where they'd pinned a big glossy photo of Randy Law to the corkboard so they could throw darts at it

"Wait a second." Mary Beth went and yanked the picture down and shoved it in front of Raul. "You're telling me that this is the man who told you that you had to kill Maria to get out from under the cartel?"

Raul crossed his arms. "That's exactly what I'm telling you."

"You're sure?"

"Yes, I'm sure."

"Absolutely certain?"

"Hundred percent," Raul said. "The guy set the whole thing up. He told me what time to be at the park and where. Told me right where she was gonna be."

Mary Beth had to sit down. This was so overwhelming, so unbelievable. But as she stewed, the pieces started to fall into place. Randy was a supposedly happily married man and a real holier-than-thou Bible thumper too, a deacon at King's Chapel who'd have been scandalized by a love child. And the city park was his hunting ground–the place where he pulled off most of his drug busts. He knew that area better than anybody. Would know exactly where to stage a private rendezvous. Then there was Bill. His reports said he stopped looking at the cartel angle because a reliable CI confirmed that they weren't responsible. Bill must have gone to Randy, just like Pomfried had, assuming he had the inside connection to cartel information. Bill trusted Randy implicitly. Only if it came from him would Bill have accepted the intel so blindly and completely closed off that area of investigation. It made sense.

Mary Beth checked her watch. It wasn't quite five o'clock. Randy would most likely still be at his dealership. She couldn't wait to see the look on the bastard's face when she slapped on the cuffs.

"Izzy," she said. "Who all do we have on right now?"

"Goforth and Jenkins are here. Skipwith's on patrol."

"Have Jenkins take Raul back to lockup. Let's get everybody else over to Law Harley-Davidson, pronto."

Mary Beth wanted to take this guy down, now. She wasn't taking any chances with him getting wind and skipping town.

"Wait," Patrick said as she tried to leave. "I'm coming with you."

Mary Beth sneered. "No, you're not."

Patrick must have realized how stupid he sounded to everyone who didn't know he'd once been–and would still like to be–her boyfriend. He fumbled for words. "Well, just … be careful, okay? Law could be dangerous."

Perhaps Mary Beth should have appreciated Patrick's concern, but it actually offended her. She'd been compared to Law so often over the past few months, and usually unfavorably, that any suggestion she wasn't a match for him kinda pissed her off. She tipped her hat to Patrick and said, "So am I."

Mary Beth organized the troops by radio on the way to Law Harley-Davidson, telling everyone to keep the lights and sirens off so as not to alert Randy to their approach. There could be customers in there and she'd need to do everything she could to get them out of the store before moving in.

When they got to the dealership, she did a quick loop around and spotted Law's truck parked in back. Mary Beth ordered Goforth to take position there to cover the rear exit, while she, Izzy and Skipwith entered from the front.

Fortunately, the dealership wasn't very crowded. Just four customers and two employees in their blue polo shirts. Mary Beth calmly drew their attention and motioned for them to exit the building which they all did without a fuss. As the last employee, a young black man, was going past she whispered to him, "Law in the back?"

"Yeah," he said.

"Who else is back there?"

"Just his secretary."

"Okay," Mary Beth said. "Get going."

The young man scurried out the door just as the first shot was fired. It came from behind the sales counter in the back of the store where two steps led to an elevated platform and a door to the business office. The bullet shattered the glass of the showroom window.

Mary Beth took cover behind a red Electra-glide that

absorbed two pinging bullets on the far side, one in the gas tank and another up by the handlebars.

Izzy and Skipwith returned fire from covered positions until she ordered them to stop. The secretary was still back there and she didn't want her to be shot by accident.

Mary Beth saw a flash of Law's white shirt as he pivoted from the door. She darted forward, advancing from one cycle to the next, using them for cover, until she heard the rear exit door kick open followed by a volley of gunshots. Law must have tried to leave out the back and found Goforth there waiting for him.

Mary Beth charged the rest of the way across the sales floor, crouching low but moving fast, then flattened herself against the showroom's back wall. Izzy and Skipwith followed in the same fashion.

She heard another series of shots, two maybe three as she slinked toward the door leading to the back office, hoping to get the drop on Randy from behind as he engaged with Goforth. But before she could get in position she heard the heavy rear exit door slam, followed by a woman's scream. She got around in time to catch a glimpse of Law dragging his secretary into his office and locking the door behind him.

"Stay back!" he yelled. "Stay back, or I'll kill her!"

Mary Beth noted the trail of blood by the rear exit. She hit her walkie. "Benny, you okay back there?"

"I'm hit, sheriff. Got me down around the thigh. But I'm okay. Think I got him with a couple too."

"Just sit tight," she ordered. "We'll have an ambulance on the way."

She nodded to Izzy who made the call for EMS, officer down.

Then Mary Beth got in position with her back against the outer wall of Law's office next to the door handle. Izzy was on the opposite side with Skipwith crouched down behind him.

"Okay, Randy," she yelled. "There's no reason anybody has to get hurt here."

"Fuck you!"

"Now, Randy. That's not very Christian like. What would Jesus say about you talking like that?"

"Go to hell!"

"I doubt that, very seriously," Mary Beth said. "Now listen. We both know there's only two ways you're leaving here. You can come quietly and you'll have access to a lawyer and a chance to defend yourself, and you'll live to see your wife and kids again. Or you can force us to come in there after you and chances are you won't be walking out at all."

"You come in here and I will blow her head off, you understand me?"

The woman screamed, "Please don't come in."

"Ma'am," Mary Beth yelled, "just try to stay calm. Nobody's getting their head blown off. Randy and I are old friends, aren't we, Randy? We just need to have everybody put the guns away and let's talk."

"No way," Randy yelled.

Mary Beth knew Randy was bleeding and she knew he was desperate. What she didn't know was how she was going to get to him without him hurting his secretary. She wanted to keep him talking. See if she could wear him down.

"Come on, Randy. Why don't you just let your secretary go? Haven't enough innocent women been killed?"

"Innocent?" Randy said mockingly. "You have no idea."

Mary Beth whispered to Izzy, "If I give you the nod, you kick the door down then follow me in."

Izzy nodded.

Mary Beth yelled through the door. "Well, why don't you come on out and tell me about it. Tell me why she wasn't innocent."

Randy huffed. "You truly are stupid, Mary Beth."

"That may be," she said. Mary Beth crouched lower, getting ready to go and the rubber sole of her boot squeaked on the linoleum floor. A gunshot blew a walnut-size hole through the lower half of the door just a few inches from Mary Beth's nose, leaving splinters in her hair.

She flattened herself against the wall again. "Take it easy," she yelled. "We're just talking here."

"Well, I'm done talking," Law yelled. "You're gonna fall back, and I'm walking out of here with Miss Margaret. If I even see any of you, she's dead."

Mary Beth looked around trying to think of how she could get a shot at him. There were no windows to Randy's office or exhaust vents that she'd noticed. Nothing like that. She tried to count how many shots he'd fired so far. Had to be at least four or five, maybe six, but she didn't know what kind of gun he was packing. With a high capacity clip he could have another ten or twelve rounds, and might even have more ammo stored in his office that he could use to reload. Maybe the best thing to do would be to fall back. Do whatever was necessary to secure the hostage's release.

"Okay, Randy," she said. "Okay. We'll leave. But first, tell me all the things I don't understand. I'm sure you've got a side to this story. What else don't I know?"

Mary Beth strained to listen and thought Randy's breathing sounded quieter. She couldn't be sure how much blood he'd lost, but his voice sounded weaker when he said, "I just want to walk out of here."

"What about Pomfried?" Mary Beth asked.

When Randy didn't respond, she yelled, "Randy?"

"What?" He sounded weaker still.

She hazarded the fastest of peeks through the small bullet hole and managed to see just enough to know that Randy was gut shot. His white shirt was soaked in blood and he was slouched on the floor with his back against the wall holding his stomach with one hand and his gun in the other. She didn't see the secretary.

"Miss Margaret, you still with me?"

"Yes, ma'am," came the frightened response. From the sound of it, Mary Beth surmised she was huddled in the corner. Normally a hostage taker would keep the hostage between him and the police which told Mary Beth that Randy wasn't strong enough to hold onto her anymore. The fight was leaving him. But he was still where he could get a good clean shot at his secretary if they rushed in and didn't get him first.

"So, tell me about Pomfried," she said. "Was he in on this thing with you?"

"Pomfried?" His voice was quiet but the dismissive tone was clear. "Who'd have thought that gasbag would turn out to have integrity. When I pulled the strings to get him appointed DA, I thought for sure he put a stop to any–." His voice was trailing off.

That's when Mary Beth gave Izzy the signal. He put one of his best taekwondo kicks on the thin door, busting it right off the frame. Mary Beth had her gun on Randy in an instant. He barely had his eyes open, looking up at her, his gun hand lying on the floor. She moved quickly to her left, putting herself between him and the secretary while Izzy and Skipwith covered her from the door.

Randy slowly raised his gun.

"Put down the gun, Randy," Mary Beth said, keeping her voice calm and even. "We've got an ambulance on the way. Let me get you to a hospital."

"You'd do that?" he asked.

"Of course I would, Randy. We're old friends, remember."

Randy cocked his head to the side, like he was having trouble holding it up, as Mary Beth inched closer to him. He gave her an ironic smile. "The things you do for your friends, huh?"

Mary Beth slid another half-step in his direction and all of a sudden his arm lurched upward with surprising speed given his weakened condition. Mary Beth was almost close enough to touch him. She lunged for his gun but before she could get to it, he had it up and in his mouth where it went off like a cannon, jerking his head backwards and painting the wall red.

36

PATRICK CONNELLY PULLED to a stop in the circular driveway of the biggest house he'd ever seen–a mansion on the outskirts of Dulcimer, Kentucky, with a columned portico that reminded him of the White House. The whole way there he'd kept scanning the radio dial, picking up snippets of news coverage reporting on the big shootout at the Harley-Davidson, telling the story of how Randy Law had been implicated in Maria Ruiz's murder and how the unfairly maligned Sheriff Mary Beth Cain had once again swooped in to save the day.

A large black man in a SECURITY t-shirt knocked on the window. Patrick rolled it down.

"Help you?"

"Can you tell Mamie that Patrick Connelly is here to see her?"

The man turned and said something into a walkie. When he turned back, he motioned for Patrick to follow.

Patrick cut the engine and trailed the security guard into the mansion past cleaning crews who were picking up lingerie and the kind of debris of empty cups and liquor bottles you'd expect to see after a rock concert. The guard took Patrick to a dimly-lit study that was lined with bookshelves where Mamie sat at a dark wooden desk. Her face was covered with a mint green mud mask. Cucumber slices covered her eyes and her head was wrapped in a towel.

Mamie removed the cucumbers and said, "You'll forgive my appearance, I hope, Mr. Connelly. This is part of my constant efforts to tap into the fountain of youth."

"How are you, Mamie?"

"I am well, Mr. Connelly. But you don't really care about that. How about you just tell me what it is you are doing here."

"Sure," Patrick said. "You mind if I sit?"

Mamie gestured to a brown leather chair.

"I'm investigating," he said. "Call it my final prosecutorial act now that the case I was brought here to handle has been summarily wrapped up."

Mamie nodded. "Yes, I heard about all of that unpleasantness yesterday. That Randy Law never was any good if you ask me."

"That's exactly what I wanted to do," Patrick said. "Ask you what you know about Randy Law. Just how dirty was he?"

Mamie shrugged. "How should I know? He certainly never had anything to do with me."

"I believe that," Patrick said. "I've been over his old arrest reports. It looks like he used to hit your operation pretty hard. Some in the sheriff's department suspect maybe he was in with one of your competitors."

"Did my daughter send you here, Mr. Connelly?"

"Oh no. Mary Beth doesn't know I'm here. I wasn't sure she could handle the answers to the questions I have."

"You shouldn't underestimate her," Mamie said.

"That's true," Patrick agreed. "She's a pretty incredible person, for sure. But I think she has a bit of a blind spot when it comes to people she cares about."

"Such as?"

Patrick pulled a sheet of paper from his pocket that he

unfolded and looked at for a moment before folding it again and tucking it away. "Bill Cain, for instance."

Mamie fixed him with her gaze. "What do you mean?"

"Mary Beth looks at all the reports from his investigation and sees a man obsessed with finding the truth. But I look at it and see a bunch of nonsense. Spending all kinds of time chasing ridiculous theories about how Maria might still be alive somewhere, papering the file with a bunch of voluminous crap like DMV records, all the while just giving up on the real areas of interest like Pedro and the cartel."

"What are you suggesting?"

"I don't know, exactly," Patrick said. "Maybe it's just my personal bias. My perpetual dislike of Bill Cain for having stolen my girl, back in the day. But it reads to me like somebody who's covering."

"Covering for what?"

Patrick considered that a moment, still not certain of his own thoughts. "I just kept thinking about how he and Randy Law were so tight. The kind of guys who'd do anything for each other. So, I figure if Randy was dirty, maybe Bill knew about it. It would have been pretty hard for one of those guys to keep something like that from the other."

Mamie picked up one of her cucumber slices from her desk and held it up to the light, turning it over. "Like I said, I wouldn't know."

"Come on, Mamie. You know just about everything that goes on in the underbelly of southern West Virginia."

"I think you overestimate me, Mr. Connelly."

Patrick smiled, seeing a little bit of Mary Beth in her coy response. "I don't think I could ever do that. Besides, I've got to leave today and there's no one else I can really talk to about this. Not without it getting back to Mary Beth."

Mamie smiled coolly. "Well, I'm sorry I wasn't able to help you."

"Really?"

"Really."

Patrick was disappointed. Apparently, he'd made the trip for nothing. He got halfway out of his chair and lingered a moment before sitting back down. He had one last little suspicion that he wasn't sure even he wanted the answer to, but since he'd traveled all that way, he figured he might as well ask.

"It just occurs to me that Randy kept hitting your operation until Bill was killed in the course of a drug bust. Then next thing you know, your daughter became sheriff, Randy Law was off the force, and your competition was on the run."

"Your point being?"

Patrick tried to put it tactfully. "Bill Cain being killed solved a whole lot of problems for you."

He watched Mamie closely, really studying her eyes, suspecting that the only information he was ever going to get out of this conversation was what he could discern from those mysterious orbs. But they remained as cold and unreadable as always.

Mamie sat her cucumber down and leaned across the desk. "Mr. Connelly, would you take a piece of advice from an old woman?"

"Sure," he said.

Mamie cleared her throat. "Well here it is: If you have any remaining hopes of ever worming your way back into my daughter's heart, you might seriously consider letting whatever is already dead and buried, remain undisturbed."

Patrick watched her for another moment, her cold, flinty, resolute expression, completely unflinching. "Perhaps you're right," he said, finally.

There was a knock on the door and the security guard poked his head in. "Miss Mamie, your guest is here."

"Thank you, Jerome. We're almost finished. Please have her wait upstairs." Mamie looked back to Patrick and said, "Well, Mr. Connelly, as much as I have enjoyed this surprise visit, I am afraid I must take leave of you now. Perhaps we might find another mutually beneficial arrangement someday like we attempted to do last Fall."

Patrick stood and shook the old lady's hand. "I don't think so, Mamie. That didn't work out too well for me. But thanks for the offer."

She nodded her goodbye, and another security guard escorted Patrick outside.

When he got to the car, Patrick asked him if he had a light. The guard fished around in his pocket and produced a gold Zippo lighter.

Patrick pulled the piece of paper back out of his pocket and gave it one last look. While Mary Beth and Izzy had raced off to arrest Randy Law, Patrick had run the test they'd need if Randy Law would have been apprehended alive, checking the DNA on file for county law enforcement against the fetal remains. It was those results that Patrick now held in his hand:

PROBABILITY OF PATERNITY: 99.9998 %
CHILD: Fetal Remains - Ruiz, Maria
FATHER: Cain, William

"Can I get my lighter back," the guard asked.

"Yeah, sorry," Patrick said. "Just a second." He hesitated a moment more then flipped open the zippo, sparked it to a flame, and put it to the paper.

37

WHEN MAMIE AMBLED UPSTAIRS, she found her old childhood friend, Mabel Honaker, the Mountain Mystic, sitting by her bedside table, next to the elevated four-poster, puffing on a Cohiba cigar.

"What was that all about?"

"You're the psychic," Mamie said.

"Very funny. You know I wouldn't have known a thing if it weren't for your man on the inside. What was his name? Clementine?"

"Quiet Clem," Mamie said. "He's so quiet, people end up telling him quite a lot. Once that Octavio Silva spilled the beans, we had all the information we needed, didn't we?"

"Yeah," the mystic said, grimacing. "But you'd have saved yourself a whole lot of time, and me a whole lot of trouble if you'd have just taken it to Mary Beth yourself."

Mamie rolled her eyes at how dense those around her could be. This was why she was always two or three steps ahead of them. "I couldn't have taken it to my daughter. She wouldn't have trusted anything that came from me. And if someone else had taken it to her, then I wouldn't have gotten anything out of it."

The mystic seemed indifferent to the explanation. "Still, I'm surprised she didn't see your fingerprints all over it. The way I knew about her childhood dream and that bullfrog business. And I thought for sure her son would tell her that it was you who sent him to me in the first place."

Mamie snorted at how ludicrous that was. "Trust me, honey, Sam would wet his little pants if his mother knew how he still comes to visit his grandma."

"Fair enough. But we were really pushing it when I just came right out and said her mother was the one who could help her find the Mexican."

Mamie clapped her hands, she was so pleased with how that aspect of her plan had worked. "Don't you see? That was the whole point. She had to be the one to come to me. Not the other way around. If I'd have just gone to her with the information I got from Clem, it would have been a very different dynamic. Maybe I'd have got some small concession. But her coming to me of her own accord–desperate for my help–and then me granting it to her, as a pure kindness." Mamie covered her heart as though it was so big it might burst from her chest.

The mystic blew a satisfying smoke ring. "I still think you should have bargained for a lot more. She was desperate when she came needing your help down in Mexico. You should have demanded right then that she let you move your operation back into Jasper."

Mamie, crossed the room, took her friend's cigar and puffed on it twice.

"That's where you're wrong," she said. "That's what the young man I was just meeting with downstairs needs to learn if he's to ever have any hope with my daughter."

"What's that?"

Mamie smiled. "When it comes to Mary Beth, you always

have to let her think it's her idea." Mamie took another puff and blew a pretty good smoke ring herself before handing it back. "Trust me," she said. "With what's headed her way, soon she'll be begging me to come back."

Patrick was packing up his office when Mary Beth stopped by and knocked on the doorframe. "Ready to get out of Jasper Creek for good?" she asked.

Patrick looked up from the books and papers he was squeezing into a banker box. "Do I have a choice?"

Mary Beth smirked at him. "Don't sound so disappointed. You always wanted to get as far away from this place as possible."

"That was before," he said.

"Before what?"

"Before I knew this was where the only two people I care about were always going to be."

Mary Beth walked close enough for him to pick up the lavender smell of her hair. He thought for a moment she was going to take his hand, but she didn't. "I do appreciate what you did here," she said. "I really do. But you need to know it's just way too late for you and me."

"It doesn't have to be," he said.

"Yes, it does."

"Why?"

Mary Beth did take his hand now and squeezed it. "Because," she said, "every time I look at you, I'm gonna think about my brother lying dead on the floor."

Patrick had a hard time thinking up a response to that. "No relationship is perfect," he said, giving her a hopeful smile.

Mary Beth smiled back wistfully. "Yeah, but I think that's a little too much baggage to put on anybody."

Patrick was dejected, but tried not to show it. "What about Sam?" he asked.

"What about him?"

"He's such a special kid," Patrick said. "Brilliant. And sweet. The way he'd talk about Maria, and Guadalupe, and you."

"Me?"

"Of course. You're his rock. A boy like him really needs someone like you. I told him that."

Mary Beth put her hands on her hips, the color in her cheeks rising to a dangerous hue. "You and my son talked about me?"

Patrick almost said, our son, but didn't dare. "Yeah," he said.

"And what exactly did you talk about?"

Patrick shrugged. "You're just a little too intense for him sometimes. He doesn't know how to handle you. But I helped him appreciate all that you do for him."

"You did, huh?"

"That's right. I told him that he could live to be a hundred, but no one in his entire life would ever love him as much as his mother." Patrick smiled. "I told him you almost always mean well. You just have sharp elbows."

"Thanks?" Mary Beth said, like she wasn't sure if that was a compliment.

Patrick pushed aside the box that sat between them. "You know if there's any way I could just be around. Just watch Sam from afar. Know how he's doing. It would mean the world to me. I promise, I'd never do anything to let him know about … you know."

Mary Beth looked deeply surprised. "You'd really want to do that? Here?"

"Of course."

Mary Beth looked stunned. She took a moment to process the thought. "And you'd never say a word?"

"Never. In fact, I'm more convinced than ever that you were right. It's best that he doesn't know."

Patrick suddenly felt the intensity of Mary Beth's probing gaze and knew she was scanning him for signs of deception.

"I'm just surprised," she said after her visual polygraph was complete. "The last time we talked, you were so adamant that we should tell Sam the truth."

Patrick shrugged. "I changed my mind."

"Why?'

"Because I know how much Bill's memory means to him. And to you."

Mary Beth looked deeply moved by that sentiment. She twisted a knuckle against the corner of her eye.

Patrick said, "You know, if I sold my place in D.C., I bet I could get something about ten times the size here in Jasper Creek."

"But you hate this place. You know you do."

"Not anymore," Patrick said. "Not enough to keep me away, anyway."

Mary Beth laughed. "What would you even do here? Go get a job as a grease monkey down at Bobby's garage?"

Patrick felt a little offended at how she had never seen him as rugged enough to make it in Jasper Creek, but he felt like he was finally making some progress with her and did his best not to let it show. "I don't know," he said. "Now that Alexander Pomfried is the DA, I think this town could probably use another criminal defense attorney."

"Hah!" Mary Beth slapped his shoulder like it was intended to be funny, but Patrick wasn't joking. "You're serious?" she said, reading his face.

"Yes, I'm serious."

"You? A criminal defense attorney? In Jasper Creek?"

"Sure," Patrick said. "Why not?"

"For one, we'd be at odds with each other all the time."

"How's that any different than now?"

Mary Beth nodded like he had a point. He could see the idea growing on her. "And you'd never say a word to Sam?"

"Cross my heart," Patrick said.

Mary Beth scrunched her lips as she thought it over. Patrick was filled with anticipation, awaiting her decision. The idea of being close to her and Sam had his heart bouncing around his chest.

"You know," Mary Beth said, smiling, "I could actually see you as a defense attorney. You caved so damn fast when Raul asked for murder two."

"Whatever," he said. "That was your decision. You're the one who agreed to it."

"Only because I knew you were scared shitless to try the case." Patrick laughed. "You're right about that," he said.

Then, just as he had Mary Beth smiling, her expression turned dour. It always amazed him how quick she was to anger. "It does still burn me up, though. Raul getting off with just second degree."

"Raul was just the weapon," Patrick assured her. "He just did what he was told. He wasn't the one who really killed Maria."

Mary Beth shook her head and he could see the raw emotion there, still close to the surface. "That will always bother me–that we never got a chance to make the arrest, get the conviction, see Randy's face when the jury returned the verdict."

There were so many things Patrick wanted to tell her. Things that might make a difference in their chances of ever having a relationship again. But they would all hurt her so much. Unbelievable hurt for someone who'd already endured more than most could ever take. Not to mention what the truth would do to Sam.

Instead, Patrick took Mary Beth's hand and was thankful when she didn't resist. "Justice has already been served," he said.

Mary Beth recoiled at the suggestion. "*Justice would* be if the man who killed Maria got the death penalty."

Once more, Patrick felt the urge to tell her all that he knew–paint himself as a better man than Bill Cain. *What good was it to make an act of sacrifice, if no one would ever know about it?* he wondered. But then Patrick took a breath and reminded himself that was exactly what made it a sacrifice.

Resolved to leave the past undisturbed, he smiled, patted Mary Beth's hand, and said, "He already did."

ACKNOWLEDGMENTS

Thanks to the great writer friends who have supported me and given me helpful feedback throughout the writing of this book: Becky Moynihan, Bill Floyd, Casey Stegman, Eryk Pruitt, J.G. Hetherton, J.M. Razinske, Lyn Hawks, Phillip Kimbrough, Scott Blackburn, Stephanie Moore, and Steve Daugherty. I would also like to give a huge thank you to all the authors who were kind enough to blurb the book. Thank you also to my agent, Mark Falikin. And last but not least, thank you to Ron Phillips and Shotgun Honey for bringing this story to the world.

RUSSELL W. JOHNSON is an attorney who got so sick of billable hours he started writing crime fiction. His first story was published in *Ellery Queen Mystery Magazine* and won the Edgar Awards' Robert L. Fish prize in 2015. Since then, he's had stories published in a number of outlets, has been nominated for a Pushcart Prize, and won the West Virginia Writers' Pearl S. Buck Award for Writing for Social Change. His Debut Novel, *The Moonshine Messiah*, won the West Virginia Writers' First Place prize for Book Length Fiction. More information on his writing is available at www.russellwjohnson.com.

ABOUT
SHOTGUN HONEY BOOKS

Thank you for reading *The Mountain Mystic* a Mountaineer Mystery, by Russell W. Johnson.

Shotgun Honey began as a crime genre flash fiction webzine in 2011 created as a venue for new and established writers to experiment in the confines of a mere 700 words. More than a decade later, Shotgun Honey still challenges writers with that storytelling task, but also provides opportunities to expand beyond through our book imprint and has since published anthologies, collections, novellas and novels by new and emerging authors.

We hope you have enjoyed this book. That you will share your experience, review and rate this title positively on your favorite book review sites and with your social media family and friends.

Visit ShotgunHoneyBooks.com

FICTION WITH A KICK

shotgunhoneybooks.com

Printed in the USA
CPSIA information can be obtained
at www.ICGtesting.com
LVHW030114240524
780933LV00010B/942

NEW CHELLE BLISS STORE

As a special thank you for reading Never Too Close, save 15% off your entire next order.

Use code **NTC** during checkout to save 15%.

ABOUT THE AUTHOR

I'm a full-time writer, time-waster extraordinaire, social media addict, coffee fiend, and ex-history teacher. *To learn more about my books, please visit menofinked.com.*

**Want to stay up-to-date on the newest
Men of Inked release and more?**
Join my newsletter at *menofinked.com/news*

Join over 10,000 readers on Facebook in Chelle Bliss Books private reader group and talk books and all things reading. Come be part of the family!

Where to Follow Me:

facebook.com/authorchellebliss1

instagram.com/authorchellebliss

bookbub.com/authors/chelle-bliss

goodreads.com/chellebliss

tiktok.com/@chelleblissauthor

amazon.com/author/chellebliss

pinterest.com/chellebliss10

LOVE SIGNED PAPERBACKS?

Visit *chelleblissromance.com* for eBooks, audiobooks, signed paperbacks, and more.